let sleeping dogs lie

let sleeping dogs lie

PATRICIA HALEY

LET SLEEPING DOGS LIE

A New Spirit Novel

ISBN-13: 978-1-58314-624-8
ISBN-10:   1-58314-624-5

www.kimanipress.com

Printed in U.S.A.

Let Sleeping Dogs Lie reveals the strain a family can be subjected to in everyday life. Dramatizing the struggles of others makes me even more grateful for my family and the bond of love knitting us together. Therefore, this book is dedicated to my amazing and very large family, one full of love, support, encouragement, and comprised of a blend between my natural and married families: Tennin, Haley, Moorman, and Glass.

With utmost admiration and respect, this is for my maternal grandparents, Clifton and Mary Tennin, Sr., and their children: my mother Fannie (Earl), James (Worley), L.C. (Marie), Clifton, Jr., (Vernell), Robert (Ruby), Mary Lou (Charlie), Luther, D.C., Arletha, Ada, Ben; their daughters-in-law, Lottie, Ivelean, Lula V., Pauline, Jessie, Minnie, Eloise, and Ollie; their sons-in-law Willie and David.

Coming from a place of love and connection this is for my paternal grandparents, Willie and Jenny Haley and their children: my father Fred "Luck," Lela (Ode), Helen (Nolan), Dorothy (James), Hilda May (Henry), Edna (Early), Essie V. (Leon), Ruby (Wade), Willie David, Jim; and their daughters-in-law Pauline and Verna.

Grateful for Jeffrey's presence in my life, this is for his maternal grandparents, Eldridge and Geneva Moorman: my mother-in-law Jeraldine, Alberta (Marvin), Louis (Thelma), Vera (Willie), Arlene (Ernest), William, and Calvin.

Honored to be part of such a close family, this is for my husband's paternal grandparents, Rubin and Mary Glass: my father-in-law Walter, Willa Mae (Bill), Hildred (John), Mildred (Gus), Roy (Cleaster), Obelia (Roosevelt), Richard (Annette), Mabel (Charles), Jessie (Johnny), and Sarah (Floyd).

To my hundreds and hundreds of cousins, aunts, uncles, other relatives, and extended family members whom I can't name one by one, this book is also dedicated to each of you.

ACKNOWLEDGMENTS

Lord, my God, the creator of heaven and earth, the creator of me, I say thank you again and again for your faithfulness in my life. Your direction and guidance enabled me to write *Let Sleeping Dogs Lie.* May this book accomplish the purpose for which you intended.

Jeffrey Glass, I am blessed to have your support, encouragement, and overwhelming love. You make this literary experience and every other aspect of my life enjoyable and memorable. You are my greatest earthly joy.

I have a long list of those who have helped me with the promotion of *Still Waters* and/or the creation of *Let Sleeping Dogs Lie.* I appreciate each and every person noted, and those unintentionally missed, but you know who you are and so does the Lord. May your kindness be returned to you a hundredfold. Thanks to my wonderful big brother—I love you Fred; to my circle of support, Bob Thomas, Lorena, Flossie & Rosa Lawson—happy 80th birthday, Freddy Deon, valedictorian Ashley Burks, Frances & Hoyt Walker, Brendon, Brice, Robert & Diedre, Kenneth, Leslie, and Lori Glass, Donald & Mary Bartel, Alesha Russey, Wanda Beasley, L.C. & Cassandra Tennin, Shirley Burks, Sheila Simms, Michele Tennin (proud of you), Leroy & Emira Bryant, Patricia Hill, Rev. Rob & Jessie Ellis, Walt Reichel, Kelly Jones, New Covenant Church (Trooper, PA), Pastor Gus & Carolyn Howell, Ravi & Dorothea Kalra, Corlette Mays, Audrey Williams, Stacy Hawkins-Adams, Kendra Bellamy, Tia McCollors, Nancy Arnold, Maleta Wilson, Michelle Sims, Ernestine Jolivet, Thelma & Freddy Gould, Frances Utsey, Maurice & Regina Gray, Trevy McDonald, Nicole Bailey-Williams, Vincent Alexandria, Susan Jarrett. Derrick and Jennifer Wooden, thank you for doing such a great job with the Web site—you're awesome. Memories of those who've inspired me with every book I've written are my beloved brother Erick, "other" mom Joan Walker, and unforgettable Aunt Ada Brown.

I'm grateful for my advance readers, who, every single time, challenge me into crafting a better story. Thank you, Emma (John) Foots, Laurel (Lynn) Robinson, Dorothy Robinson, Dr. Leslie (Eldridge) Walker-Harding, Attorneys Tammy and Renee Lenzy, Kirkanne Moseley, Katy (Dean) Boshart, Rena (Roscoe) Burks, Ade Bakare, and my incredible husband who puts the "H" in *handsome.* T. Davis Bunn and Sands Hall, thank you for helping me to sharpen areas of my craft, particularly with point of view.

Thank you, sisters of Delta Sigma Theta Sorority: my chapter—Valley Forge (PA), Schaumburg-Hoffman Estates (IL), Rockford (IL), Blytheville (AR), Augusta (GA), Texarkana (TX), Quaker City (PA), Columbus (OH), Houston, S. Jersey, Milwaukee, and Atlanta. Special thanks to Freda Hopkins-Whitehaven Library (TN), House of Knowledge (Texarkana), Deltas of Durham, the Simmons at Trinity Faith (NC) Anita & Brenda—Beulah Grove Baptist (GA), Bethany Baptist (NJ), a long list of independent booksellers, and book clubs, especially Good Girl online, Sistahs with a Vision (NJ), Sisters Empowered & Making A Difference (DE), Prominent Women of Color (FL/GA), Books Ends (GA), Beulah Grove Readers (GA), Page Turners (OH), Sisters Turning Pages (OH), Booking Matters (GA), and African-American Women's Book club (PA).

Special thanks to Linda Gill and Glenda Howard for your enthusiasm and creativity surrounding the development and release of *Let Sleeping Dogs Lie.* It's been a pleasure working with you on this project.

As always, I acknowledge you, the readers. I write to glorify God while striving to provide an entertaining read for you in the process. Thank you for compelling me to write—may each of you be blessed in return.

Above all, love each other deeply, because love covers over a multitude of sins.

—I *Peter* 4:8

Prologue

His office, slightly larger than a walk-in closet found in luxury homes outside town, was crammed with stacks of books and mounds of papers—quite a departure from the meticulous order he'd come to appreciate in boot camp forty years ago, a period of his life he labored to forget. An empty spot was hard to find. A five-by-seven photo with his wife, daughters, Angela and Sylvia, sat next to the picture of their only son, the one who had followed in his father's military footsteps against his mother's protest.

The walls followed the motif of the room—crowded, covered, concealed, except for the images of his family. They were his reason for living, the force driving him to excel at his job. Maple, oak, fake wood and gold-trimmed metal frames containing two degrees, awards, commendations and honorable mentions plastered the room like wallpaper. A dozen "Educator of the Year" plaques filled the room, with a few on the wall and the rest piled on the credenza. Success was abundant, but nothing was more prominently displayed or gratifying than the eleven-by-sixteen family photo—his favorite. The picture represented the last time he, his wife and all three of their children were together for a picture, not to mention he was fifteen years younger at the time. Every now and then, the dream of returning to that time in his life was the refuge he sought, void of mistakes and before the secrets became a key ingredient for his survival. He knew too well the man he was, but his family didn't have to. He gazed around the room, reflecting on who he was today, reaffirming that the past was behind him. No room for dwelling on what was, or for getting organized. Another impressionable teen entrusted to his care had found her way into his office requiring personal and immediate attention, the kind he was an expert at giving.

"Latoya, I can't permit drinking on school grounds."

"But it wasn't mine," she responded, standing in front of the desk with the timidity of an elementary school student and the body of a high school senior.

"Latoya, I've been more than fair with you, but I can't keep letting you slip past the rules, otherwise the other eighth-graders will feel like I'm showing you favoritism."

"I don't care what they think," she said in the sultriest voice a fresh new teen wanting to be an adult could muster, while leaving her seat and sauntering around the corner of the desk. She approached the chair with her age-eighteen-year-old-looking hips following behind. He knew how to handle her type.

"It's my job to care. I'm the principal."

"I know, but give me another chance," she said, not backing away from his chair.

He didn't budge; it wasn't the first time he'd found himself in this situation, and most likely wouldn't be the last. He knew exactly what she was after. Staying alert was key. "No more chances, Miss Scott. You're suspended for three days."

"What? Three days? My mother will kill me."

Sultry turned to a boldness, a sign she was sure of herself, but he was still determined to let her know he was in charge and meant business this time.

There was no doubt in Latoya's mind. Her mother wasn't going to put up with another problem. She'd made that clear. What if her mother finally kicked her out like she'd threatened to do two or three other times? "Please don't suspend me. I can stay after school and do my homework, or clean the classrooms, or anything you want—please, anything. Just don't suspend me."

They were all the same, boys, men that were so-called daddys, teachers, those at the church, baby-sitters and even family. He was the principal, but she was convinced they could work this little situation out. She'd heard rumors about him, anyway. He wouldn't be any different, just like all the rest, once she made it easy.

"I'll do anything, anything for you."

"Anything?" he repeated, leaning back in his chair, remembering why work and home occupied separate and not-so-equal spaces in his life, with rarely the two worlds crossing. He'd learned the ability to compartmentalize the thinking, feeling and loving family man that he was from the machine programmed to survive in the war. What happened in 'Nam—the drips of good and the craters of tragedy—stayed in 'Nam. His family didn't know that man, had never met him, and that's how it had to be. Daily he had to make decisions affecting the livelihood of many young students, and his family needn't be exposed to the fallout. Looking at Latoya and contemplating his options, he knew what happened at school would stay at school.

Chapter 1

Block out the painful sting of reality and concentrate on creating a night of fun, laughter and a good time—an oasis away from the damaging attack she and Reese were undergoing in their marriage. Angela grabbed the shopping list from the seat of her SUV and placed it neatly in her purse. She would concentrate on her parents' anniversary celebration, pushing past the cold reality that there wasn't much worthy of praise in her marriage. If she let go of the party, she'd have nothing positive to hold on to. An hour at the party store was the spark she needed to jump-start a festive mood, hopefully lasting a few weeks until the next sprig of hope surfaced. Angela pushed a cart down the first aisle, pausing to pull the list from her purse and get a plan of attack established. Invitations were the priority. The event was in four months and family coming from out of town needed plenty of notice.

The rickety, hard-to-manage cart strolled awkwardly down the aisle under Angela's control. Mayhem and dysfunction were becoming staples in her life. Catching a glimpse of the invitation sign hanging from the ceiling located in the back corner of the store, Angela hurried the cart along, struggling to manage resistance from the disfigured wheel along the way. Without warning, she slammed into another cart crossing the aisle at the intersection, sending the infant into an instant screaming fit.

"Oh, I'm…" Angela began to say, and then let her voice drop.

"Angela, I'm sorry," the woman said, extracting her big infant from the cart and drawing him close to her bosom.

Could life get any worse? Angela wondered. Couldn't she have an hour at the party store to herself, one hour to try to put the pieces of her life back together? So what if planning the anniversary was a farce; she wanted—no, deserved—a moment to have what his deception had stolen, a taste of unprecedented happiness. At least the taste she desired wouldn't be a price anyone else had to pay.

"Felicia, I didn't expect to run into you here." Or anywhere else she wanted to add but caught the words before they escaped. Standing this close to her wasn't easy. She was trying to be the good Christian wife, daughter and sister, but it was proving to be more than she could handle. Forget about religion. Reese was relying way too much on her dignity, the part preventing her from going off on him and Ms. Felicia, the woman who was now standing right there in arm's reach, the one who had stolen a piece of Reese's affection. Angela could just strangle Felicia right here and close out that ugly, painful, dark spot in her life.

Felicia wouldn't make consistent eye contact, but continued rubbing the baby's back as he kept both arms tightly wrapped around her neck. "Junior's turning one next month."

A year already. It seemed like only yesterday to Angela when she'd found out about the child. On the other hand, it seemed like an eternity. She struggled to hold her rational thinking together. No matter how much the words sliced to her core, Felicia would never enjoy the benefit of seeing Angela crushed. She was the wife, sitting in the place of dignity, and Felicia would never know different. Angela could probably wish the boy a happy birthday. Besides, he was an innocent child who hadn't contributed to the fiasco of events surrounding his birth. Regardless, she couldn't do it, wish Felicia and her baby a happy birthday. Why should she? The two of them, Felicia and the baby—Reese, too, for that matter—had made her world unbearable this time last year, questioning her worth as a woman and wife and espe-cially her decision to wait a few more years before starting a family. Pretending had its place, looking the other way had it's time, too, but lying to this woman wasn't a farce she cared to engage in. She had to accept reality some time, and this felt like one of those moments.

Chapter 2

A warm, comfy blanket on a cold, dreary night is what his embrace should have felt like, but instead the contact was smothering, agitating. The love Sylvia wanted, she had, but why did the affection feel so wrong?

Her parents were probably home by now, but she could hear their words just as if they were standing in the room. "Between the two of you, there won't be any place left to hang another award in this family. The two of you are so much alike," she could hear Mom saying.

"That's right. This is Daddy's girl," he echoed, with pride pouring out in every word. "And when you're sixty you'll still be my little girl."

"Herbert, let's go home," she envisioned her mother saying, locking arms with her father.

"Okay, okay. Baby girl, I've already told you this twenty times today, but I'm so proud of you. I always knew you'd be a star."

He reengaged his hug, tighter this time, and whispered, "You're my favorite, but don't tell anybody. It's our secret."

Those words tore through her body like acid, burning, singeing, violating her flesh and sense of security.

"Sylvia, hello, earth to Sylvia," she heard someone calling out with a raised voice. The talking pricked her consciousness, abruptly terminating what must have been a dream and instantly drawing her back into the room, back into a conversation with her four friends present.

"Where were you?" Mike asked, taking her hands and drawing her into his embrace.

Her natural reaction was to repel him. "Forget about me. You wanted to celebrate, so let's celebrate," she said, instantly responding while grabbing a Waterford goblet. "I'm fine."

"Do you have anything in here besides sparkling water and Sprite?" Karen asked.

"No, and at forty dollars per case, the water suits me fine," Sylvia added, shaking off her feeling of unrest and throwing herself into party mode. She couldn't help but think about her sister for a quick moment. Angela was the party planner in the family. Angela would be the one to get a gob of beverages for everyone. She was already planning the menu for their parents' anniversary party, which wasn't until May, Sylvia acknowledged, but not having the interest or time to pine over a party plan.

"It wouldn't matter to me if this was two hundred dollars a bottle—water is water, and for a party you need something stronger, at least some sparkling cider, wine or something. You know that, and don't tell me your born-again adventure has changed your taste for wine?"

Church hasn't changed me, unfortunately, she wanted to say but didn't. Her infrequent visits were most likely a factor, but her friends didn't need to know about her religious challenges. Besides, religion was such a small part of who she was. "I didn't get a chance to run to the store. I didn't know your partying behinds were coming here after the award ceremony."

"I don't know why not. We've been here every other time you've received an award, and with as many as you've gotten, you should know our routine," Karen said.

"She knows we practically go every place she does, except church," Beth clarified.

"Yes, you're right. You're on your own with that one. I'm not ready to get my act together," Karen said roaring into laughter. "I like being a, what is it?"

"Heathen," Beth answered.

"Yes indeed, heathen, and loving it," she said, opting for a glass of Sprite.

Sylvia took another sip, allowing her body to relax into the moment, feeling secure among her friends, her other family, not to be confused with her bloodline, the Reynoldses, whom Beth, Tim, Mike and Karen knew little about. On rare occasions she'd let them interact with the Reynoldses: once at the graduation party after earning her master's, again when she got her Ph.D. and maybe at the celebration her family forced after winning her first Governor's Award. It was hard to keep track of who knew what and had been where with her family, but Sylvia thought she'd done a better job of shielding her friends from those people. She might not be good at everything, but Sylvia was an expert at keeping the world she shared with her friends far away from the one she tolerated with the

Reynoldses, all except her father. He wasn't petty and pretentious like the rest of the Reynoldses; he was honest and a man she'd been able to rely on all her life, in spite of Angela's drain on her parents' emotions with her in-and-out-of-marriage catastrophe. Enough with her sister's issues. This was Sylvia's night with her friends in her element.

"Can we forget about drinks and religion and anything else that's standing in the way of us having a good time?" Sylvia suggested.

"That's right. We're here to have some fun," Tim said, nudging her shoulder with his, a comfortable touch.

Merriment saturated the living room with abundance, sufficient to drive out that lingering, nagging feeling buried deep, deep inside. Heaps of merriment and good times were bound to cover up the annoyance, whatever it was that refused to let her be at peace with her feelings for more than a day, especially when it came to her family.

Another award, more accolades piled on top of a yearning desire to achieve, to please, to emulate her role model and earn the title of special child in his eyes, her daddy, Herbert Reynolds. Sylvia wedged the crystal figurine of a trophy into the remaining space on the mantel.

Mike resumed his attempt to pull her close. This time she bit her lip and let it happen, easier than struggling and far better than having to explain. Besides, she knew how not to resist, a behavior she'd practiced to perfection.

"It's rare that you get beauty, brains and b—" Mike said before getting interrupted.

"Ooh, I know you're not getting ready to say what I think you're going to say. You're nasty," Beth jumped in to say.

"Well, it's the truth. She's bold, that's what I was going to say."

"What you mean is that she has a mouth," Karen added with a giggle.

"Come on, people, you're talking like I'm not standing right here. As tall and black as I am, there is no way you can miss me. Mike, thank you for the compliment, at least I guess that's what it is," she said, suppressing a budding smile.

"No doubt."

"You, too, Beth and Karen, thank you, but I'm ready to call this an evening."

"You're not upset, are you?" Beth asked.

"No, no, for what? No, not at all. I'm tired. It's been a long day, that's all," she said, leaning against the mantel and removing her shoes, dropping her from five ten to five eight.

"That's right, we're tired," Mike abruptly cut in, and told their friends.

"You don't have to tell me twice. We don't have to go home, but you're saying that we have to get out of here. I hear you loud and clear," Tim said, causing a roar of laughter to erupt within the group. Tim, Karen and Beth set the goblets on the coffee table. A slew of goodbyes, good-nights and hugs ensued until the last friend had exited the town house, leaving only Sylvia and Mike.

Chapter 3

Angela stomped into the family room, having refused to let her anger diffuse during the thirty-minute ride home. Reese's gaze was locked on the big-screen TV hosting his alma mater's football game.

"Hey, baby, you're home already," he said, turning the volume down on the game. He got up to give her a proper greeting, but everything about her body language said there was a problem. She slung her purse over the back of the couch. The last couple of months had been dicey for them, but he was still determined to make the marriage work. There was a lot of repair and hurt that had to be handled. He would have to continue being patient and deal with the consequences of his mistake, and Angela had made it clear—regaining her trust wouldn't come easily. She was a different person. Not the same bubbly Angela he'd once known. She'd changed in many ways, one being her desire for him, but he had to keep trying. He reached out to pull her close. She pulled away.

"I ran into that woman and your baby."

The flow of hope left his body. His neck hung down, and his gaze danced across the floor, unable to rise up and make eye contact with Angela.

"He's celebrating his first birthday next month."

"Really?"

"I'm surprised you didn't know. You mean she didn't call and invite you to Reese Junior's birthday party?"

"Let's not do this, Angela."

"Why not? No sense keeping it quiet now. The truth is out."

"He's not my son and you know that."

"I don't care what the paternity test said, you had sex with her. He might not have your blood, but he sure has your name."

"I can't do anything about his name. His mother can name her son whatever she chooses. We can't let his name cause any more damage than I've already done."

"You mean you couldn't stop your woman from stealing my child's name?"

"Here we go. Do you think we'll ever be able to work through this?"

"I'm trying, but it's kind of hard to look the other way when your husband not only cheats on you, but the woman has a baby, and I run the risk of having to face that woman and her child every day. I shouldn't have to hide in my own town just to avoid being hurt. You blew our shot at happiness. It doesn't matter how you try to justify it. The name Reese Jr., that name belonged to our child."

"What child?" he blasted back at her. "I'm the only one who wants a baby in this relationship. You don't even want children. Doesn't matter to you how much I want to be the father of your children. I want that for us and you don't."

"So, what, does that give you the right to have another child outside this relationship just because I'm not ready for children? Don't try to use me as your excuse for cheating. If I never have a child, so what? We're still supposed to be faithful to each other."

Reese walked past his brooding wife, having experienced this scene, or some variation of it, repeatedly since he returned home and countless times prior to leaving. Acknowledging his error and getting her to give him another chance to make amends didn't have a connection. Sure, she'd invited him back into the house, but not into her heart. He was beginning to wonder if reconnecting with Angela in a meaningful relationship was a realistic possibility. For now, distance was best before something was said or done that caused both of them to want out, again. "I'm going for a drive."

"Go ahead, run away. Remember, taking your so-called drives is how we ended up in this situation in the first place."

There was so much he could say in retaliation, but what would be the point? Nothing good was coming out of this argument. Walk away and think was his plan.

"Go ahead, leave, and whatever you do, please don't bring another baby in here."

He tried to crawl away without detection, but her words were cutting, deserving of a retort. He'd made a mistake, but Angela had to choose or move, he decided, turning to face her.

"Yes, I cheated. Okay, is that what you want to hear? I've said it a thousand times, and apologized a million times, and have begged and pleaded for your forgiveness, but I don't think you can let it go because you don't want to. I don't know if there's anything I can do to fix this. That might be the cold, hard reality. Maybe we need to consider being apart."

"We've already separated for six months and a lot of good that did for us."

"I'm not talking about separation. I'm talking about divorce."

Chapter 4

The town house was empty, guests gone, except for Mike. "Finally, just the two of us," he said, swooping Sylvia into his grip.

Automatic, like a knee jerk, she wiggled free from his embrace. "I need you to be patient."

"Patient, come on now, we've been dating more than a year. I'm starting to wonder about you."

"What do you mean?"

"Maybe it's not me. I have to say, it's crossed my mind that you might have a lesbian thing going on. I don't know."

"What are you talking about?" she said, pushing back and claiming her space. "Because I respect my body and won't let the first smooth-talking man have me, that makes me gay? I've told you from the beginning, I'm not doing anything until I'm married."

"But we've been together a full year. Don't you think it's

time to revisit your rules? It's obvious that we're serious about each other. You know you can trust me in this relationship. I'm not going anywhere, but we need to take this to the next level," he said, still trying to ignite a mood of affection.

"You seemed to be fine with the rules, at least that's what you said. I believed you," she said, protecting her space.

"A year ago, yes, but I have to be honest. I need more than what you're offering. If we're going to keep our relationship going, we have to do some of what I want. We have to keep both of us happy, not just you. I can't sit back and let you have complete control of what happens between us anymore. I have needs," he said, closing the gap between them again, his voice losing a pinch of bass. "We're two mature adults. I need you to act like one," he said, making his move.

Taking another three steps away from him, she responded. "I trust you with my feelings, with my heart, and this is how you treat me, trying to manipulate me?"

"Call it what you will, but you know I'm right. You know me. I'm the same man you met last year, nothing has changed. I wanted to be with you then and I do now, no difference."

"Then I guess you're not who I thought you were after all."

"You can't put this on me. This is all about you and whatever hang-up you have about getting serious with a man."

"I'm not going to let you talk about me, all because I won't go there with you, not yet."

"I can't win with you. What am I supposed to think? You don't want to get close unless we're married, but each time I've brought up the idea of marriage, you put me off."

"Because we're not ready."

"Personally, I've been ready from the first day we met, but

I'm a man, baby, that's just the way it is. But still, I've followed your rules whether I agree with them or not. I respect you and so I've gone along with this situation because I love you, I really do. That's kept me here, but man, can a brother at least get a little affection?"

"I show you affection all the time."

"Let's be for real. I try to kiss you, you turn your head. If I hug you a second too long, you pull away. Now that I'm thinking about it, you're not affectionate with anyone, except your father. He's the only person I've seen you hug."

"I'm not the touchy-feely type. No one in my family is. That doesn't make me wrong because I don't hug everybody. Hugging doesn't mean anything unless it's sincere, anyway."

"Look, I know I'm a catch. I have plenty of women who are interested in me, but you're the one I want."

"Am I supposed to take that as a compliment or a threat?"

"Either way, whichever gets you thinking and let's you know I'm serious. You're an award-winning psychologist, can't you figure this out? We need a change in our relationship and soon."

"If change is what you want, that's what you shall have." She stepped to the door and cracked it open. "Get out."

Mike chuckled. "You're kidding me, right?"

"I'm standing here freezing with the door open in the middle of January. Does it look like I'm joking? I want you to leave."

"Are you serious, after a year of dating? That's it? Get out, without any discussion?"

Responding would keep the confrontation going. Sylvia kept quiet, feeling badly about obviously hurting his feelings. But what was worse, to stay in a relationship she wasn't satisfied with and build their future on a lie, or to be honest and let him go now? Having the relationship end so abruptly felt tacky, and really Mike deserved better, but what was done was done.

"Fine, if that's the way you want this. You're good at helping other people work out their relationships, what about your own?" he said, snatching up his coat from the back of the sofa. "I guess it's easier to give advice than it is to take it." He stopped and turned to her and said, "This is a mistake. I've done nothing to you."

"It's not you. It's me. This serious relationship isn't working for me. I need to step back and regroup, sort out my feelings. I'm sorry."

"I really don't understand you. After we got involved, you started harping on getting in touch with your feelings and your spirit, which is why you've supposedly been going to church. I was okay with the church thing, but now you've really changed. I don't know who you are anymore or what you want."

"Maybe not, but I know what I want," she said, reopening the door that she'd temporarily closed.

"Are you sure?"

"Quite sure."

"You'll regret this."

"You could be right." He walked out without looking back. She closed the door behind him, then twisted around, letting her back lean against the door with her hand still gripping the knob. A year-long relationship, another one down the tubes. A bucketful of thoughts could spring forward at such a moment, but the most prevalent one was hearing her mother's voice. Contrary to what appeared to be the truth, she did want to be committed in a relationship heading for marriage. Mom didn't understand her, not as well as she understood Angela, which didn't make sense because they were both her daughters, requiring a motherly touch of wisdom from time to time. Mom would never admit it, but Angela got her share and part of Sylvia's.

Dad was easier to talk to about relationship matters. She gazed at her watch—ten-fifteen. Too late to call him tonight, but tomorrow she'd convince him to steal away for lunch later this week when her schedule was free. That was if Angela wasn't in the middle of another crisis requiring his attention. Angela would just have to put her whining on hold and let Sylvia have the spotlight, at least until she could get some manly, fatherly advice about dating, the game she was clearly ill equipped to win.

Mike was right—religion hadn't done much for her. She was sure there were powerful words of encouragement in the Bible about relationships, but she hadn't invested enough time to find out. She wasn't proud of the realization but didn't feel pressed to make a change, either. Life was pretty good and she was getting by.

She schlepped along the path to her bedroom, glad to be alone. She needed to break out of her cycle of engaging in dead-end relationships. The nagging feeling, buried in her gut, was resurrecting, the feeling she got from time to time, particularly when one of her numerous boyfriends pushed for more of a relationship. Psychology was her field, her passion, her lifeline, and she was good at it. She could help everybody solve their problems, except someone who needed it most: her. What was her problem? More important, what was the answer? In pursuit of understanding herself she'd wound up with a Ph.D. in psychology, still with no answers, followed by two solid years of intense therapy, and last year, out of desperation, she accepted Christ. She'd hoped the church route would be a quick fix, but progress was moving a bit slower than expected, quite a bit slower. Might help if she went more often, but increasing her attendance wasn't in the plan.

The ringing phone yanked Sylvia from the closet of her despair and back into the dim light. The caller ID read R. and A. Jones. Great, exactly what she didn't need, to hear from her sister at an already bleak moment. She pressed on the talk button but didn't let up to complete the connection. Tomorrow would be a better day. Angela was probably calling about their parents' anniversary, anyway, which amounted to another four months of grueling planning. Hoots with planning, get the event over. Having to spend an entire day with the Reynolds clan would require a month of therapy before and at least five months after. Sylvia had completed a round early last fall after the family reunion and had initiated a fresh round in early December in preparation for the holidays. How much more family could one person stand? Come next week, she'd be closer to finding out.

Chapter 5

Understanding, compassion and honesty were Angela's desire. Reconciliation was most likely what God preferred, and she was going through the motions in her mind, but the heart hadn't committed to change. Maybe her faith in what God was able to do was the reason for her getting back with Reese, but was it strong enough to keep them together? When they were separated, she committed Luke 1:37 to memory: "For nothing is impossible with God." She meditated on the scripture day and night, clinging to every word until Reese came home, and then somehow the urgency of reciting the verse daily didn't seem necessary. Receiving him back into the house was easy, back into her trust was a struggle, but there was hope. There had to be, because the alternative was more dreadful than living with him, angry and hurt, but at least still married. More time, less distance, hopefully the combination would net a marriage worth cherishing. For now, delving into the planning activity for her parents' thirty-sixth anniversary and settling for the warmth swirling in someone else's relationship was sufficient.

She sorted the piles of envelopes into separate stacks. How had her parents done it? A priceless secret, had to be. How else could two people survive thirty-six years of marriage? They had earned more than a party, they were entitled to medals.

"Are you coming upstairs?" Reese called out on his way upstairs.

"In a little while. Both the mayor and superintendent's offices like a six-month lead time and we're already two months late. The month of May will be here before we know it."

His response was faint, but she could hear Reese's heckling. Words didn't need to be exchanged. She knew what he was thinking. Troubles they had, but the sound of d-i-v-o-r-c-e tearing across his lips earlier in the evening felt like molten liquid pouring into her life. Bad enough dealing with the shame she suffered during the outrageous child-support hearing last year. Could the stigma of being a divorcée be worse? She had no intention of finding out. "I promise I'll be up in less than an hour."

"Perfect, I should be asleep by then," he said with an edge.

"Reese, let's not make this a big deal. It will take me less than an hour to finish and then we can spend time together before you go to sleep."

"Don't put your family on hold for me. I wouldn't dare ask you to set aside a Reynolds event for me. Asking to be on your priority list would be crazy. I know better."

"Reese, that's not fair. I don't put my family ahead of you. I never have."

"Funny, then, I've been confused for the past five years. Nothing new, add that to the long list of details Reese doesn't know about this marriage or about his wife," he said, descending halfway down the staircase and stopping.

"This is ridiculous. We've been back together two months and we're already arguing every day." This couldn't have been what God intended for her when He softened her heart, allowing room for the mere thought of reconciliation.

"You're right, it's ridiculous. You were full of the Bible when we were separated. What happened to all of that you were saying to me? What was I thinking to come back here and expect you to change?" he asked. He might not want an answer, but she was giving him one, anyway.

"Change," she said, rushing to the stairs. "You have some nerve preaching to me about change and what the Bible says. You came back because I asked you to come back. Don't forget who cheated in the first place."

"How could I forget? You remind me every opportunity you get. Why did I come back? What was I thinking? I was out of here and maybe I should have stayed out, and left you and whatever interpretation of the Bible you're reading to yourself."

"We're married. Commitment should be your reason for coming home, and don't try to make this all about me and my family. You have plenty of issues with your little family that need to be addressed. You don't see me throwing it in your face, do you?"

"Here we go. Less than five minutes in and you're already bringing up the subject. I'm definitely going to bed now. So much for forgiveness. I'll see you in the morning, or not."

"Don't tell me about forgiveness," she yelled out. "I know it too well. 'Forgive...from your heart,' Matthew 18:35, and Luke 6:37, 'Forgive, and you will be forgiven,' and I have a whole bunch more for you."

Reese gave a round of deliberate, taunting claps. "Whoop-ee-do, so what? You know a handful of scriptures. Big deal, they don't mean anything if all you do is quote them. How about applying them? But then don't listen to me, I'm just a sinner in your eyes with little or no value to add to your life," he said as she watched him ascend the stairs without stopping this time.

She'd let him return home because that's what a woman of faith was expected to do, believe for the impossible, always open to miracles and restoration, despite her emotions. That's what her spirit of faith chanted, but her heart of hurt wasn't buying the speech. She fumbled with the notebook, trying to submerge herself into the planning details. Hiding might work for some, but her marital woes were too big to squeeze into a party book. The marriage needed work, and the time would come when she had to face the challenges. Reese's words were hard to swallow, but he was partially right. She knew the scriptures very well, and she wanted to apply them in the marriage, but hurt and hope were still dueling inside her soul with neither having the edge. What did God want her to do? She had no idea, truly none, or maybe she did but didn't want to hear what He had to say. She'd have to get some direction from the only one who could give her guidance through the quagmire of a troubled marriage. For now, dreaming about her parents' anniversary and their ideal relationship provided enough fuel to keep her hope light burning, at least for the next hour.

Chapter 6

The long leather couch with the big pillow was a myth. She didn't use one and Dr. Jan didn't, either. Two armchairs with a small circular coffee table ample to hold a silk flower arrangement, a desk, a few built-in bookshelves was the extent of her therapy sanctum.

"Sylvia, so how have the past two weeks been for you since our last session?"

"It's been tough. I ended my relationship with my boyfriend."

Dr. Jan didn't respond immediately, and Sylvia knew why. Sitting in the therapy seat never got easier. The propensity to dissect the session and psychoanalyze the therapist was an internal battle constantly waging during her fifty-minute visit. As a psychologist she valued the concept of counseling and helping individuals work out challenges in their lives. Receiving advice was much more difficult than giving.

"How did the breakup make you feel?" Dr. Jan asked, with legs crossed and fingers locked, resting on her thighs.

Sylvia had the inside track on the leaders in her field. Selecting a therapist took time, tact, and whoever she chose had to come highly recommended with credentials and experience, no rookie counselors for her, the seasoned New Jersey psychologist bearing the governor's stamp of approval. Discretion was also a factor Sylvia had to be concerned with, where other clients didn't. She couldn't have her business loosely leaking into the public forum. Dad taught her about decorum and the importance of protecting a reputation. He would often say, "Your reputation speaks on your behalf when your mouth has been silenced."

Dr. Jan met Sylvia's criteria. However, they could fast-path through the basic analysis of how to deal with a recent breakup. She could self-medicate and save her fifty minutes for better use. Sylvia wanted help in digging deeper, discovering the true source of her unrest. The prickling feeling that kept her awake periodically, some nights more than others, the agitation that made her avoid affection, the uneasiness she knew existed but couldn't touch.

"Mike will be fine and so will I," she said, waving off the thought. Dad could provide the male perspective for no charge or maybe the price of a lunch, but definitely not the two hundred and twenty-five dollars she was paying an hour, actually for fifty minutes of conversing with the last ten minutes reserved by the counselor for notes, same as what she did with her patients. "I would like to spend our time exploring my issue with affection."

"We touched on affection last session and ran out of time. Do you think you have a problem?"

She could give the direct answer, which would be that every boyfriend during and since college had told her that she did, right after or right before she called off the relationship. Five boyfriends in twelve years said something was wrong. "I'm having a difficult time with expressing affection."

"With men, women?"

"Definitely men, with the exception of my father, who always forced me to hug him from the time I was a little girl. Hugging other men is uncomfortable for me."

"Does that include male friends, boyfriends, colleagues, relatives?"

Sylvia didn't have to think about the answer. She'd had the problem for a while and knew the extent of her discomfort, not the source, but the impact. "Pretty much all men, relatives included."

"You used the word *uncomfortable*. What does that mean to you?"

"Eerie, creepy," she said, intentionally shaking in her seat. "I just don't like people touching me, in an affectionate way. Bumping me or shaking hands, regular contact, is no problem."

"Does your discomfort extend to women also?"

"Most of the time, although I'm not repelled by a hug from my mother or sister, I don't think. I'm not quite sure since my family doesn't hug a lot. So, with my family this isn't really a problem. I'm seeing the manifestation of my issue in relationships."

"Do you see discomfort with hugging and affection a problem as opposed to merely a preference?"

"What do you mean?" Sylvia asked, entertaining the idea of letting herself off the hook and taking the easy way out instead of probing further.

"As you know, some people prefer their space. They shun an excessive amount of hugs, touches and general attention. Doesn't necessarily mean they have a problem with affection, then again it might."

"My natural response would be to accept the preference theory, but I know better. I need to understand the source of my issue. Once I've discovered the problem, then I can consciously decide to ignore it, but not knowing is driving me insane."

"Okay, let's dig in for some hard work." Dr. Jan picked up the small wood-framed clock on the table, barely larger than an egg, and said, "This is where we'll pick up at our next session in two weeks."

The session concluded and Sylvia went to her car, feeling as if she hadn't made much progress, but was hopeful Dr. Jan would bring more insight than she'd gotten so far. Counseling was good, she thought, when it worked.

Chapter 7

Early afternoon in the heart of winter, Angela envisioned leaving school, making a nice dinner, drawing a bath, and when both the bath and food were done, she'd throw a log into the fireplace and enjoy her meal, her husband and a rare time of relaxation and bonding. She wanted to make an effort with Reese. She was willing, but God would need to do more work on her heart to keep the desire burning. "Have faith in God…" no matter what the circumstances, would be her new motto extracted from Mark 11:22. Uncomplicated clear advice is exactly what she needed to get out of her cloud of confusion and get back to the basics with her spirituality.

Angela entered the school office and greeted the secretary. "Is my dad around?" she asked.

"No, he's not, Angela. He's at an offsite meeting. What brings you by? Your sister stops by quite often, but we don't get to see you very much."

"You know, busy with this and that," she said, pushing open the gate separating the staff from the students. "Can I leave my dad a note?"

"Sure, go right on in," the secretary said, pointing to his office. She hated missing out on lunch with Dad, a rare treat. So much for her impromptu plan to swing by Wilmington Junior High and take him to lunch, but on the other hand, her evening with Reese could get started sooner. For the first time in months, she was excited about spending time with her husband and couldn't wait to get home.

Angela jotted a few lines onto the paper and placed it on the desk, next to the photo of her, Sylvia and Mom. A bit of her enthusiasm leaked out. Probably best that Dad wasn't in, anyhow. He wasn't fond of her springing up at the school unannounced, but she happened to be in the area for a training class that let out early and she figured lunch would be nice. She wanted to spend more time with him. Sylvia was his favorite, she was Mom's. They'd never admit to favoritism among any of their three children, including Donny, but if her parents wanted to pretend that both their remaining children had equal attention, fine. There was still enough love to go around and no one was complaining. Then why was she jealous? She was too embarrassed to tell Mom or anyone. She didn't need anybody telling her that being envious of her sister was wrong. She knew her thoughts weren't acceptable, but the fact was, she was jealous of Sylvia's education, her job, her group of dedicated friends, her adventurous spirit, her awards and, of course, her special bond with Dad, the one that no matter how hard she tried didn't shift in her direction.

"Where is he?" a woman shouted. Everybody in the suite of administrative offices could hear her. Angela was in her father's office using the phone when she heard the commotion but didn't surface immediately.

"Who?" the school's secretary asked at a normal voice level barely audible inside the principal's office.

"The principal. Who else would I be looking for in the principal's office?"

"Ma'am, this is not only the principal's office, this is the main office."

"Whatever. Where is Principal Reynolds?"

"And who are you?"

"I'm Ms. Scott, Latoya's mother. I don't have all day to be answering your questions. Where is the principal? I need to speak with him right now. Get him out here and stop wasting my time."

"Ms. Scott, Principal Reynolds is out of the building today."

Unable to stand the curiosity any longer, Angela approached the doorway in eye's view of the woman.

"Well, where is he, at another school? Because I can go to another school to see him."

"I'm not at liberty to tell you where he is, but if you want to leave a message stating the nature of your visit, I'm sure he'll get back to you when he returns tomorrow."

Angela considered going out to the counter to see if she could help but decided to wait unless summoned by the secretary. She knew how the school operated where she taught, but wasn't familiar with how problems were handled at Wilmington Junior High. She and her father never really talked about his role as principal. Wasn't a secret, but then it was, kind of in the sense that she didn't know much about the job her father had held for twenty-five years.

"Oh no, I'm not waiting until tomorrow."

"Then I don't think we'll be able to help you."

"Let me put it to you this way, he has one hour to get in touch with me." She scribbled a series of phone numbers on the crumpled receipt extracted from her purse, and laid it on top of the chest-level countertop separating the administrative team from the rest of the world. "Either he talks to me or he talks with the police." She leaned into the counter. "Personally for him, he will be better off if the police get to him first. He doesn't want to deal with me," she concluded, snatching the purse from the counter and stomping out of the office.

"What's going on with her?" Angela asked, emerging from her father's office.

"I'm not sure, but she sure was mad. I thought I'd have to call security. I hope she doesn't come back. My heart is racing."

"I know. She looked dangerous. There are times when these parents truly make us question our jobs. I'm glad my father wasn't here," Angela commented.

"He deals with irate parents often enough to be a pro at handling these kinds of matters."

"Maybe, but in situations like this it's hard for me to see him as a principal who deals with people like her. He's just Dad."

"I hate to tell you this, but you might as well expect parents, teachers and students to come in here outraged about something. It happens all the time. I admit that sometimes I get frightened, but mostly these are people venting. They're harmless."

"I hope so," Angela said without a great deal of confidence.

"See, aren't you glad you're in the exciting world of education where craziness thrives, especially for us here at WJHS."

"I guess we probably have the same challenges at my school, but as a teacher I spend most of my time in the classroom. I don't see what principals see. So long as you're not worried about my dad, I'm not, either."

"I'm not, at least not about Ms. Scott. Her daughter, Latoya, is a troubled young lady with problems. Your father has been working one-on-one with her since last spring. I'm not sure it's doing her any good, but your father is a wonderful man with a good heart. He reaches out to each of the students here and to their parents, whether they ask for help or not."

"That's just like my dad. He's a saint."

"Hard to find one of those, your father must be the last one."

Chapter 8

Sylvia peeled off her gloves and handed her coat to the attendant. "Reservations for two, last name, Reynolds," she told the hostess.

"Is the second person here?"

"Not yet, but he'll be here in a minute."

"Would you like to be seated now?"

"No, I'll wait for him to arrive," Sylvia said, stepping from the doorway. Waiting for him was no problem, the only man she didn't mind going out of her way to please. Her gaze was drawn to the gigantic water fountain shaped like a wall, as big and as tall as an executive desk with two credenzas stacked on top. Watching the water stream down, aimlessly, without a care or concern was enviable. A sense of freedom, unencumbered with the challenges of dating, of pleasing, of succeeding, of surviving.

"Would you like a drink from the bar while you're waiting?"

"No, thank you." She didn't need a beverage. She needed advice, a consoling word and peace of mind. She joined church last year in search of spiritual peace, but becoming a member and attending on occasion wasn't meeting her need. Thank goodness for Daddy.

Periodically she peeped between the blinds to see if he was coming down the street. Hurry, she thought. Her strength was fading. She needed an upbeat jolt. She wasn't depressed. Psychologists didn't get depressed. Melancholy is what she was, but the six-foot-tall man who had just walked through the door with skin like dusk was the cure.

"Daddy," she said with jubilation, as if he'd returned home from war.

"Hi, baby girl," he said, shedding his coat with her help. "I'm so sorry about being late. I never can find a parking place downtown."

"Why didn't you let the valet park for you?"

"The sign says twenty-five dollars. I'm not paying twenty-five dollars. Downtown Philadelphia is expensive. The most I have to pay in Delaware is ten."

"Oh, Daddy," she said, latching onto his arm, "I would have paid."

"And you know I wouldn't have let you."

"Well, we're not going to argue about the lunch bill. I'm paying. This is my treat and don't argue," she said, following the hostess to their seat positioned directly in front of the gigantic Buddha. "I'm paying and that's all there is to it. Besides, paying is the least I can do with you driving all the way downtown in the middle of a workday."

They took their seats and the hostess handed them menus. "Your waiter will be Doug and he'll be right over."

"Don't you worry about me," he said as the hostess left. "I was at an offsite meeting today, anyway." He opened the menu and perused his choices, lifting his glance long enough to say, "Wouldn't have mattered where I was. If my baby girl needs me, I'll be there. You know that, right?"

"Yes, I do," she said, letting the weight of her fears and the sadness about her recent breakup fall away. Daddy was there and she was safe.

Chapter 9

Angela sat on the floor of the family room, letting the warmth of the fireplace thaw her chilled heart. Reese deserved more, but when she made the effort, like tonight, he would do something stupid to dampen her hope, like not showing up and not bothering to call although he had gotten off work hours earlier.

She peered into the fireplace, mesmerized by the burning embers. What the two of them wanted from the relationship wasn't clear, but truth didn't minimize her discontent. If he could acknowledge that she was trying to make a difficult situation work. If he could give her some credit, because the average woman wouldn't have thought twice about refusing to take him back, but she had let him come home. Her spirit said it was right, the part of her that was maintaining a pure connection with the Lord through the Holy Spirit, but her battered emotions weren't as accepting or connected to what seemed right.

She stretched her body out across the rug, flat on her back, and stared at the ceiling. Speaking of faithful, why couldn't he be like her father? If her husband had qualities like him, then their marriage could survive into the double digits.

The ambience in her sanctum was broken when the phone rang. Angela answered the call to find her mother on the other end.

"Slow down, Mom, what did you say?"

"Your father has been arrested" were the words stinging her ears.

"I'm sorry, I didn't hear you correctly."

"Your father has been arrested."

The last time Angela heard crippling news of this magnitude was when they found out her oldest and only brother, Donny, had been killed during his first month overseas.

Chapter 10

The forty- or fifty-mile-per-hour speed limit didn't matter. Angela was determined to go as fast as her Nissan could travel. She zoomed in front of her parents' house, eclipsing the curb before plopping the wheels back onto level ground. The engine was shut off, keys removed and door open within seconds. She ran up the walkway to find the door already open.

"Mom, I got here as fast as I could. What's going on?"

"I told you, your father has been arrested. I tried calling Sylvia, but I haven't been able to reach her."

"I tried calling her, too, on my way over here and couldn't get her, either."

"I need to get to the police station downtown."

"Wait, Mom, why was Dad arrested? What happened?"

"I'm not sure, Angela. All I know is we were eating dinner and the police came banging on the door. You would have thought your father had killed somebody."

"But tell me, why was he arrested?"

"We don't have all the details, but it has something to do with a student named Latoya Scott."

"Latoya or her mother?"

"Latoya."

"Are you sure?"

"That's what the police said, why? I don't have time for all these questions. You can stay here and try to get in touch with your sister or you can go downtown with me," Mom said, clutching her purse and grabbing the doorknob. "I have to find out what's going on and see what I need to do to get him home."

"This must be a mistake," Angela said as they darted to the car.

"Well, it's an awfully big one, but the way those policemen banged on our door, I'm telling you, they meant business."

"Latoya's mother came to the school today, yelling and screaming, looking for Dad," Angela said, bolting the car away from the curb and into the street.

"What did she want?"

"We never found out. She left in a huff and I thought everything was fine until you called. I will say that she was mad and making threats right and left about how Dad better call her in an hour or he'd be sorry."

"It's no telling what lie that woman has cooked up."

"Has he mentioned their names before or anything about them?" Angela asked her mother, hoping to find a shred of information pointing to what could possibly be going on.

"No, your father doesn't bring work home, never has. That school takes on another life with him."

Angela suspected her mother's answer but had to ask.

"What I do know is that your father goes out of his way for those kids at the school, most of the time doing more for them than their parents, and this is the thanks he gets. After we get this trouble sorted out, I'm going to push him to retire. He's been with the school board ever since returning home from Vietnam. He'll be sixty this year. He hasn't been in trouble his whole life. He certainly doesn't need this kind of foolishness to deal with at this age. Take the back way, down through Rodney Square."

The Nissan was blowing through every yellow-and-already-turning-red light there was along the five-mile trek from the house to downtown, but somehow challenging her mother's route didn't seem wise. Let her give directions.

Angela maneuvered through the traffic and didn't truly use the brakes until she reached the parking garage.

"Wait, let me out here and you go ahead and park. Meet me inside," Mom instructed.

"Where do I go?"

"I'm not sure, but you'll figure it out," Mom said, wasting no time jumping from the car and starting her jaunt toward the courthouse entrance.

"I'll call Sylvia and leave her another message and then I'll be right in," she had to yell from the window. "Don't worry," she shouted, not confident her mother heard.

First floor, first row, prime parking spot. Since it was after eight, the court crowd was gone and the garage was empty. She didn't know if the lateness of the day was good or bad for her father's ability to get released tonight. He'd never spent time in jail. Probably the closest he'd ever come to ac-commodations anywhere near what she was imaging would have been the time he spent overseas. She cringed, thinking of what her father was probably enduring right at this minute, and fought back the tears, determined to stay strong and focused for her mother. She whizzed off a prayer, unable to move without asking God for some type of help, although she didn't have an overwhelming sense of confidence that her prayers were capturing the magnitude of the situation. Feeling distracted and not fully prayed up, but at least covered, she was ready to take on the courthouse and legal jargon that was sure to inundate her and Mom.

Oh, yes, there was still the matter of contacting Sylvia. Angela speed-dialed Sylvia one last time as she juggled her cell phone between her shoulder and ear on one side, purse, gloves and keys in her hands, while briskly bouncing toward the courthouse entrance, feet barely touching concrete. Sylvia answered. "Finally, I got you."

"I was out, what's up?"

"Daddy was arrested."

"What? You're lying."

"I wouldn't lie about something this serious. I wish it was a lie. Mom and I are at the police station downtown trying to get more information."

"I had lunch with him not more than seven hours ago. When did this happen?"

"Maybe in the last hour or so."

"Why was he arrested?"

"Not sure."

"Was he arrested or taken down for questioning? There is a big difference."

"I don't know, but you better get down here as soon as you can. I'm on my way inside with Mom. She's probably going crazy in there."

"You know Louise and Herbert can't be apart too long," Sylvia said.

Sylvia was right. The only time her parents had spent any significant time apart was during Dad's tour in Vietnam, a time neither parent spoke of. "Look, just get here if you're coming. I have to get inside," she said, entering the courthouse. Angela knew her mother was in torment and wanted her daughters by her side. "I'll see you when you get here."

She concluded the call and laid the phone, purse and gloves into a tray on the conveyor belt and walked through the security monitor preparing for the worst. Reese entered her thoughts. She could have called him, but the gesture would take time and energy, neither of which she felt like spending on him tonight. Wasn't her fault he hadn't come home on time and gotten the information firsthand. Besides, she didn't have details to share with him. When she knew more, maybe she would give him a call then, after her family was taken care of. Dad had to come first, although he had gone to lunch with Sylvia instead of her.

Chapter 11

The constant sound of keys and clanging wouldn't stop. The doors slamming shut behind her. She was descending deeper into the dungeon. There wasn't a smell, but the noise was deafening. The screams became louder, but they didn't overcome the heckling. What were they saying? She had to find him, cell after cell she passed with men whose backs were to her, faces hidden. She was scared but had to keep pressing on in order to find Daddy. He would protect her from these men, the ones who were luring her to the door of their cells by whispering her father's code words, "Daddy's girl." They were fooling her with kindness, but she knew they meant her harm. The jingling keys, screams and rattling of the bars became unbearable. She was swirling around in the middle of the hallway, separating one row of cells from the other. Her fear became unchained. Holding her head back and clutching her fists, she let out a wail that woke her instantly.

Sylvia shot straight up in the bed, scanning the room with high-speed glances, trying to get her bearings, a glimpse of familiarity, of security. Finally after three quick trips around the room with her piercing gaze, she caught the bedpost and gained composure and her sense of place. She threw the comforter back, catching the sheets in the process, drenched and clammy.

Not another nightmare, she thought. They'd been intense during her teen years, trailing off in college and not totally gone but infrequent during her twenties. She hadn't awakened in the middle of the night from a nightmare in at least five years. She had insomnia plenty of times, but once her body accepted sleep, an uninterrupted night ensued. At least she understood the source of tonight's nightmare. Having Daddy behind bars was a nightmare when she was awake let alone giving the demons of sleep an opportunity to get involved. She had to get him out, no matter the cost. He was the last man on earth capable of such a crime and he had to be freed. She would see to his release. After all, she was Daddy's girl, and he would be counting on her. She'd never let him down and wouldn't start now. She'd earned a Ph.D., the one he didn't get to finish because of his dedication to the family and unwillingness to put his responsibilities on hold in pursuit of his dream. Her degree was as much for him as the degree was for her. She'd used the same relentless determination earlier in the evening in retaining the best attorney on the East Coast.

Too tired to change the bed linen, she would opt for changing her soaked pajamas and shifting to the other side of the bed. Tomorrow she would have more energy for dealing with the bed and with Daddy. For now she would find a safe harbor in her sleep, a place becoming more difficult to find.

Chapter 12

The fitted suit was her one splurge item last year. With the separation, Angela hadn't gotten many opportunities to wear the suit, but today was important for the family to put on their best face, holding their heads high. The arrest of a prominent educator in the community, her father of all people, was bound to be big news in Wilmington, attracting journalists from New York to D.C. What would people think? What would they say? She tugged at the jacket, easing it down around her hips—perfect fit. Could the rest of the day go as smoothly? When she arrived in the courtroom with Mom at eight o'clock, it wasn't jammed yet, but a few reporters had already secured seats.

"Mom, are you all right? Can I get you some water or something?" Angela asked.

"No," she responded, "just your father."

Mom fumbled inside her handbag and pulled out a tissue.

It was hard to believe she had tears left. Angela had slept at her parents' house last night after leaving the courthouse around 1:00 a.m. At one point, Angela was sure the guards were going to physically remove Mom. She refused to leave, although the night jailer made it clear the arraignment would not occur before morning and Dad was spending the night. Mom refused to accept that her husband would be locked behind bars like an animal all night for nothing. He was an honorable man of distinction. He deserved better and Mom was determined to put up a fight. Mom had plenty of God in her. Finally, reason kicked in and she agreed to go home, with the understanding that she'd return first thing in the morning.

Sylvia was another story, a new babe in Christ who didn't go to church on a regular basis. She yelled and screamed and demanded access to Dad. She threatened to sue for false imprisonment. Her antics and connections probably got her in to see Dad when his own wife couldn't. Sylvia always got what she wanted. Nothing was off limits to her. Too bad what she wanted most of the time was more than she could handle or should have. Lord, Angela was letting this thing with Sylvia get to her again. The feeling was wrong. She knew it. Sylvia was her sister, and they were the only remaining children of Herbert and Louise Reynolds.

"You look tired," Sylvia said to Angela.

"I am. I didn't sleep well at all. I was too worried about Mom."

"Daddy, too?"

"That goes without saying," Angela said, pulling on her

suit. "I said 'Mom' because I stayed with her last night and it was hard hearing her crying all night."

"Well, you know her, she's strong. She can get through anything."

"That's because she knows the Lord," Angela said. "With Daddy's situation, we better all know somebody. These are serious charges." If Angela's comment was a dig at her not frequenting church as often, the comment had no effect.

Seeing her father shackled across the ankles with his hands cuffed was unbearable. Herbert Reynolds, a tower of strength, integrity and honor, chained like a ravenous animal wreaking havoc on a playground of children. What kind of mistake could allow a decent man like her father to be arrested for such a heinous crime? He was innocent. Yet, his words had slept with her through the night and rose with her this morning. When she was allowed to spend five minutes with him last night, he was insistent upon two things: one—that she tell Mom how much he loved her; and two—that he was innocent and would never do such a thing.

He kept repeating, "You have to believe me, baby girl." Right before she left the makeshift visiting room, he said, "I knew you wouldn't let me down. You're Daddy's girl. You always have been and always will be."

The words should have been comforting, consoling, re-assuring at a time of overwhelming doubt and fear, but oddly they seared the nugget of peace she'd acquired and began cutting into her insides, going deeper, claiming more than their share of her security.

There was no explanation for why she felt the way she did, but something was wrong and had been for as far back as

Sylvia could remember. She just didn't know what, and therapy hadn't discovered the culprit. Her last two therapists, the ones before Dr. Jan, had both taken the easy way out after hours of counseling netted zilch. They both resorted to the possibility that she'd been sexually abused by a male figure in her childhood and had most likely suppressed the trauma. Since her brother was dead and her father was the ideal dad, the old abuse theory held no validity. One day she'd figure out her problem, but for now, Daddy's problem was bigger. He'd been accused of committing indecent acts with a minor, a felony. How could anyone dare think he'd do such a thing?

Chapter 13

Every Reynolds that could get off work or that was out of work flooded into the courthouse. She preferred not telling them about the charges until Daddy was home, on his own turf, but Sylvia found out a few hours earlier that Angela had gone and called Aunt Mabel for information about an attorney last night. Just because her sons, Lee and Tony, stayed in trouble didn't make Aunt Mabel the premier source for good legal counsel. Once she got wind of the situation, apparently Aunt Mabel insisted on her lawyer showing up for the bail hearing, refusing to take no for an answer, at least from Angela. Sylvia was ready to call her back right before court and tell her not to bother bringing an attorney, but Mom disagreed, feeling badly about turning the attorney down without meeting him. Paying him was a waste of money, but what could Sylvia do about it now? Nothing.

Angela should have known better. Talking to Uncle Sam

would have been a better choice. He knew too well how to keep information away from his wife, or so the rumor went. First Aunt Mabel came, then Aunt Kay with Aunt Ida Mae. Seeing Aunt Ida Mae was always a calming feeling. She was the next best thing to having God standing at the defendant's table. Daddy needed all the help he could get. Sylvia couldn't offer religious support, but Aunt Ida Mae's surplus would comfortably offset her spiritual inadequacy.

"Sylvia Reynolds, I'm Lloyd Jackson," the attorney said, standing in the back of the courtroom wearing a dark gray suit that hung on him as if a tailor had made the suit specifically for him, falling perfectly on top of his high-polished black shoes. He had on a crisp white shirt with black-and-platinum cuff links that eclipsed his watch. Sylvia recognized the Rolex by its large face. His hair was short, groomed.

"This is my mother, Louise Reynolds, and my sister, Angela."

"Mrs. Reynolds, pleased to meet you," he said, shaking the hand of both Mom and Angela. "I spoke with you on the phone this morning."

"Yes, thank you for coming down from New York on such short notice."

"Glad I could help."

"And you are?" Mom asked Aunt Mabel's attorney.

"Jim Logan, Mrs. Reynolds," he said, extending his hand after letting go of his briefcase, which plopped to the floor, making a thud. When he bent over, his polyester-looking suit was stretched to capacity in critical areas. His hair was long and in need of a thorough washing. His shirt was paper thin and she could see his chest. His shoes appeared comfortable, although worn. "I came at the request of Mabel Reynolds."

"Thank you for coming to the bail hearing, Mr. Logan," Mom said, and was then pulled in different directions by several family members.

Right before nine, Lee showed up with one of his girl-friends and walked up to the attorney.

"Hey, Mr. Logan," he said, extending his hand.

They shook hands, and the attorney responded, "Good to see you, Mr. Reynolds."

"Good to see you, too, on this side of the table," he said, chuckling along with the attorney and a few others, excluding Angela, Mom and her. Laughing wasn't an option for them until Daddy was out. "So, you're going to represent my uncle?"

"We haven't made a decision yet," Sylvia said, jumping in. "Attorney Jackson, you'll be the lead counsel for the hearing." Aunt Mabel and Mr. Logan both looked baffled. She didn't know why. Aunt Mabel might have forced her lawyer on the family, but his tenure on Daddy's case was going to be brief. He should have saved the parking lot fee and just parked out front with the motor running and car door open. Mom could be polite if she wanted, but this was serious business. She didn't need a small-town jackleg attorney defending her father. The charges he was facing could land him in prison for the rest of his life. For a fifty-nine-year-old man, a twenty-year sentence could easily make the dire prospect a reality.

"Who are you?" Lee asked the other attorney.

"I'm Lloyd Jackson," he said, extending his hand to Lee, who reciprocated, surprisingly.

"He was recommended by a friend of mine out of New York," Sylvia responded.

"Oh, New York, the Big Apple. What, you must be like a Johnnie Cochran or somebody."

Sylvia glanced her sister's way and knew Angela was probably thinking the same thing: how fast could they hide under the table?

"Mom, Uncle Herbert has the dream team, right here in Wilmington," Lee said, getting loud as his mother inched into the crowd. "I should have known you'd go big time on us, cuz. You're no joke. You know how to take care of business," he added, trying to hug her. "Where's that husband of yours?" he asked Angela.

"He's at work. He couldn't get off."

Sylvia was amused. She knew work was a foreign concept to Lee, at least for more than a few months. One year he worked long enough to qualify for unemployment and Aunt Mabel bragged for the next six months, until the funds ran out, as if he'd cashed in on a seven-figure retirement plan. Lee was tacky at times but overall harmless. She liked him, a lot. They were a year apart and had basically grown up together. Donny was her big brother, but with six years' difference in their ages, she was in school with Lee all the time and he became her surrogate big brother. Everybody in the neighborhood and at school knew Lee and Sylvia Reynolds were cousins. He was always in and out of trouble, even back then, but still, the other students knew that messing with Sylvia meant messing with Lee, and they weren't about to go there. The other kids thought he was crazy. Sylvia never saw him as crazy. He was tough, almost like a bully, and refused to back down to anybody except Aunt Mabel. Tony was older than Lee by seven years and didn't interact with

Sylvia much, other than times he babysat her after school when she was a young girl. He'd watched Angela, too. When Donny started sixth grade, he took the bus to school and stayed after to play football and basketball, and any kind of sport he could. Afterward he got to stay at his friend's house until Mom picked him up on the way home from work, at least that's what Mom and Daddy said. Sylvia couldn't remember. Childhood was pretty much a blur, oddly enough, seeing that her adult memory was keen.

"Will the court come to order," the bailiff commanded. Seats were filled and the chitchat stopped. The all-rise-for-the-judge followed by the be-seated routine. A door on the side of the courtroom opened. There stood Daddy, chained around the wrists like a slave, not the same adventurous man she'd introduced to seaweed salad and sushi yesterday at lunch. He didn't fully embrace the concept of eating bite-size pieces of raw fish with rice, but Daddy did try the rolls with smoked salmon and found them enjoyable. Her broken heart threatened to leap forward, to surround him with a protective covering. He hobbled to the table, negotiating his pride and cuffs. The stubble on his chin, the darkness in his pupils, and the bags under his eyelids spoke volumes. She could feel his shame, and in an effort to spare him, she wouldn't make eye contact. That way he couldn't be forced to acknowledge his temporary reality or the bitter sensation of fear.

The judge spoke a list of legal jargon, which amounted to Daddy being ridiculously accused of sexually violating a child. It was difficult deciding which was more tragic: having him chained and sitting in a cell, or grappling with the thought that a child could make such an accusation about her father and people would remotely believe there was any truth in it. "In the matter of Herbert Reynolds, how do you plead?" the judge asked.

"Not guilty," Attorney Jackson responded.

"So entered. Then there's the matter of bail," the judge stated, perusing the paperwork in front of her.

"Your Honor," the prosecutor said, standing up, "we're asking for a million-dollar bond."

Daddy's attorney began countering when the judge interjected.

"That's unusually high," she said, peering at the prosecutor. "Any reason?"

"Yes, Your Honor. Mr. Reynolds is a prominent individual in this city."

"Which is why the bail should be more reasonable. His family, his job and his reputation are based in this area," Attorney Jackson pointed out.

"He could be a flight risk, Your Honor."

"My client is not a man of substantial means. He is, however, a highly regarded individual in the community. He does not pose a flight risk," Attorney Jackson said.

"I disagree, Your Honor."

"Bail is set at $250,000."

"Your Honor, we request that the bail be raised. The defendant is being charged with the sexual assault of a minor."

"Your Honor, my client is an upstanding citizen, a decorated military officer with no priors. We ask for a bail of $100,000."

"Your Honor, we have physical evidence."

"Bail stands at $250,000," she concluded, slamming the gavel onto the wooden pallet.

"Herbert," Mom cried out, clawing at his jumper as the bailiff led him from the defendant's table. "Don't worry, Honey, I'll get you out. Oh, Lord, take care of him," she wailed, covering her mouth but not the pain reflected on her face.

Chapter 14

The bunch spilled into the hallway outside the courtroom.

"The first question we have to address is whether we need two attorneys," Sylvia had to ask, unimpressed with Mr. Logan's demeanor and double-vented suit.

"He's our family attorney," Aunt Mabel said.

"I don't know you, sir," Aunt Mabel said to Attorney Jackson, "but, Louise, I know what Mr. Logan can do. I'm sorry, Mr.—" She paused, searching for his name as if it would fall from the ceiling.

"Jackson," Angela reminded Aunt Mabel.

"Jackson, right. I'm sorry, Mr. Jackson, but we're all family here and we look out for one another." She shifted her conversation to Mom. "Louise, you might want to keep Mr. Logan. He's local. He knows the judges in Wilmington and how the system works down here. No offense to you, Mr. Jackson, but I'm thinking down the road."

"No offense taken," he responded, direct, commanding.

Sylvia continued being impressed with Attorney Jackson. Considering their other options made her cringe inside. Mr. Logan stood there, trying to hold back a ridiculous smirk, probably because he didn't realize who was making the ultimate decision and who was going to pay the bill. Mr. Logan could keep listening to Aunt Mabel if he wanted. The best he could hope for was getting paid for his few minutes of service, even though he hadn't spoken a word during the hearing and added no value. Because of Aunt Mabel, Sylvia knew that she and Mom were going to have to throw a couple of hundred dollars away paying a so-called family attorney. They'd pay him for the day and say goodbye. No way was Aunt Mabel's prepaid legal attorney, who was provided by benefits from her uncle's job, going to hold her father's innocence in his hand. For all she knew, Mr. Logan was defending a jaywalking defendant yesterday.

"Mr. Logan has kept my sons out of prison more times than I care to admit."

"He sure has," Lee substantiated, with what couldn't possibly be a tone of pride.

"Maybe we should keep them both, Mom?" Angela suggested.

"We don't need to pay two attorneys. Attorney Jackson has assured me he is comfortable with the Delaware system," Sylvia clarified.

"But you're from New York. Don't you need a license in Delaware to be a lawyer here?" Aunt Mabel asked, as if she was making the decision and paying the bill.

"My firm is based in New York, but I'm also on the bar in other states, including Delaware."

Angela wanted to rub her aunt's face in the attorney's response, but there was no need. If his stature didn't indicate his abilities, then his credentials did.

"He also comes highly recommended as a leading criminal defense attorney." Mr. Logan kept quiet, as he should. At times, it felt as if he was invisible, the last attribute Sylvia wanted with an attorney representing her father in a felony case. She needed a lawyer who could take charge and make his presence known, not someone whom Aunt Mabel could dominate as she did with Tony and Lee.

"I'm not sure. What do you think, Mr. Jackson and Mr. Logan, about working together?" Mom asked.

Attorney Jackson spoke first. "Mrs. Reynolds, I will do whatever you like. I'm sure my colleague here can serve as excellent representation for your husband. Whoever you get, make sure they've handled a high-profile case like this before and have the track record you're looking for. I have that record."

"What about you, Mr. Logan, how many cases have you defended like this?" Sylvia asked.

"Only one and we were able to plea-bargain my client down to a second-degree felony, which amounted to a reduced maximum sentence of seven years instead of twenty-eight."

"I'm sure you represent many guilty defendants, but my father is innocent. So, plea-bargaining is not an option," Sylvia said, leaving no room for doubt and then turning toward Attorney Jackson. "What's your record?"

"I have defended fifteen high-profile cases. Fourteen of

those resulted in full acquittals and one was a plea bargain with the charges reduced to a third-degree felony or what you'd call a Class A misdemeanor. The sentence was time served, twelve hundred hours of community service and five years of probation."

"I like your odds better," Sylvia said.

"Me, too," Angela agreed.

"Mr. Logan, I'm sorry for taking your time this morning, but it sounds as if we've made a decision. We're going to use Mr. Jackson," Mom confirmed.

"I understand. Good luck to your family," he said, preparing to leave.

"Mr. Logan, I'd like to settle my bill with you right now for today's hearing. Can I write you a check?"

"No need, Mrs. Reynolds, it was my pleasure," he said, doing a round of handshakes. "If you need my assistance with any other legal matters, don't hesitate to contact me. I have enjoyed working with your family."

"Thank you for retaining me," Attorney Jackson interjected after concluding his professional courtesies with Mr. Logan. "Mrs. Reynolds, I will work hard on your husband's behalf. As you saw, I got the bail as low as I could. As we discussed this morning, we'll need ten percent of the bail amount set in order to get Mr. Reynolds released and have him free until the trial," he directed to Mom and Sylvia. "Mrs. Reynolds, you told me on the phone this morning that you could pay up to $20,000 in cash for bail. Will you be able to secure another $5,000?"

Aunt Mabel jumped in as if Daddy was her husband and said, "We can all put in a little bit. There's no problem coming up with $5,000. Sam and I will put in $500, up to a thousand if you need it."

"Thank you, Aunt Mabel," Angela groveled.

"Thanks, Aunt Mabel, but I'll pay the difference," Sylvia said, unwilling to let anyone do more than she was going to do as Herbert Reynolds's daughter.

"Oh, that's right, I forgot. You have Oprah-money. I guess you don't need our help. You don't need our attorney or our money."

"I'm sorry, Aunt Mabel, but that's my father locked up. I'm not taking any chances."

"Wait a minute now. I'm making the decisions today," Mom interrupted. "Thank you, everybody, for your help, but right now I have one thing on my mind, getting Herbert out. Nothing else is more important to me right now. Mr. Jackson, who do I make the check out to?"

"Mom, I have the money," Sylvia reassured her.

"I have some, too," Angela added.

"I'm not worried about the money. Whatever I don't have the house will cover the rest."

"You don't want to put your house up," Aunt Mabel said.

"I sure will without blinking an eye. Our house is paid for and it's not worth a nickel to me if I can't use it to save my husband."

"But not your house, we're family. We can help. Sam and I have been there for you from the time your kids were born. We were there for you when Herbert was gone for months at a time during Vietnam. We didn't have any money back then, but Sam came over every chance he got to help out. We're always going to help, that's what families do for one another."

Aunt Kay's gaze wandered around the room, appearing to avoid contact with Aunt Mabel and Mom.

"If God blessed us with one house, He'll bless me with another. He will supply all my needs. I'm not worried. Just let me know, Mr. Jackson, what me and my daughters need to do to get my husband home today," she said emphatically.

"Since money is not a factor for the bail, I'll get the paperwork under way."

"Wonderful, we'll wait here and Herbert can ride home with us."

"Mrs. Reynolds, posting bail could take a while."

"How long?" Mom asked, with an anxious tone in her voice.

"I hope to have him out by midafternoon."

"I'm not sure why it takes so long, but I'll wait right here at the courthouse with you."

"No, Mom, let's go home," Angela said.

"I agree, Mom," Sylvia added, fully expecting a protest.

"I'm not going anywhere."

"Mrs. Reynolds, I will need you here for the financial transaction with the bail bondsmen."

"Then I'm staying, too," Sylvia quickly jumped in to say.

"No, you're not. I want you to go to the house and get something ready for your father to eat. He's going to be hungry and tired. I'm going to take care of this."

Angela didn't move and Sylvia couldn't.

"Go ahead, now," Mom said, embracing each daughter one at a time. "I am not alone. The Lord is with me. Now, go on home and take the rest of the family with you," she said with a dab of humor.

She didn't want to leave Mom there alone, and she definitely didn't feel right leaving Daddy, but Sylvia did as her mother requested, at least today.

Chapter 15

Angela wanted Reese by her side, at her parents'. The reason was simple, to keep the family from suspecting they were having problems. Keeping up appearances wasn't so bad if she really tried, and tried she did.

"I was planning to wait until Herbert got in, but we don't know how much longer this is going to take," Aunt Kay said, drawing attention to the clock displaying four-thirty.

"Posting bail money can take all day," Aunt Mabel said.

Poor Aunt Mabel was very familiar with the process, because of Lee and Tony, but thank goodness they had parents willing to bail them out each time. Some parents would have left them to figure out life and circumstances on their own, but not the Reynoldses. That's what she loved about her family. They were dependable, no matter what the circumstances. Angela breathed a sigh of comfort, looking around the house, seeing the family packed in like sardines, each one offering their version of support, some in the way of finances, others in kind words, others with their presence. Reese needed to see, to taste the sweet feeling of a family, a unit that knew how to stick together, to work out their problems together, instead of turning to outsiders. Angela leaned back against the refrigerator and folded her arms, believing nothing would ever rip her family apart, which was more than she could say about her marriage.

"Angela," she heard Sylvia calling out, "your cell phone is ringing."

"Grab it for me," she said, maneuvering around people and furniture, making her way down the center hallway to her parents' room. "What are you doing back here?" she asked Sylvia, who had the cell phone to her ear.

"Take care of yourself. Hold on, here's your wife," Sylvia said, handing the phone over.

At least she was somewhat isolated from the crowd. Hopefully Sylvia would leave the room, too, and give her complete privacy, but her sister didn't budge, lying across the bed with the remote propped on the side of her thigh and the TV on Mute.

"Hello, hon," she said, cringing inwardly and knowing the pet name didn't feel or sound legitimate, given how upset she was at him, had been for several weeks. It wasn't anything Reese had said or done today, or yesterday, or the day before that. Her disappointment in him was an everyday occurrence. "Are you coming over?" she asked, trying to ignore Sylvia's presence in her conversation with a husband she was barely talking to at home. "Dad should be home any minute now. Everybody's here, except you." She couldn't stand the intrusion any longer. "Sylvia, do you mind giving me a little privacy?"

"Girl, go ahead and talk to your husband. I'm not paying attention to your conversation. I'm thinking about my daddy, not what you and Reese are talking about."

"Please, just for a few minutes."

"Oooh, what's so secretive between the two of you that I need to leave?" she muttered, sliding to the foot of the bed and then standing up, tossing the remote back onto the bed. "Just tell him to come on over here. Then you can get off the phone and go back out there and entertain your people."

"Please, Sylvia?"

"Hello," Angela heard blaring from the cell phone.

"Hold on, Reese."

"I can't believe you're sending me out there with Aunt Mabel. That's just downright mean." Sylvia dipped her head in front of the mirror and touched a few of her twisty braids and pulled her jeans up, tucking in her shirt. "You owe me," she echoed, exiting into the hallway.

"Hello, Angela," she heard Reese calling out to her again, louder this time.

"Thank you," she muttered to Sylvia without actually yelling the words into the phone.

Sylvia turned back around and stuck her head in the doorway. "If she says one thing to me, it's going to get ugly." Before Sylvia walked away again, she asked, "Is Denise here yet? Because if she is, I'll be okay."

"The two of you act more like sisters than cousins." Closer than the two of them, she felt but refused to accept it as truth. Even if Sylvia and Denise were sorority sisters, Sylvia was her blood sister, the only sibling she had left. They had a bond no one else shared. They were the children of Herbert and Louise Reynolds, which made them both special. In a tone that carried an edge of affection not often evidenced between the sisters, Angela said to Sylvia, "Aunt Kay and Aunt Ida Mae are in there. Go ahead, you'll be fine. They'll be your reinforcements."

"Thank goodness for Aunt Ida Mae. She's the sensible one."

"Aunt Kay, too."

"Most of the time, but you know she can work a nerve, too. You better take that call before your man hangs up on you. I hope you don't put him off like that all the time," she said, leaving the doorway this time and not turning back.

"Okay, I'm back." She didn't hear a peep. "Reese, are you still there?"

"Yes, but I shouldn't be. You've had me holding for about five minutes."

"There are a lot of people here and it's crazy around here."

"Of course, what else. I don't know if I should come over there if it's that crazy."

"I need you."

"Really, you need me, for real?"

"I said it, didn't I?"

"We've both said a lot of things that I'm not so sure we really mean."

"Yes, I need you. Having my father arrested is tough on me and my mother and my family. I need as much support as I can get."

"Then I'll be there in twenty minutes, and, Angela…"

"Yes."

"I'm glad to know you need me. It means a lot. I was beginning to think you didn't want or need me."

"I'll see you in twenty minutes" was the most she could offer, not wanting to slip into a deep and possibly disruptive conversation. He was on his way, let that do for now.

"Have you eaten?"

"No, I'm not hungry. I can't eat," she told him.

"You have to. Letting your body run down and getting sick won't help your father or us. I'll stop by Caprioti's or Boston Market and pick up something to eat. I'll get enough for everybody."

"Thanks, Reese. I'll see you soon," she said, ending the call. Thanks to the Lord, she was feeling a bit at ease. Given the gravity of the obstacle sitting in front of her family, any tidbit of peace was priceless. Thank goodness she didn't have to deal with Dad's situation and the problem with Reese at the same time. She could have said thank-you, Jesus, for answering her prayer, but recognizing she hadn't sincerely prayed for reconciliation in the marriage for more than a month meant she couldn't hypocritically take claim. Family in the kitchen might hear her quoting scriptures or sitting in church, but they didn't know the battered condition of her walk of faith. God did, and there was no sense in faking with Him.

Chapter 16

Angela owed her retributions. She could have stayed camped out in her parents' room watching TV away from the crowd where her aunt, the ringleader, was hosting the show. Whenever Daddy got home, she could usher Aunt Mabel out of the house and finally have some peace and quiet. Aunt Ida, Aunt Kay, her uncles and even Lee and his girlfriend could stay. They were funny and overall good company at a time when she didn't really want to be alone, but Aunt Mabel never knew when to shut up.

"This is a downright mess. Does anybody know the little girl or her mother?" Aunt Ida asked.

No one answered. "Lee, you don't know them? I thought they might run in your crowd," Aunt Kay said.

"Oh, no, Lee doesn't hang around any trash like that. Oh, no," Aunt Mabel answered for him. It was a wonder Lee knew how to burp and wipe his own behind. If it wasn't so shameful, she'd probably still be doing those basic functions for him.

"I thought you didn't know her, Mabel," Aunt Kay asked.

"I don't, but I know her kind. Her mama's probably the type who doesn't watch her fast-tailed daughter, and one day she pops up pregnant and they try to pin it on the first successful man they can find with a good-paying job."

"Is this girl pregnant?" Aunt Kay asked with obvious concern.

"I don't know, she might be," Aunt Mabel couldn't wait to say. That was her routine, start a conversation, draw her listeners in like a spider, get them caught up, and then release a seed of gossip or plant a flat-out lie, letting her listeners be the ones to give her tale life.

"Nobody said the girl was pregnant," Sylvia clarified, smashing the rumor.

"What do we know?" Aunt Kay asked.

"Not much, not until the attorney gets a chance to talk with Dad and review the evidence, I guess."

"I don't know what evidence they could have. Daddy didn't do this," Sylvia said.

"You never know what kind of evidence they make up. Like I said, these fast-tailed, desperate girls lock in on a paycheck and that's all they see. They don't care if their lies ruin a person's reputation or destroy his family life. They don't care, so long as they can get what they want."

"Which is what?" poor Aunt Kay asked, being pulled into the web.

"Money or the man. I know what I'm talking about. Women are always trying to pin their pregnancies on Lee and Tony, trying to get some money."

"Lee, do you have any money?" Sylvia couldn't resist the temptation.

"Not like you, cuz, but I have a little change from time to time. It seems like they always catch me when I'm getting my unemployment checks. Mama's right, they get wind of that good money rolling in and try to get a piece of it, but I'm too smart for that. I protect myself."

"How good is your protection? You have five kids, and they're not all by the same woman," Sylvia said.

"Yeah, you're right, cuz. I got caught a few times, but I was young then."

"Weren't your twins born last year?"

"Man, cuz, you should have been a lawyer. You don't miss anything."

"Aunt Mabel, when are you going to make Lee and Tony get married?"

"Here is my fiancée right here," Lee said, boasting with pride and pointing toward his friend. She giggled, believing his gesture was sincere and unique. With Lee's five illegitimate children and four baby mamas, many young women had heard those same words, and none of them had lasted long enough to attend two consecutive family reunions.

"Oh, I didn't know you were engaged. Congratulations," Sylvia told the young lady whose name she couldn't remember and how could she? The women in Lee's life were like the local commuter train, somebody getting on and off every five minutes. "Let me see the ring," she said, inching to them.

"I didn't get the ring yet," Lee responded quickly. "But she's the one for me. Isn't that right, Nina? We're getting ready to settle down. Nina has a big house already. I'm going to get custody of my other children and I'm going to take care of my family."

"I'm ready for my boys to settle down. It's time now."

Comical is what Sylvia was feeling. Among Aunt Mabel's sons, the term fiancée was tossed about glibly and carried no significance. Nina wasn't aware of the code, but Sylvia knew the term meant living with the woman with no intention of getting married. One day, if ever Lee purchased a ring and set a date, then she'd take his fiancée gesture seriously. In the meantime Nina was just another girlfriend providing a roof over Lee's head so he wouldn't have to stay with Aunt Mabel and Uncle Sam.

"It's getting late, and I need to run a few errands," Aunt Mabel said, standing. "I'll probably come back after Sam gets off. I know he'll want to come by and see his brother."

"I need to go, too," Aunt Kay said, standing up and stretching her spine. "Aunt Ida, you want me to give you a ride home?"

"That would be wonderful."

As the house emptied, Aunt Ida said, "Call me when they get home and don't hesitate to let me know if you need anything." The words of kindness stirred a soft emotional spot and produced a tear. "Everything's going to be all right. We have to carry one another's burdens and struggles, that's what a family is all about. We'll get through this, don't you worry. We serve a risen Savior who is bigger than any court case."

"That's right," Aunt Mabel and Aunt Kay reiterated.

Watching all of them finally leave wasn't as refreshing as she'd hoped. She stood in the doorway, shivering inside from the fear of what was to come more so than from the forty-degree January weather. Before she could reenter her parents' place, Reese eased his SUV up to the curb across the street.

"Angela, your husband is here," she called out to her sister, wishing the same words would have applied to her about a man showing up with a supportive heart and gentle words.

Chapter 17

Daddy was free on bail and had been for the past week. He had to be worn out, but didn't let it show. Herbert and Louise Reynolds stepped off the elevator and down the hallway, arm in arm, with strength and dignity, leading their family into uncharted waters. The rest of the Reynoldses would have come but they hadn't been invited. Daddy had the support he needed, the three women who loved him unconditionally and had no doubts about his innocence. This was a protective moment. Sylvia didn't want people, including family, surrounding Daddy to raise a peep of doubt or voice an iota of negativity. She didn't expect him to admit the gravity the charges had on his soul, but Sylvia realized he was devastated. That's why she had to protect him. Doubters had to be kept at a distance, no exceptions.

They entered the office in the bank building, finding

Attorney Jackson positioned behind the tightly stuffed four-person table with no extra chairs.

"Come in, Mr. Reynolds, Mrs. Reynolds," he said, shaking each of their hands and concluding with the daughters, Angela last.

"Please call us Herbert and Louise."

"Herbert and Louise, pleasure to see you again. Please have a seat," he invited. "I apologize for the cramped quarters, but this is the only available shared office space within five miles of the train station and the courthouse. I hope this arrangement will be acceptable to you?"

The Reynolds family agreed in unison. In spite of the challenges her family faced, Sylvia couldn't help but acknowledge and appreciate in her own way how the Reynoldses united time and time again during a crisis.

"I have reserved the room for two hours," he said, setting his Mont Blanc pen on top of his designer Coach portfolio. So, let's get down to business, Herbert, shall we? I want to talk with you first, answer any questions you might have, and then I'll bring my legal assistant in to scribe," he said to Daddy, and then turned to let his gaze rest on the Reynolds women. "Ladies, Louise, can I please ask you to take a seat in the reception area out front while I speak with Herbert?"

"Why do we have to leave?" Sylvia questioned without a moment of hesitation, not giving Mom and Angela a chance to respond.

"It's to protect your father's rights."

"I don't mind if they stay," Daddy admitted.

"Herbert, I believe you and your family retained me with the expectation that I would provide the very best defense possible, which means I can't interview you and talk about strategy with your family present. I apologize in advance, but I have to protect his rights."

"I don't understand. How would our presence put him in jeopardy?"

"Several reasons, Louise. One, you may become a witness for the prosecution."

"I would never testify against Herbert."

"You're right, as his wife you wouldn't have to, but your daughters could be subpoenaed by the prosecutor. So, I couldn't have them privy to details of our defense."

"But I have nothing to hide. I'll tell them everything, anyway," Daddy said.

"That might be so, but having them present during our interview would jeopardize our attorney-client privilege."

"What does that mean?" Mom asked.

"Louise, that's the legal way of saying no matter what's said in this room between Herbert and me, the content is confidential and can't be used against him in the court-room. The concept is meant to encourage open and honest communication between client and attorney. Since the privilege doesn't cover your daughters, any information discussed in their presence becomes potential ammunition for the prosecutor, and that's certainly not what we want."

"Mr. Jackson, we trust your judgment," Mom said, lifting Daddy's hand and holding his in hers. "However you want to proceed is fine with us. Between the Lord's guidance and your experience, justice will prevail and my husband will be vindicated from all charges."

"Please call me Lloyd."

"Out of respect for your position, I prefer to call you Mr. Jackson," Mom said, and Dad nodded in agreement. "We'll wait for you in the hallway."

"Thank you," Attorney Jackson said.

Sylvia meandered down the hall not completely convinced leaving her father alone was the best decision. She gave the situation a little more thought and barreled back down the hall.

"Where are you going?" Mom insisted from a few steps behind, with Angela trailing behind her.

"Daddy needs us."

"I trust Mr. Jackson. I believe he's protecting your father. We need to wait and let the lawyer do his job."

"We can look to him for guidance and direction, Mom, but we should be a part of all major decisions," Sylvia conveyed.

"You picked one of the best criminal attorneys on the East Coast with a great record. How come you can't trust him to do his job? If he's as good as we think he is, then we should listen to him. He'll be good for Dad's case."

Sylvia had no doubt. His win-loss record was impeccable and he was worth every penny if he could ensure a victory, but he wasn't family to Daddy, not like they were. He didn't love him like they did, like she did. Daddy's freedom was too important to completely surrender their decision-making ability to anyone, even to a distinguished lawyer such as Attorney Jackson. She burst into the room, greeted by Attorney Jackson's astonished look. "I'm sorry, Mr. Jackson, but we need to be here. We're willing to deal with the consequences."

"I understand your desire to support Herbert and that's commendable, but my legal advice is to let me conduct my interview with him alone. Otherwise I can't represent him."

"But I have a lot of questions," Angela said.

No, she didn't have questions, Sylvia thought, unless Angela had money to contribute. At three hundred dollars an hour, petty comments were out of the question. Forget about that for the moment and stick to the key issue. "Daddy, do you want us to stay?"

"Of course I do."

"But it's not what we want. It's what Mr. Jackson recommends," Mom stepped up and said.

"Mr. Jackson, is there any way they can be present?" Daddy appealed.

"Okay, here's what we can do. I'm willing to answer general questions related to the process, but I must reiterate, discussing details of the case in open forum, even with family members, will put your father at risk. I know it seems like I'm being incredibly stern with you, but this really is in your father's best interest. One reason for my success in the courtroom is that I don't take chances outside the courtroom. I plan to put forward the best possible defense for Herbert, and I will need your help by supporting him outside of the interview room and not talking about the case with others. Even an innocent phrase said in jest can be damaging."

"We will watch our tongues," Mom responded with firmness, glancing at both her daughters as if to say, "I've spoken and that's the end of that."

"Fine," Sylvia acquiesced. "Has the trial date been set?"

"The trial is set for May 15."

"That soon, that's only four months away," Angela stated.

"And they may feel like the longest four months of your life leading up to the trial, but we'll be ready."

"Is that the only time we'll have to go to court?" Angela asked.

"There will be a pretrial hearing, but nothing to be concerned about. May is the date you should concentrate on."

"How difficult are cases like this?" Sylvia asked.

"Any case can be challenging."

"But my husband is innocent, so it seems like the case should be easier."

"Whenever a minor is concerned, there is an added layer of complexity."

"Herbert has an impeccable reputation in the school system and in the community."

"Of course your stellar reputation is a plus, but we'll have to strike the right balance between presenting your impeccable reputation without demonizing the minor. Some jurors might take offense."

"What kind of evidence does Latoya have?" Dad asked.

"The D.A's office is still building its case, but as of right now they only have her statement."

"That's good, right?" Angela asked the attorney while cutting her glance toward Sylvia.

"That's as far as I want to go with discussing the details of the case, agreed?"

"Agreed," Sylvia responded.

"But I still have a lot of questions," Angela interjected.

"We can jot our questions down and forward them to him later," Sylvia recommended firmly.

The look in Angela's eyes said she wanted to retort but was backing off, thank goodness. Disagreements in the presence of a high-priced attorney were too costly for words.

"I never thought Latoya would do anything like this," Daddy whispered.

Watching the light in his eyes dim created an indescribable ache in her heart, which poured out in the form of a few tears. Daddy reached out to her. "I'm sorry, Sylvia."

"Don't worry about me, Daddy, I'm fine."

"My daughter is a well-known psychologist in New Jersey. She's won the Governor's Award for her work two years in a row. Angela here is a teacher, and a good one."

"I've testified in other criminal cases as an expert witness. If you need me to testify, I will."

"We're all willing to testify," Angela added.

"Thank you for the offers, but I wouldn't be able to use your testimonies. The prosecutor would attack your opinions on the stand because of your established bias. You wouldn't be viewed as credible."

"But I have a strong background in my field."

"And that's not in question. What I mean about credibility is that you will be viewed as someone willing to say or do whatever it takes to save your father. Using you or any other family member would be too risky on cross examination. However, I would love to use your psychological opinion in establishing profiles for both an abuser and accuser, if you're willing."

"Of course," she said in a renewed, chipper voice. "Whatever you need me to do, consider it done."

"Wouldn't she be in a conflict of interest? I can imagine some members of the jury saying 'but that's his daughter,'" Angela asked.

"Good question. I will have other psychology and child-molestation experts in court. Sylvia can help behind the scenes. Your background will be very helpful to us. We have to capitalize on your credentials and standing in the psychology community."

Angela slumped back in her chair, while Sylvia pulled in closer to the table, waiting for the next ray of hope to keep her pumped about her father's inevitable acquittal. Attorney Jackson was correct—whatever she had to do, she'd do to get Daddy released.

Chapter 18

Sylvia wanted to turn down the dinner invitation but Karen refused to let her decline.

"What would make a girl lie about your father like that?" Karen asked.

"I have no idea."

"Her mother's boyfriend probably molested her and she's afraid to tell on him. So, she picks a nice man like your father to blame."

Sylvia had heard the word *molested* spoken hundreds of times from her patients, in continuing education classes, psychology seminars, discussed among peers during analysis, but the word never sounded as heavy and as personal as right now, causing her to tense.

"I can't imagine being molested, by my father, mother's boyfriend, neighbor, cousin or anybody else," Karen said.

"Happens all the time. You'd be surprised at how many children are violated and the offense is never reported."

"Right, and that's how we get all of these screwed-up adults. They keep the secret and then they grow up and pass the secret on to someone else."

"I don't know Latoya's story, and I'm mad about her lying on my father, but what courage for her to step forward. Clearly this is a cry for help."

"Or a way to get her mother off her behind for being promiscuous. Some of these teenagers are sexually active by choice and looking for an excuse to justify their promiscuity."

"Perhaps, but I see this as a cry for help. Latoya has a problem, and I wonder what it is?"

"Maybe, but why did she have to drag your father into her problem?"

The discussion stayed on a light note, nothing too heavy. Dinner was short and Sylvia was home climbing the stairs to her bedroom. She had paid her dues for the evening and welcomed sleep or at least the idea of resting.

Two clinical psychology periodicals, hot chocolate, the Bible, the first chapter of the *Iliad* and meditation didn't pack the same sleep potency as they had two months ago when her insomnia resurfaced. She didn't know which was worse, not being able to get to sleep or getting to sleep and being tormented with nightmares. Daddy's arrest had set off a chain of emotions she couldn't harness. As long as she lived, the image would plague her soul, seeing him sitting across a table handcuffed and shackled the night she saw him in jail.

Sylvia sat up in the bed with her back against the headboard. She turned the TV on using the remote and surfed the channels, not finding much at 1:00 a.m. but refusing to give up. Latoya Scott kept gnawing at her. What was she like? Was she a fast teen who'd lied about Daddy to cover her own promiscuous tracks with some little boy, or was she trying to protect a real predator in her life? Sylvia had made the full circuit around the 425 cable channels before starting again. She was a therapist and a good one. The textbook said Sylvia had the classic signs of suppressed molestation, but her environment didn't support the theory. She was raised in a loving, safe, God-fearing environment. The only man in her security circle was Daddy and she was his little girl, and as awkward and unnerving as those words sounded being whispered by him into her ear, she was her father's favorite, their secret.

Surfing channels, reading a periodical, looking at the clock, over and over with the images of a Latoya being violated by a man didn't leave her thoughts for very long, regardless of how hard she tried to drown them with busyness. She wanted to sleep, to escape. Besides, she needed rest and plenty of it in order to come close to mustering the tenacity required to endure the knuckle bashing in store for tomorrow, an afternoon with the Reynolds women, Aunt Mabel in particular.

Last look at the clock the time was 2:14 a.m. Sylvia saw the little girl with her yellow dress in the dark room with a tall-looking man whispering in her ear. Then the little girl was crying. Sylvia jumped up, realizing she'd dozed off, gasping for air. Same dream she'd experienced on and off for nearly twenty years. This time was different. She fumbled on the nightstand for her bottle of water. Same girl, same dress, but for the first time in the hundreds of times she'd had the dream, she could make out the room. It was the big walk-in closet at their old house. The man was leading her into the closet in her parents' room where she loved to play with her dolls. One day she stopped playing in the closet. She couldn't remember when and why. She'd forgotten about that closet, but after two decades, it was back. The memory of her childhood refuge should have fostered warmth and joy in her heart, but no. Reflecting on the closet made her feel scared, ashamed and dirty. Who was he? She couldn't see his face.

Sylvia refused to give way to the conversations swirling in her head. Wasn't possible, couldn't be. There was no way Latoya could be telling the truth, could she? No, squash the idea. No room for doubt. She turned off the TV, nightstand light, then slid under the covers.

Fill her mind with topics, keep occupied, just don't let doubt and those images push to the front. She wanted to run but didn't get far in her thoughts. "Daddy's girl" chanted in her head like a hundred-person choir, louder, irritating, louder, crippling, louder and now undeniable. Enough. Latoya was a liar, that's what she was. Didn't matter why, she was. Latoya had to be, otherwise Sylvia would be drawn back into the closet and forced to look into the face of the man holding her hand and whispering in her ear. She buried her head in the pillow, unwilling to cry, to panic, to break down or show any signs of weakness. She was a therapist, a good one, and that would be the image ushering her into sleep, however minuscule.

Chapter 19

Family is good. Family is good, Sylvia recited as she dragged up the walkway, wondering why they were planning an anniversary party now that Daddy was facing criminal charges. Their collective energy and time should be spent on Daddy's defense, let alone finances, but who was she to say anything. Keep repeating the phrase long enough and the concept was bound to sink in. Family wasn't bad, but why did she have such abundance: a goulash of personalities, idiosyncrasies, problems and who knows what else. Toughen up, put on her shroud of tolerance and get in there. The sooner she was inside, the faster she would be bolting back toward the New Jersey bridge, away from the strangling clutches of Delaware, away from the notion of Latoya Scott. She sucked in a deep breath of fresh air, and held it in her lungs as long as she could before slowly releasing it and knocking on the door.

"Come on in here," Angela greeted. "You're the last one to get here."

"That's our Sylvia, always late. You and Angela are total opposites when it comes to being on time," Aunt Kay commented with a spirit of light-heartedness. Opinionated Aunt Kay was, but mean-spirited she wasn't. At times the distinction was small. Her comment didn't sound right, but Sylvia didn't believe she meant any harm.

"That's because she lives all the way over there in Jersey, when the rest of her people live right here in Delaware. See, your sister has stayed near her family."

Thirty seconds in the door and Aunt Mabel was flapping her gums. Why did that woman always have something to say about everything and everybody? Aunt Kay had her issues with perfection and bossiness, but overall she was decent and easy to get along with, even for long periods of time. She could be tolerated. Aunt Mabel was a handful. Dealing with her on a regular basis required a cast-iron stomach and a bottle of super-strength ibuprofen. To make matters worse, Sylvia realized she'd left her 250-count bottle at home. She hadn't dealt with Aunt Mabel nonmedicated in a long time, more reason to do her part and get out of the house, fast.

"There's nothing wrong with living in New Jersey. She has her own house, and I'm glad when the children in this family do well. We should be proud. Now, come on, let's get this work out of the way. We're already starting fifteen minutes late," Aunt Kay said in her normal take-charge—even when it wasn't her party—kind of tone.

"Lee has a nice house, too, over there in New Castle with Nina."

"As long as my children can take care of themselves, I'm pleased," Mom added, making sure Angela was protected from her busybody sister-in-law, and preserving Sylvia's integrity came along as a bonus, an afterthought. The middle child was the one who got the leftovers, hand-me-downs and scratches of their parents' affection. Sylvia knew she wasn't officially a middle child, actually she was the baby, but she was made to feel like a middle child, except for her father's attention, which there was always plenty of, when she thought about it, maybe even more than her share, considering her ability to squeeze into his busy school schedule for lunch or late-night calls for advice whenever she wanted.

"Is Denise coming?" Sylvia asked Aunt Kay, hoping for reinforcement from a family member that hadn't been completely programmed into the Reynoldses' stifling way of life. Denise was another free spirit who set her own path, unmarred by tradition and pretension.

"I don't think so. She's running around with that brother of hers."

"How's he doing?" Mom asked. "I haven't seen Deon in months."

"He's doing fine, I think. Something's been bothering him lately. I don't know what it is. You know how children are when they get grown. They don't tell you about their problems. I should count that as a blessing, but I don't," Aunt Kay said.

"Well, if there is anything wrong, he'll tell Denise," Mom reassured Aunt Kay.

"That's for sure."

"They've been close all their lives," Mom said with an

element of sadness. Everyone present knew why but didn't nurse the moment or elongate the pain of her loss. In fourteen years, they'd had their moments: Mom, Daddy, Angela and her. There would be other times when the loss of Donny would surface without notice. This was one of those times for Mom, and it would pass as quickly as the blip of grief had arrived, so long as it wasn't nurtured.

"Denise is another woman with a lot of education and no husband or children. Women nowadays, I don't know what they're waiting for. All these degrees, but what about some babies to keep the family going? Louise and Kay, I feel sorry for both of you. When you become grandmothers like me you're going to want your babies nearby."

"I don't know if my daughters are ready for children yet, especially Sylvia."

"Oh, that's right, she's one of those working women, a doctor and all. Well, let this older woman tell you a little something about life. Don't wait until you get old to have children. An old man can have children but a woman can't. Your education and job is all well and good, but you need a man in your life like Angela. She's on the right track," Aunt Mabel said.

Angela squirmed in her seat. Aunt Mabel was unaware of Angela's separation from Reese. The fact that she didn't know was a small miracle. Information in the Reynolds family spread like a forest fire. How Angela and Mom had kept the separation from the rumor mill was amazing. Exposing Angela's business to the family crier would be more brutal than anyone deserved.

"Right now, children, education, Jersey, Delaware doesn't

mean a thing to me. My only concern is getting the charges against Daddy dropped."

Silence blanketed the room.

"Your father comes from good, strong stock," Aunt Mabel said. "He's going to be all right."

"That's right, in the name of Jesus," Mom added.

Their confidence and well wishes were helpful, but Attorney Jackson was her hope. She hadn't been able to count on church to make a significant difference in her life over the past year and wouldn't rely on religion for Daddy's predicament. Might have helped if she'd gone to church more than once a month and attended a few Sunday school classes, but that was a whole other discussion for another time.

Angela didn't speak. She was unusually quiet, inserting a chuckle here and there with a short comment periodically, but not engaged. Between Daddy and her marriage, her mind was occupied and anniversary plans couldn't be extremely high on her priority list.

"You girls have been a blessing to your father. He's so proud of you both, and I am, too."

"That's why people need to have children, exactly my point," Aunt Mabel interjected. "In your old age, you need somebody around to bring you a cool drink of water in your hour of need."

"Mabel, I'm not sure my daughters are quite ready to have children. Sylvia's not married and Angela and Reese need some time together just for the two of them to enjoy before loading up with children. You are blessed, because I don't ever expect my girls to give me quite as many grandchildren as Tony and Lee have given you," Mom said.

"I know Denise and Deon won't," Aunt Kay added.

"They only have nine between them. Lee with five and Tony has four."

"You'd think that after all those kids and baby mamas, somebody would want to get married," Aunt Kay commented.

"You met Lee's fiancée. Tony will be next."

"How can they afford to pay so much child support?" Sylvia had to ask. Aunt Mabel could stand a dish of humiliation, the same kind she fed to others so generously.

Aunt Mabel let her glance hit the table with the zeal in her voice trailing. "They're not the best with child support. The mothers are constantly calling me looking for one or the other."

"Is that why they've been in and out of jail so much?" Once the words hit the airways, Sylvia couldn't reclaim them. "Oops. Mom, I'm sorry. I forgot about Daddy. I didn't mean to say anything out of line."

"You didn't, don't worry. I'm fine."

"They haven't been in trouble for child support, have they, Mabel?" Aunt Kay asked.

"Those boys," Aunt Mabel said, waving her hand in the air, "what can you do with them? I'm so happy that they've gotten beyond those wayward years and are staying out of trouble."

Actually, Sylvia knew Lee had recently spent thirty days in jail on a DUI. Denise had told her, who had found out from Deon, who was the one Lee had called for bail money. If Aunt Mabel preferred to act like all was well with her trifling sons, so be it. Initiating a pointless conversation with Aunt Mabel would only prolong her time in the house and away from her place of peace.

"I don't know what their problem is," Aunt Mabel contin-ued, since no one else had anything to say about Tony and Lee. "They need to talk to their father about how to pick the right woman, like he did with me, and settle down."

"I don't know how Sam's put up with you all these years," Aunt Kay said.

"Put up with me, huh. Sam's not going anywhere. He knows how good we have it. Thirty-eight years of marriage and still going strong."

Mom and Aunt Kay shifted their weight and let their gazes drop, appearing to avoid eye contact with Aunt Mabel. Amazing how delusional one person could be when it came to a marriage and body language, but that was Aunt Mabel, living in a world she painted and to heck with reality.

"If you ask me, you can have all the Reynolds boys, includ-ing mine. Louise, I believe you got the best out of the bunch," Aunt Kay said. "This police business is a mistake. We all know Herbert is innocent."

"You're right about Herbert being innocent. We know that's true, but I can't agree with you about the Reynolds men. You can't make all the brothers bad just because Arthur doesn't have the good sense that God gave him and left you to go live over there with that young woman and a house full of kids who aren't his. Oh, no, don't lump my Sam into his nonsense. My husband is a good man. We have thirty-eight years and going strong, like I said."

"Oh, Mabel please. Let's not get into any serious conver-sation about the Reynolds men, because you and I know the truth." Aunt Mabel must have understood what Aunt Kay meant, because she didn't speak, but the tightening of her lips, arching of her eyebrows and the squirming in her seat did the talking. "Now, let's get back to this anniversary celebration. Angela and Louise, what do you need us to do?"

Forty-five minutes in and Sylvia was fully aware of the inadequacy an ibuprofen would have been. Dealing with her aunts and the constant comparison to Angela were the proper ingredients for a headache, but they weren't the source of her ambivalence this time. Mike was. She'd invested a year into their relationship and really was hopeful about the outcome. She didn't merely break up with him. She literally kicked him out.

Sylvia dreamed about the idea of discussing her relationship woes with the women in her family, the matriarchs, the women of wisdom who could help her navigate through the romantic times and the pitfalls, but not with this group of women, her mother excluded, although she, too, rubbed Sylvia the wrong way at times when she pressured her about commitment and staying in a relationship long enough to see it succeed or fail. No way would she offer her latest heartache as prey for this bunch. She didn't feel comfortable going to God for help since she hadn't spent much time with Him or the church in the past year. He felt like a casual acquaintance. There was always the Bible, which she could read on her own for direction, but where would she start?

Daddy would yet again have to serve as her listening ear, maybe. The conversation they started nearly two weeks ago was a distant memory given the arrest and her nightmares, but Daddy was the only person who truly understood her perspective. He was probably a bit of an enabler, which as a seasoned psychologist she recognized but chose to willfully ignore. He would side with her, because in his eyes no man was right for his baby girl. Reflecting on his unwavering acceptance eased her tension and brewing headache. She'd get through this party hoopla and escape, with the first stop along her journey to recovery being a phone call to Daddy. Besides, he was cheaper than the therapy she was already undergoing. What else was a psychologist to do, make problems even when there weren't any to begin with?

Chapter 20

No more stalling. Time to pull herself up to that bed, the sanctum of their marriage, the place they vowed to cherish, to share and to commit their trust and love to each other, the place Reese had defiled. Night after night, crawling into bed next to him was a constant reminder of his betrayal, his lack of ability to believe in her, his selfish desire to have a child any way he could.

She slipped into the room and into the bed without a sound, daring not to awaken him just in case he wasn't already awake and pretending to be asleep.

Reuniting had been as much a dose of hard labor for him as it had been for her, at least that's what he had led her to believe, but equating his hurt and humiliation to hers wasn't feasible. When he left last spring, the emotional part of her heart had been ripped from its chest cavity and was in desperate need of a transplant. Although, she had to admit the pain of separation came a bit easier only because the initial devastating blow had occurred four months earlier when she found out about Felicia and her claim to be carrying Reese's baby. She still couldn't remember the full brunt of the episode; thank goodness for the ability to suppress painful, unimaginable, unbearable memories.

Reese turned his body over, facing her, causing Angela to stiffen, not move and not breathe. She didn't want him awake. He turned his face back to the window and she let the air she'd been holding in her lungs seep out, quietly. Too long Reese had believed the lie, too, that those who'd made a commitment to Christ didn't hurt the same when their hearts were broken, that it was simple for them to forgive, forget, let go and move on. If the concept was true, then she needed serious adjustments in her faith. She wasn't Louise Reynolds with the faith of a lion tamer, nowhere near, but forgiving, she had to do. The words in Matthew 6 dashed in. She couldn't remember the exact verse, but the words were something like forgive people when they wronged her in order to receive God's forgiveness from her sins. She knew forgiveness was God's requirement. Besides, forgiving was the easy side, a sheer once-and-done act of her will to forgive her husband and herself, absolute, done.

She couldn't forget the evangelist at last year's retreat emphatically stating that unforgiveness doesn't travel alone. Wherever unforgiveness dwells, anger, resentment, meanness and bitterness were soon to follow. The bunch traveled in a pack, a sure recipe for personal unhappiness. She could and had forgiven Reese, but forgetting was the challenge, even with Christ in her heart. Lying close to the man she'd married felt distant, with half of her wanting his caress and the other half afraid to trust him again. Forgetting was the part where she had to acknowledge her wound, the hurt suffered by the man who promised to honor and protect her, the one who elevated another woman to her position of recognition in his life and in his bed. Forgetting meant letting the hurt heal and there lay the problem. There was no time limit on how long the healing would take, but Reese wanted to rush the process. He needed to be patient. At least he was home. That's where he claimed he wanted to be. Time would have to tell if his heart had returned, too.

Chapter 21

Reese sat in front of the TV with the remote close by. The heated match between the 76ers and Miami with Iverson and Shaq both having phenomenal nights didn't hold his attention. How much longer could he continue to live like this? Last night, words weren't spoken when Angela eased into the bed around midnight, touches weren't exchanged; ignoring the problem, another wasted night is what they had. He was wrong, had been, but this was a new start for him and Angela. She was entitled to some mad-at-him time, but at some point Angela had to let go and move on, with or without him. He heard the back door opening. For the past two months, she'd been a seesaw, up one minute, happy, and down the next, angry and downright mean, talking about God's grace and then the next day ready to put him out. The yoyo affect wasn't working and couldn't continue. He'd take a stand and tell her tonight, but first he needed to get a read on her mood.

"Hi, babe," he greeted, halfway expecting a not-so-positive reply based on the distance between them last night. Before the separation and before Felicia's baby came into the picture, they talked on and off throughout the day from work. Now he was lucky to hear from her once a day after they said their goodbyes in the morning.

"Hello, Reese," she said, without batting an eyelid or tossing a tiny glance his way, indicating this wasn't the best time to approach her with a suggestion on how to improve the marriage, but then there wasn't a perfect time with Angela these days. Between her father's situation, and that anniversary she was harping on, there wasn't any time left in her life to work on the marriage. One fact was for sure, time had run out. A drastic change was mandatory.

He approached her, determined to complete the moment. "Look, Angela, we have a problem. I know it, you know it and we have to do something, otherwise we're headed for divorce."

She paused and sighed. "Do you want a divorce?" she said, folding her arms and leaning against the counter with her coat still on.

"No, I don't. You know that I don't."

"I'm not really sure what you want, Reese. I believed you wanted me six years ago, but I was wrong. So, I'm not guessing anymore about what it is you want from me or from this relationship."

"Why not? I'm here, aren't I?" he asked Angela while she removed her coat. He tried to help but she jerked away. "Angela, I screwed up. I take full responsibility for my mistake."

"Full responsibility, what does that mean? Doesn't change

what happened, doesn't prevent me from running into Felicia and the baby."

At least she didn't say "his" baby this time. It wasn't much, but her choice of words was a glimmer of hope that maybe she could let go.

"You're right, I can't get rid of Felicia and I can't do anything about her baby. What I can do is show you how much I love you and how much I'm committed to our relationship," he told his wife, taking one or two steps closer without caging her, afraid she'd run away and hide like an injured and frightened kitten.

"Didn't you love me two years ago when you met Miss Felicia," she said, starting to walk away, not willing to wait for an answer, but he couldn't afford to let the conversation drop just because the topic was becoming uncomfortable for Angela.

"Angela," he said, resting his hand on her shoulder, "don't walk away. We have to get these issues on the table. We can't fix what we don't address."

She wiggled his hand off her shoulder but didn't leave the kitchen, which was more than he could hope for at the moment.

"We have got to make changes, Angela. You know it and I know it. We have to. I love you. I do, I love you and I want this marriage to work. I don't want anyone else. You're the one for me."

"Why didn't you see that last year or two years ago?"

"Last year was last year, this is now. This is where we are. In order to move forward, I can't make you forgive me. I can't make you trust me again. All I can do is ask for your forgiveness and pray that you find it in your heart to forgive me."

* * *

Angela could hear the words in the Bible from Matthew, Mark and Luke speaking to her about forgiveness and redemption. She let the words dwell in her head but not in her spirit, the place igniting change. Ignore her spirit, her sense of right and wrong, and continue to be moved by her emotions and hurts. Besides, she had at least taken a step in the right direction. She'd forgiven him. She had to, a basic requirement of her faith. The part of her faith she was struggling with was the piece about restoration. In her spirit she knew God was able to fix a bad situation, but in her heart she didn't know if she wanted him to. Maybe she just wanted Reese to hurt for a while, like she had night after night, during the separation. She wanted him to feel her pain. After he'd suffered long enough, then they could talk about true reconciliation. Her extended punishment was wrong. She was taking God's rightful place of judgment into her own hands, which she acknowledged as dangerous and flat-out wrong, but her spirit, which was where her faith resided, allowed her flesh and need for revenge to dominate her actions.

"I'm willing to put the past behind me, but you can't rush me. I'm in the middle of healing. I'm trying, but now with Dad's arrest, I have to walk slowly. I'm on the emotional edge."

"I'm not pressuring you, but will you at least consider counseling?"

"You didn't want counseling before."

"Like I said, that was then and this is now. I'm willing to do whatever it takes to get you back."

"I'm not sure if I want to go to counseling." Too risky. What if the counselor takes the focus off Reese and puts it back on her, the whole issue about her not wanting to have children, at least not yet, although Reese desperately wanted to be a father. She wouldn't take a chance of becoming the villain in their marriage.

"We can get a referral from Sylvia. She's good with that stuff."

"Sylvia's not the only psychologist in town," she responded, walking toward the closet with her coat tucked under her arm. "If we go to counseling, we'll find our own person. I don't need Sylvia's help to get a counselor. Good grief, you people act like Sylvia is superwoman. She can't do everything."

Reese threw his hands in the air. "Sorry for the suggestion. I just thought she'd be the logical person we'd ask for help."

"Well, you thought wrong, again," she said, slamming the coat-closet door. "Are you watching TV down here or upstairs tonight?"

He hesitated, as if she was asking a trick question. "Why don't we watch some TV in the family room together?"

"You watch it in the family room. I'll be upstairs," she said, leaving the room. "Oh, and don't bother waking me up when you come to bed. I was sleepy all day today and I'm looking forward to getting a full night's rest tonight."

She glided up the stairs, feeling the gap between them expanding, wanting to bridge the divide on one hand but not ready to deal with the consequences on the other. After they fixed Reese's infidelity problem, then they'd be back to her shirking the discussions about having children. She couldn't win. Angela entered her bedroom with a heavy heart. Sylvia, Sylvia, Sylvia. Sylvia's money wasn't enough.

The attorney wanted Sylvia to help behind the scenes with her psychology. Reese wanted Sylvia's input on a counselor. She had a six-year jump on Sylvia regarding marriage, yet if the past was any indication of the future, Sylvia would be married and have two children before her. Life came easy for Sylvia. She turned on the TV and plopped onto the foot of the bed. For two people with the exact same genes, same mother and father, they were as different as night and day. Sylvia was dark like the dusk but always got the best the day had to offer. Angela fell back onto the bed, hoping sleep would be kind and whisk her away before Reese ascended the stairs, yet again forcing her to deal with reality, the place she was trying to avoid. Between Reese and Dad, nothing else could go wrong, she couldn't take any more bad news.

Chapter 22

The oak floor was covered by an old rug strategically placed between the bed and the dresser to cover the harsh, cold floor, particularly during the winter months. So many times Louise had stood in the center of the rug, feeling warm, safe. Herbert was home. She was warm and safe having him close. His arrest, being in jail, and the allegations made against him reminded her of the time when he'd come home after Vietnam. There weren't any long, deep conversations about what he'd experienced then, either. She knew he'd done what he had to do in Vietnam and had come home un-ashamed, which wasn't the case for her. They never talked about that dark time of separation and moments of guilt, no need. The past was the past.

The pending charges were a lie. Herbert was innocent and she didn't require any additional information. She knew exactly how to pray for his deliverance and ultimate victory.

By faith, her husband wouldn't spend another day in jail, not a single night away from his home, his family, his love. No matter how much fasting and praying she had to do, doubt and negativity would not graze her being. She flipped through the pages of her eight-and-a-half-by-eleven-inch Bible, which read Large Print Study Edition on the cover. The corners of the pages were worn from constant rubbing. She got to 2 Corinthians 12 and stopped. The reassurance she needed leapt from the page in verse nine. "My grace is sufficient for you…." Six words supplied the dose of strength and encouragement she needed to keep going. Her spirit was renewed.

Louise embraced every aspect of her being, including the softer color in her skin, three parts cream and one part chocolate. She had learned to accept both the good times and the challenges equally. The phone rang, and she extracted the cordless receiver from the corner of the nightstand by the second ring. Seeing the caller ID read Arthur Reynolds, she instinctively handed the phone to Herbert, who seemed a bit drowsy lying in the bed next to her.

"It's your brother."

"Who, Sam?"

"No, Arthur."

"How can you tell?"

"Because…" she said, "the ID says Arthur Reynolds. He's been my brother-in-law for thirty-six years. I recognize his name, honey. Now, take this phone." It had stopped ringing by the time they concluded their caller discussion.

"But you've forgotten that he's living with his new woman." He sat up in the bed with phone in hand and back pressed against the backboard. "I shouldn't say 'new woman.' It's been almost a year now, right?"

"I think so, at least six or seven months, because he brought her to the family reunion for the first time last year with her children. What a time that was." Louise sat on her side of the bed. She reached for her husband's free hand and continued the conversation. "I don't know how Kay can put up with him living with another woman."

"She doesn't have much to say about it."

"She's still his wife."

"I know, sugar, but they were sleeping in separate rooms for two or three years before he moved out."

"I understand that, but if he doesn't want her, why doesn't he get a divorce and then go and be with whomever he wants to, instead of leaving her wondering what's coming next? I just can't understand for the life of me how two grown folks, married for thirty years, can't work out their problems."

"I don't know, darling," he said, shortening the distance between them by scooting closer to her side and easing her back onto his chest and embracing her while still holding the phone. "Arthur isn't so bad, but Sam, now, he's something else. He takes the cake." Louise's shoulders gave a slight quiver, which he must have taken as a signal to embrace tighter. "Arthur has another woman, while he's separated, but Sam has another whole family, at least one that I know of. God forbid if my brother dies. I have no idea how many children will show up at the funeral." Louise quivered again, fainter this time. "He's something else. Shoot, if he wasn't my brother, I wouldn't trust him around you," he said, laughing, she imagined, at the ridiculousness of his own comment. "My brothers have a funny way of handling their relationships, but one thing is for sure, you don't have anything to worry about with me."

"I know that, Herbert," Louise responded, with the zeal of a deflating balloon.

"No, I really mean this, Louise, you can trust me. I've never cheated on you. I've never touched any of my students or any other woman, never. I would never do that to you."

"I believe you," she said, layering her arms on top of his and falling into his embrace, wishing she could say the same.

The phone rang again. This time he answered without hesitation, not caring whether it was his brother calling from his home with Kay, from a cell phone, from his girl-friend's house or whatever you called a married man living with another woman.

"Hey, fella, why you hunting me down so early on a Sunday morning?" The chipper tone faded with each word that Arthur deposited into his ear after the initial shocker. "Dead, are you sure?" he asked pulling away from Louise and springing to his feet. "Okay, I'll be there. You're at Kay's, right? Okay, don't worry. I'll be there. Do you need us to call anybody, Sam and Mabel, or Aunt Ida Mae?" He waited for the answer. "Well, if you think of anyone, let me know, but we should be there in a half hour. I'm hopping in the shower right now. Hang in there, brother."

Déjà vu, the tragic news he received fourteen years ago about Donny getting killed by friendly fire rushed back, with almost the same force that it carried back then. He knew how Arthur was feeling. He'd stood in the shoes where his brother was now standing, a father trying to accept the loss of his only son, an unimaginable reality. Through his current legal troubles, Arthur was there for him and he would return the brotherly favor.

"What is it?" Louise asked timidly, wanting to know, but with the instincts of a mother, especially one who already heard the I'm-sorry-to-inform-you speech. Please, God, don't let anything be wrong with Angela or Sylvia. On top of the impending trial, losing another child would be too much to bear.

"Deon is dead."

"What, how, what happened?" she said, springing to her feet, too, but still on the other side of the bed.

"Denise found him early this morning. They think it's suicide."

"What, not Deon. Everything is going so well for him right now."

Herbert hustled toward the bathroom, putting the phone back in its cradle. "They're not sure if it was suicide or not, but it was an overdose. That much they know, some kind of sleeping pills."

She erupted into tears, crying for Deon and the family, but mostly for Donny, her son, the one who left to support his country, and never came home. Herbert held her until the sobs weakened.

"I want to get to the house as quickly as we can," he said.

"You're right. I know Kay is going to need me. I won't even worry about a shower, I'll just throw something on and meet you downstairs," she said. "I'll call the girls, too." Before walking out of the room, she turned to her husband and said, "Herbert, we're going to get through this together, we always do."

"Yes, but we have a lot going on," he said, letting his gaze plummet to the floor. "It's too much at one time."

"God says He never puts more on us than we can bear."

"That might be true, but I'm feeling mighty loaded up right now. My brother's only son just killed himself and I can't give the kind of support that my brother's going to need because I have this case hanging over my head. It's pretty much all I think about. How could this happen? I became a principal in order to help children, especially ones like Latoya. How could she do this to me? The school needs me and I can't go near the place. I can't believe that I'm on leave until this is resolved."

"At least you're getting paid. That's a positive. If someone down at the board didn't believe in you, you'd probably be suspended without pay."

"You're right," he said, coming to her. "What did I do to deserve you?"

"You must have been living right before you met me," she said, carving a path into both their souls that resulted in laughter; at least a chuckle seeped into the room. There was much dimness in the family, but God's light could find its way into any situation with a bit of faith and positive thinking. That's what Louise believed and refused to let her circumstances or anybody tell her otherwise.

Chapter 23

Laughing, crying, talking, shouting, young, old, drunk, sober, the house had reached capacity fifteen family members ago. More had arrived since Sylvia did the ad hoc head count, and there was surely more to come. Tragedy and accomplishments were the quickest way to get the family together. There wasn't a written communication plan for disseminating information among the Reynoldses, but the order was understood, a call was made to the elders in the family and each had their set of calls. Sometimes the news traveled so fast and so far she had to wonder if some in the family were using smoke signals, messages in a bottle or carrier pigeons. Whatever the method, the communication was effective. The family found out about everything, even at times when they didn't need to know certain business. Death and funerals were the exception. Family was showing up whether invited or not, from Delaware to Alabama and each state in between. It was an understood rite of passage among the Reynoldses. The deceased was due a family gathering—a time when old stories were shared, pictures passed around, and a few arguments were bound to surface, too.

"I still can't believe he's gone," Denise muttered amid a flurry of tears. She couldn't stop crying. No one was shocked at her depth of grief. Deon and Denise were close. They shared a house together, a venture Sylvia couldn't see ever happening with Angela. They were too much alike, as her mother liked to think—but Sylvia knew better. They were too different to be able to share the same space. Their only common thread was their bloodline. Every other aspect of their lives was opposite. Angela was married. Sylvia was still single. Angela wasn't ready for children. Sylvia wanted a house of kids. Angela's skin tone was like Mom's, lighter, and Sylvia's, like Dad's, darker, richer, stronger. Angela loved being around the Reynoldses. Sylvia could take them in small groupings, small doses. Sylvia had spared no expense, time or commitment in getting a top-notch education and subsequent training from prominent institutions. Angela wanted to stay close to home and was satisfied with a local college even if she had to settle for a limited choice of curriculums. Thank goodness for her they offered a degree in education, which is what she supposedly wanted. Sylvia pledged Delta in college, uniting herself with more than two hundred thousand sisters, driving a larger distance between her and Angela. Reflecting on the relationship she had with her sister made the compassion for Denise and her loss more sincere.

"I'm on midnights at the hospital this week. If I had just gone home. If I'd just…"

Aunt Kay eased her daughter's head onto her chest, rocking slightly and letting her own tears have way. "There's nothing you could have done."

"That's right," Mom agreed.

"This isn't your fault," Aunt Kay said. "This isn't any of our faults."

Sylvia understood the mixed emotions the family was feeling. She'd counseled enough suicide-surviving family members to recognize the signs, anger mixed with grief, and heavy doses of both, equal portions.

"How did this happen?" Denise said, gasping to get her breath, while the room remained quiet, as if they were watching a monologue.

"You never know what a person is thinking. I've never understood suicide," Aunt Mabel threw in.

Denise jerked her head from Aunt Kay's shoulder. "Nobody said anything about suicide. He didn't commit suicide. He took too many sleeping pills and overdosed. That's it. Please don't start any rumors and lies," she said, practically yelling at Aunt Mabel.

The room was already quiet, pretty much allowing the immediate family to have their say, but Denise's comment created utter silence. Aunt Mabel was more than a handful in large lumps, and no matter how much of a bother she could be, no one from a younger generation dared raise a voice to an elder. That was a no-no, had been since their childhoods. The Reynolds children had their own set of parents, but the overall rules on how to act were the same across households. Aunts and uncles were like parents when the task of discipline became necessary.

No one attempted to break the silence in the dining room, unsure of what was coming next. Denise had violated the respect-your-elders rule, but there was a good chance she'd get extra grace given her brother had just died. Pretty much death, dismemberment and some cases of mental illness were the only situations warranting a grace pass, and they were dealt sparingly.

"Oh, I'm sorry," Aunt Mabel said, drawing her body away from the table. "I was only saying what I was told."

"Let's not worry about how and when and why. Let's get ready for the funeral director. He's going to be here any minute," Aunt Kay said, attempting to diffuse the tension.

Uncle Arthur came in the front door and Aunt Kay motioned for him to follow her into the back bedroom area. They didn't go far from the dining room because Sylvia could hear their muffled conversation without trying.

"The funeral director is coming any minute. When we put together the obituary, I don't want your woman and her kids mentioned anywhere, no special friend, no family friend, because she is no friend of mine," Aunt Kay told Uncle Arthur.

"Kay, why do you always have to create problems when there aren't any? I haven't said anything about putting my woman, as you call her, in the obituary. I'm not even thinking about that. All I have on my mind right now is my son and my daughter."

"You're talking about our kids?" she questioned.

"Who else, those are the only kids I have, the ones with you."

"I don't know that, not with the way you Reynolds men get around. I have no idea, but let me tell you something and hear me good, I don't want any trouble at my baby's funeral."

"Ah, come on, Kay, give me some credit."

"Look, I'm not beating around the bush. I'm not turning the other cheek. I'm flat out telling you not to bring that woman to the funeral."

"How can you tell me who can and can't come to my son's funeral?"

"I'm telling you that her and those kids better not show up at the funeral. Deon is my son."

"And mine, too, don't forget."

"I've said what I have to say."

"After two years of separation, you're still bossy and self-righteous. Still see yourself as the perfect woman. Nothing has changed. You still have to push me around like I'm a child. I'm a man, not your son, that's what you need to remember."

"I'm done with it." Sylvia heard Aunt Kay's footsteps approaching the doorway and Uncle Arthur hadn't finished talking.

The doorbell rang.

"That's probably the funeral director. Let's go, and remember what I said. Unless you want her to get embarrassed, you better leave her at home," Aunt Kay said, reentering the dining room with a stoic expression as if the conversation with Uncle Arthur hadn't occurred, and for everyone else in the room, other than Sylvia, it hadn't.

Chapter 24

Normally when a family member passed, their house became the condolence-gathering headquarters with traffic in and out from church members, friends, coworkers, neighbors, family and so on. Deon had a house, but since he was single, the protocol defaulted to his parents' house, which was why Aunt Kay's had been jammed with a flurry of people for the past three days, nonstop, a constant barrage of food, beverages, cards and sentiments.

"I would have gone to the funeral home with Kay, Arthur and Denise, but she said they could handle the arrangements," Aunt Mabel said, eating a slice of sweet potato pie.

"My goodness," Mom added softly. "I remember that dreadful day when Herbert and I had to make the trip for Donny."

"Thank God I've never been through that before," Aunt Mabel said.

"Losing a child is not easy. Even when you know the Lord, it's quite a cross to bear," Aunt Ida said, finishing a small piece of pound cake.

"I don't know if it gets any harder than losing a child, but preparing for the funeral helps, keeps you busy."

"You're right. At times like this, Kay doesn't want much free time on her hands," Aunt Ida said.

"Putting together the obituary, picking the flowers, working out the details for the repast, none of the other details broke me down the way picking out the casket did. That was the hardest," Mom said, crisscrossing her arms across her chest and bowing her head.

"Well, you did a great job with the arrangements, top of the line. I'm not sure what Kay and Arthur are getting. I don't know if they have any insurance. We'll probably all have to chip in. I haven't heard them ask yet, but I'm sure it's coming. Otherwise they wouldn't hold him out so long. The funeral isn't until Saturday, almost a week. That's too long. Doesn't take that long to bury anybody, not when the money is right."

"Mabel," Aunt Ida said, turning her entire body toward Aunt Mabel, "you know how big this family is. Some family members can't jump on the plane like you. Some of our family in Alabama said they have to wait until Friday. The earliest they can pick up their checks is around noon. They'll get on the road and drive straight through the night to get here Saturday morning. You've been in this family long enough to know how we operate."

"Too much driving for me."

"Maybe, but you can bet they'll all be here. That much you can count on."

"I still say it's too much driving for me."

"Whatever we have to do to help out, me and Herbert will do it. The family offered to help us and we have to do the same."

"Me, too, Mom," Angela said, feeling a bit down.

"That's right," Aunt Ida Mae affirmed, "we have to stick together. A little money isn't enough to lose sleep over. There are enough of us in this room to bury Deon if necessary. As a matter of fact, they shouldn't have to ask us. We should be asking them. It's enough to deal with Deon's death as it is. The last thing they need to worry about is where the money's coming from. We're a better family than to let one of us pass the hat for funeral funds."

"That might be true, Aunt Ida Mae, but everybody should have some kind of insurance, though."

"Here you go again. Mabel, times aren't like they were when you were coming up. Everybody had a Metropolitan policy," Aunt Ida said.

"Remember that? The agent would come to the door every month and collect a few nickels on the policy," Mom said, trailing off with laughter.

"And with all those payments and so-called policies, we still had to pass the hat when somebody died because the face values were never more than a thousand dollars or two, and you can't bury anyone with that kind of money, not even twenty years ago."

"With child support and who knows what these young people spend their money on nowadays, I went ahead and took out adult life insurance policies on my sons when their Jack and Jill policies ran out. That way Sam and I don't have to worry about how they're going to get buried when the time comes. Whether they need the policy a year from now or a hundred years from now, it's there."

"Everybody's not as able to buy policies for their adult children as you are, Mabel," Aunt Ida said.

"That's true, but times are tight for some of us. People can't always chip in as they'd like when it's on short notice."

"But times aren't tight for you, not with all the spending you do, or at least you're always talking about spending, Mabel. I don't want to hear any sob stories. When it's time to come up with the money, I'm expecting you to do your part, like the rest of us. Just remember that we are all one situation from being in our sisters' and brothers' shoes. Don't stand too mighty over someone else's misfortune, because you never know when your turn's coming. Being too proud is a slippery slope. You need to sow some seeds of compassion so there will be some waiting for you down the road, Mabel."

"Aunt Ida Mae, you can put us in our place without raising your voice," Mom said, leaning over and giving her a kiss on the cheek. "You know how to handle Mabel."

Seeing Mom amused was refreshing, Angela thought. Battling her own trauma with the case looming over the family, but yet, she stepped forward with a ton of compassion for Aunt Kay. There were plenty of good women in the world, but none quite like Mom: integrity, grace, style, faithfulness and an incredibly giving heart. God hadn't made any more like her. She was the real deal, a born-again believer who lived her faith more than preaching it. One day Reese might get the benefit of her genes. There was still a shred of hope.

Chapter 25

February could have been brutal to the family gathered on the steps of the church waiting on the funeral director, but mercy came in the form of a mild Saturday morning. Unfortunately the kind weather couldn't erase the bitter, chilling bite January had taken out of the Reynolds. Saying goodbye to Deon was difficult for Sylvia. He was her favorite male cousin. Her plan was to whisk by Deon without taking a glance, remembering him as he was—smart, funny, good-looking, successful and loving, not whatever look the funeral director had conjured up. She'd keep her Deon intact, where his image counted, in her heart and mind.

Small pockets of chitchat were going with low volume, not loud enough to interpret neighboring conversations. The order of entry was set in standard pecking order: immediate family, extended family, family friends of distinction, and then close friends that considered themselves family.

Any others could follow the family into the service only if there was sufficient room left on the family side of the church. A family the size of the Reynoldses was sure to overflow the right side of the church and pour into the left side. People who came early to secure seats on the guest side of the church ended up mad, because they arrived at Mount Calvary with the intent of getting front-row seats and would end up sitting in the back or in the overflow downstairs.

She couldn't worry about the other people today. Sylvia committed the day to the memory of her beloved cousin, and anybody close to the Reynolds knew not to sit in the first ten rows on the guests' side. Deon was well liked and had many friends, colleagues and acquaintances. It would be safer to avoid the first twenty rows, leaving only five for visitors.

Deon wasn't into the church, not regular, but the idea of having his service at the funeral home was immediately swatted down by Aunt Kay and Aunt Ida Mae. For them, something about the funeral-home setting made the service incomplete, as if the funeral location and burial spot had any reflection on where his soul was resting. No need to argue the point. Every member of the Reynolds family had only two choices for their funeral: the church where they held membership, or Mount Calvary, the family church. Whether eight or eighty, Mount Calvary was the Reynoldses' church home. No one had tried, but most likely violation of the unspoken rule would result in stringent penalties, possibly being ostracized. Some dared to stray away to other congregations but not without severe tongue-lashing and brow-beating for abandoning the family. Since God was everywhere, what did it matter what church a Reynolds worshipped at?

The general quiet and spirit of mourning was broken when a loud commotion came from the back of the line. Pinpointing the noise was difficult because the family was bunched together like a group of football fans storming the entry gates. The voices got louder, drawing more attention from the front of the line, not quite reaching Aunt Kay and Uncle Arthur yet, but it was coming.

"She doesn't have any business here. She's not going in that church."

"You can't tell me where I can and can't go," the voice retorted, getting closer but still not visible.

"What are you doing here, Keisha?" Aunt Mabel asked as the woman came into view, quite recognizable. "You shouldn't be here. This isn't right. Why don't you go on back home before Kay sees you and this turns ugly."

"I'm not here to start any trouble," Keisha responded, with her four children close to her hip. "We know Deon and we loved him. We came to say our goodbyes and that's it."

"This isn't right," Aunt Mabel repeated.

"She doesn't need to be here," Lee added.

Chatter had erupted into fully formed rumbling in the crowd. The Reynolds family had a strange way of getting on one another's nerves and pitting themselves one against the other, but outsiders didn't have a chance. If one family member was under attack, the entire family was. Having an intruder disrespect the funeral protocol was a big no-no even if she did live with Uncle Arthur.

"Please leave before you start some mess, please just go," Aunt Mabel spouted.

"It's almost ten-thirty. We'll be going in any minute," Mom

said, probably wanting Keisha to leave, too, but not as willing to speak out and cause conflict.

Keisha kept pushing toward the front. "Art knew I was coming. He is Deon's father, too. If it's okay with him, then it's okay with me and should be okay with you," she said, cutting her glance at Aunt Mabel, which was the wrong move to make.

Aunt Mabel had tried to be as nice as her meddling heart would allow, but Keisha had crossed the line and it was evident in Aunt Mabel's scowl. "Arthur might be Deon's father, but you're sure not his mother. That would be Kay and she's up front with her husband. Now, why don't you and your children go on back home and leave this family business to our family, and," Aunt Mabel said, rolling her gaze up and down Keisha's frame, "you are not family."

"I am."

"Oh, no, you're not, Keisha. I don't want to go there with you. You need to keep pushing on and get out of my face and out of this line. Just because you're shacking up with Arthur doesn't make you Kay, do you understand? You're the other woman, so stay in your place," Mabel said, letting the *c* in *place* trail off and sizzle like a hissing snake.

Keisha would not be deterred.

"This isn't good," Mom whispered to Daddy, and she was most likely right. "She could have come to the visitation anytime between nine and ten-fifteen to avoid this. Why did she wait until ten-thirty when everybody knows the family arrives a half hour before the funeral begins. This could have been avoided, and now we don't know what's going to happen," Mom said, latching onto Daddy.

"I can't believe she came," Angela whispered to Sylvia, most of her outrage surfacing from her own situation with Reese. If his other woman showed up at a family event or anywhere, she'd just die. Bad enough knowing the woman existed, but it was deathly destructive to the soul having to face her anywhere, anytime, and have to give credence to her existence. "Felicia is out of line."

"Felicia, you mean Keisha, right?"

Blood rushed to Angela's face. "Right," she said, probably hoping Reese hadn't heard.

Couldn't there ever be a funeral in the family without some drama? Why did funerals have to bring out the worst in the Reynolds?

Against all attempts to prevent Keisha from touching the top step of the church, the one holding Aunt Kay, Denise and Uncle Arthur, there she stood, in the middle of a sure-to-be war zone. Yet, when the lines of diplomatic interventions broke down, or in the case of Aunt Mabel's not-so-diplomatic attempt to divert the war, then certain wars were inevitable.

Keisha tried to sneak past Aunt Kay and enter the church. Maybe her intention was to ease in undetected, which was cavalier and perhaps unwise with four kids in tow and a line of family members that had a high probability of recognizing her as Uncle Arthur's live-in girlfriend. Maybe Keisha's bond with Deon was a strong one, and she felt compelled to come. Maybe she felt obligated to support her boyfriend, or whatever it was that she called Uncle Arthur, seeing that he was still married to Aunt Kay. Maybe, just maybe, she wanted a confrontation. Whatever the reason, it didn't matter now. Keisha was standing on the steps of her destiny, prepared for a good old fashioned beating from Denise, if Aunt Kay didn't get to her first.

"Wait a minute," Aunt Kay said, jerking her arm from around Uncle Arthur's waist. "What in the..." Aunt Kay couldn't get her words together.

The funeral director opened both doors in preparation for the family's processional. Thank goodness there was a vestibule separating the sanctuary and seated guests from the family outside. *Embarrassment* and *humiliation* were terms too weak to reflect the family's impending mood if a fight broke out in front of a church full of people.

Denise jumped in to finish off where Aunt Kay had started yelling at Keisha. "You're not going in there."

The rhetorical tongue Keisha exercised with the family slicing through the line kept silent in front of Aunt Kay and Denise, first wise move she'd made in the last five minutes.

The funeral director, unaware of the catastrophe in motion, beckoned for Uncle Arthur and Aunt Kay to come forward. Aunt Kay didn't see him standing right in front of her because she had her sight locked in on the target. Uncle Arthur tried to be of use and escort his wife into their son's funeral but it was too late for discretion and tact. He'd most likely blown the opportunity by not stopping Keisha from coming to the funeral long before now. He had his chance to keep his dirty secret, but the wind was blowing his dust Aunt Kay's way and she was poised for cleanup.

"Move," Aunt Mabel said, forcing her way up the steps as if she were the cavalry.

Keisha and her children were surrounded by Aunt Mabel,

Aunt Kay, Denise and several cousins, who were always looking for a fight, as well as a few friends who wanted to be family and must have felt the need to prove themselves worthy of a seat in the reserved section. The funeral director became more demanding, most likely wanting to stay on time. He might not have understood the full gravity of the confrontation, but the air was so thick everyone present got the sense something bad was happening.

"Kay, let's just go in," Uncle Arthur tried to interject.

"Don't tell me what to do," she said, lashing out at him and elbowing him from her side. "Your woman is not going in this church and I mean it."

"That's right," Aunt Mabel echoed, with both fists pitted into her waist. "We've asked you nicely to leave. Asking is over."

Johnson Brothers was known in the community as being the premier funeral home. Supposedly they did a phenomenal job with the preparations, not that Sylvia ever expected to get a firsthand look, but with their experience and reputation, they'd probably seen situations break out from finances to fraud, from fights to frolic. The director must have clued in to what was happening because he stepped in. "Ma'am, this is a family matter."

"I am family."

"She's not part of my family," Denise said, stepping in front of Uncle Arthur and getting closer to Keisha. What a disaster. Her children were crying and the smallest one had a death grip on Keisha's thigh. No mercy was given for the children's presence. Once Keisha had decided to bring them with her, she automatically put them in harm's way.

The director stood in front of Keisha, with his arms circling the children but not touching them. The family was already dealing with an outstanding matter pertaining to a child supposedly being touched. They really didn't need any more problems. "Ma'am, I'm going to have to ask you to leave."

"That's right," Aunt Mabel said, continuing to heckle.

"But I just want to get a program and say goodbye to Deon, that's it, and then I'll leave."

The request sounded reasonable under normal circumstances, but the director clearly didn't know Aunt Kay and the Reynolds family.

"I said she's not going into this church to see my son, period."

"Are you sure we can't resolve this by letting her go in and leaving through the back door," the funeral director suggested.

"The only way that's going to happen is if she beats us down right here," Aunt Mabel jumped in and said, as if it was her fight.

Aunt Kay must have gotten tired of the conflict, or been overcome by her impending grief, or thought about the heavy cloud of humiliation hovering, and caved in. "Let her go in and leave out the back door. I don't want to see her face during the funeral. I wouldn't be able to take it."

"What," Aunt Mabel yelled, "you don't have to let her in, Kay. I'll stand behind you. Don't worry about nothing going down because I'm right here."

"Leave it alone," Aunt Ida Mae said. "Leave it alone."

"Thank you," Keisha muttered, trying to maintain a protective wrap around her children.

"Don't thank me. I'm not doing this for you." Aunt Kay shot her gaze to Uncle Arthur. "I'm definitely not doing this for you. I'm ashamed at how little respect you have for me." Her gaze shifted back to Keisha. "This is my baby's funeral. I will not let his memory be disgraced by someone like you. Today is about Deon. So," she said, flicking her hand in midair and gesturing to Keisha. "Please go and hurry. My family has a funeral to get through, together," she said, latching her arm with Uncle Arthur's. He didn't say a word, not a single word.

"We have to hurry, ma'am. The family should have been inside and seated fifteen minutes ago." The director turned to Aunt Kay and Uncle Arthur. "Don't worry. I'll take care of everything." He beckoned for one of his assistants to come and escort Keisha in and out, clearing the way for Deon's legitimate family, or at least that's how Aunt Mabel would define the people gathered on the steps of Mount Calvary Baptist Church. Thank goodness February and its weather was kinder than January had been.

Chapter 26

The upholstered chairs in Aunt Kay's dining room had hosted many behinds over the past week. Now with the funeral officially over, friends and guests were gone and close family were the only ones remaining—Aunt Mabel, Mom and Angela. Daddy and Uncle Sam were outside. Denise, Aunt Kay and Uncle Arthur weren't home yet.

"Yes, you just never know. You raise your children the best way you can, and no matter what you do, they end up like Deon," Aunt Mabel said, shaking her neck. "You know they say he was that way."

"What way?" Mom asked.

"You know, funny."

"Oh, Mabel, I don't want to talk about anything like that. I don't even want Kay to hear those kind of words discussed in her house."

"I know, but Tony says it's the truth."

"How would he know?" Sylvia jumped in, trying hard to contain her ongoing irritation.

"I don't know, but you know how it is on the street. They hear things. Tony also said he heard Deon was probably sick. That's why I doubt if he had insurance. You know they can't get insurance once they get sick. Poor Kay, I don't know which is worse, having to deal with a drug overdose, suicide or that funny cancer. Umph, umph, umph. Oh, my goodness, I'm so glad Tony and Lee are okay."

Aunt Mabel could barely ooze the words out before Denise darted into the family room like a tornado. Her presence alone caused instance silence. Aunt Mabel had a big mouth, saying the wrong thing at the wrong time to the wrong people for the wrong reason. She deserved to be exposed, but this wasn't the time or place. Her hurtful words would be too cruel for Denise to bear. Hopefully Denise hadn't heard Aunt Mabel, but with the fury she carried entering the room, there was a slim chance.

"You have some nerve sitting in my parents' house and talking about my brother."

Stunned, the family froze in their spot as if a power plug had been pulled.

"Who do you think you are?"

"Girl, you better lower your tone. I'm not your cousin."

"No, you're a bragging, fake woman who doesn't care about this family. You just want to spread lies to make yourself and those worthless sons of yours look good. Do you think people really listen to you? They just laugh at you and tolerate you, including Uncle Sam."

"You better look in my face and see who you're talking to."

"Everybody lets you run your mouth and say whatever you want to say, but I'm sick of it. I'm sick of it and you."

"I'm going to give you a pass because you're going through something right now. Your brother committed suicide, but you can't take it out on family. We're here to help you, child."

"Really, you're here to help me. Well, Aunt Mabel, how do you think Tony knows so much about Deon, did you ever wonder about that?"

"What are you saying?"

"You know everybody else's business, figure it out."

"Denise and Mabel, stop right now. I'm not going to allow the two of you to be so disrespectful to each other," Aunt Ida Mae told them.

"Somebody better get her. She might be my niece, but if she's grown enough to get in my face shouting and screaming, then she's woman enough to take this beating I'm about to put on her."

"Come on," Denise said, approaching Aunt Mabel, while a room of stunned family members watched, unable to move. "If you hit me, I'm hitting you back. I'm not taking your crap. I don't have to."

"Go get Arthur or Sam or Kay, hurry," Mom whispered.

"You all need to stop this," Aunt Ida Mae said, stepping in. "This is wrong and no fruit can come from this."

"Excuse me, Aunt Ida Mae and Aunt Louise, I don't mean to disrespect you, but she has it coming. What kind of family is this if we keep pretending and lying as if everything is okay when it's not?"

"We all need to cool down, before this goes too far," Mom pleaded.

"She's already gone too far," Aunt Mabel bellowed.

"Family shouldn't act this way toward one another," Aunt Ida Mae said.

"We're always talking about family and sticking together, but where was the family when Deon was little and Tony molested him, over and over."

"What are you talking about? You have really lost your mind now," Aunt Mabel shouted.

"I know exactly what I'm talking about and you probably do, too. Deon told me about it a long time ago. So, if he is whatever 'funny way' you're insinuating, then Tony is, too."

"Stop this," Aunt Ida Mae pleaded.

"Now I know you've gone too far," Aunt Mabel said, standing to her feet with Aunt Ida Mae standing in the middle. "Don't try to blame Tony for what happened to Deon. That's his cousin. He's never done anything to Deon but treat him like a brother."

"Yeah, right, keep telling yourself that."

That nagging, pricking feeling of unrest in Sylvia's soul stirred. "Where is Kay and Arthur?" Mom yelled out.

"They're not back yet," Angela answered.

"Then get Sam, find him."

"I don't know why you want to start this kind of nonsense on the day of your brother's funeral. This family already has plenty to deal with. We don't need any more lies and rumors stirring."

"This family is built on generations of lies and secrets, lies on top of lies. It's about time we started telling the truth and getting some of this fake family bonding on the table."

"This isn't the right way," Aunt Ida Mae said.

"There is no right way. The truth is the truth and we need to hear it."

"I'm not going to stand here and listen to you talk about me and my family as if you're somebody's mother in here, little girl. You're about to mess around and let your mouth write a check your behind can't cash."

Aunt Kay dashed into the room with Angela on her heels. "What in the world is going on in here?"

"Your daughter is being disrespectful and I'm tired of listening to her. She can't blame the whole family for Deon's passing," Aunt Mabel said, pushing toward the doorway.

"Wait a minute, Mabel, let's everybody settle down," Aunt Kay pleaded, sliding in front of Aunt Mabel to deter her exit.

"Let her go. Don't stop her."

"See what I mean? She has a mouth on her and I need to leave before I take a belt to her behind like I did when she was five years old."

"Try it." Sylvia knew Denise wasn't going to take a whopping from Aunt Mabel at twenty-five. Denise had talked to her many times about feeling mistreated by Aunt Mabel growing up, feeling that she received a harsher whopping from her than the other Reynolds children. The unresolved resentment must have brewed for years, and without warning, the lid on Denise's tolerance for Aunt Mabel finally reached the point of explosion, right there in the dining room.

"I'm leaving," Aunt Mabel said, pushing past Aunt Kay this time. "I'm going home. Call me if you need me."

"You don't have to leave. Denise, I didn't raise you to act like this."

"Mom, I'm just telling the truth. Why wouldn't we want to hear the truth?"

"Some things need to be left alone. Sharing certain kinds of information does more harm than good," Mom said, surprisingly.

"Can't do Deon any more harm than these lies and secrets already have. Why should my brother be dead and Tony walking around like he owns the world?"

"If this is something we need to deal with as a family, we will, but let's not talk about this here. We have enough to deal with today," Aunt Ida Mae said.

"That's why we had a day like today. If this family was more honest and stopped keeping secrets, then we wouldn't have had the fight at the funeral. That's what happens when lies keep building and building, lies on top of more lies. Eventually they get exposed, and as far as I'm concerned, it's exposing time," Denise said, walking out. "Say whatever you want about me, but I'm going to be brutally honest."

"No, you don't mean that," Aunt Ida Mae retorted. "There's nothing loving about the word *brutal* especially among family. That's all I'm saying. Now, let's get back to making the best out of this time we have together and let this tension and hatred go. One loss today is enough."

Chapter 27

Denise and Aunt Mabel were lucky. They got to leave without the round of goodbyes and endless conversations leading up to goodbye. After their fight, proper etiquette dictated they leave without haste, and they did. A few other members of the family had gone, but mostly everyone else remained, talking in large and small groups, others helping Aunt Kay straighten the populated areas in the house. Daddy, Uncle Sam and Uncle Arthur were bunched together in the corner conversing as only brothers can do.

"Sylvia," Daddy said, breaking away from his brothers, "can I speak with you outside for a minute?"

"Sure, Daddy," she responded, sensing Angela's stare, but not causing her to tense. Sylvia extracted her coat from the pile stacked on the easy chair closest to the front door. Outside, the sun hadn't gone down and wouldn't for another hour. The unusual sixty-degree weather was waiting for sunset, too, before taking a leave, letting winter resume its rightful position in February.

"I wanted to tell you that I'm sorry for what I've done to you."

"What do you mean?"

"For years I've done the same thing to you. I've harped on you about staying away from public controversy and keeping your record clean. You've always done everything I've asked of you, even when you were a little girl, and this is how I repay you."

"Daddy, this isn't your fault."

"The charges against me will ruin my reputation. I'm concerned that yours will be affected, too."

"Daddy, don't worry about me. I'll be fine," she told him but wasn't sure. Having this conversation with her father, the man she adored, the man she trusted, the man she had to believe was innocent, couldn't be any more painful, watching him ask for her forgiveness.

"You're right, you'll be fine. You're Daddy's girl, right?" he asked, probably not expecting an answer. His words landed wrong in her soul. Each time she'd heard them in recent months, a stirring in her gut manifested. Not a good feeling—one of fear, tightness, oddly, a sense of shame. Why? She didn't have to be ashamed to be Daddy's little girl, but she was. She could ask him to stop saying those words, but her heart wouldn't allow him to be hurt any further. He'd already been betrayed by one person he dared care about—Latoya. He wouldn't feel another painful sting from Sylvia.

He extended his arms and let them envelope her. His embrace should have felt reassuring, comforting, but instead the contact was smothering, agitating. The love she wanted from her father, she had, but why did it feel so wrong? The moment felt irritatingly familiar.

She pulled away, not sure by his facial expression if he sensed her uneasiness with his touch. "Don't worry, Daddy. This will work out for all of us."

His grin eased her concern about hurting his feelings. The two of them went back inside Aunt Kay's house, back into the clutches of family and unrest.

Chapter 28

The air in Aunt Kay's dining room was clearing. Denise had left visibly upset, but not before Aunt Mabel stormed out in a huff. Uncle Sam and Dad ran to the store to pick up a list of items requested by Aunt Kay. Since Dad was in the car, there was a good chance Uncle Sam would go and come right back, not making one of his popular off-the-record stops at the liquor store that he was known to make. Uncle Arthur left a while ago with no mention of if and when he'd be back—Reese, too. Angela looked around the room, drawing wisdom from the women seated around the table, the ones who always seemed to carry the family during tough times, the ones who ironi-cally knew the Lord—Aunt Ida Mae, Mom, and Aunt Kay to some extent.

"I'm glad this day is over," Aunt Kay said.

"Johnson Brothers did a beautiful job," Aunt Ida Mae

added. "They've always been good to this family. You all know when my time comes, that's who I want to take care of me."

"Aunt Ida, you're going to live another fifty years," Mom said, lightening the last bit of heaviness lingering from the episode earlier with Aunt Mabel and Denise.

"At least," said Aunt Kay, who seemed to be feeling a little better, "because as you can see, this family is a wreck without you. We can't get past ourselves sometimes and it's truly frustrating. We should be closer than we are, as much as we get together. I'm so sorry about what happened here today."

"You don't owe us an apology. We need to be apologizing to you. We were supposed to be here to support you, Arthur and Denise, all of us," Mom said.

"Sometimes that means we have to learn how to hold our tongues. Every thought doesn't need to see the light of day," Aunt Ida Mae preached in her wonderfully insightful way that only she could do, drawing her listeners in for more pearls of wisdom.

If her marriage wasn't such an embarrassing set of circumstances, Angela would have gladly sat down with Aunt Ida Mae and garnered advice on what to do about Reese. She was praying and seeking God on occasion, nothing heavy. Honestly, she wasn't quite ready to hear His instruction. Reese deserved to squirm for a while in the chaos he'd created. She had.

"Amen," Mom agreed.

"I know you're talking about Mabel," Aunt Kay said, watching everyone's gaze look away, "but you know how she is. Mabel is always there when we need her and sometimes when we don't," she said, having to talk louder in order to be heard over the low-key laughter running around the table. "After thirty-some years of being in this family, I have to love my sister-in-law for who she is."

"You're right, that's Mabel," Mom concurred.

"I do hate that Denise and Mabel got into it. I don't know what got into Denise. She's headstrong, but I didn't think she'd go up against Mabel that way," Aunt Kay said.

"Mabel can push your buttons," Mom acknowledged.

"That's why family has to be careful with their words. Takes one word or one good argument to destroy years of unity. When everybody has to be heard and nobody is willing to take the low position in the conversation, there's going to be a problem. Denise and Mabel are family. I love them both, but they're a whole lot alike. That's why they can hardly stay in the same room together without biting off each other's heads," Aunt Ida stated.

"I hate to admit it, but Aunt Ida Mae, I think you're right," Aunt Kay confessed.

"Aunt Mabel and Denise probably wouldn't agree," Angela said, finally feeling comfortable diving into a conversation with the gathering of the Reynolds matriarchs.

"This has been a tough winter for the family. We all need a break, so Herbert and I have decided to cancel the anniversary party."

"Why, Mom, no, don't cancel the party. We canceled your thirty-fifth anniversary last year when Uncle Sam had his heart attack. I really want you and Dad to have this one."

"Louise, don't cancel on my account. It's going to be rough for me losing Deon, but I'm going to make it with the

Lord's help. The funeral is over, so there's no reason for you to cancel your anniversary."

"I agree. We need a reason to celebrate, and your thirty-six years of marriage is the perfect reason. I'm sure you've had your challenges together, but no separation, no scandals. Herbert hasn't been sneaking around with other women. Two beautiful daughters," Aunt Ida said, reaching for Angela's hand. "You have much to celebrate."

"That's the truth, especially the part about your husband not sneaking around with other women. With a Reynolds man, that's a miracle all by itself," Aunt Kay agreed.

"Don't cancel the anniversary party, Mom, please."

"I don't know. The trial is scheduled for May and I believe the party and the trial will be too much in the same month," Mom said.

"That's a good point, Angela," Aunt Ida agreed.

"Mom, planning the party has helped me not to dwell on the trial. We need the party to keep us distracted and to have something positive to look forward to."

Aunt Ida patted Angela's hand. "We're not going to let the devil steal our joy, are we? May is three months away, Louise, plenty of time to heal wounds and show up like family ought to, ready to celebrate and act like we love one another. Keep moving, that's what this family needs to do. So, keep the party on, nothing has changed. If it's the Lord's will to let me see May, I'll be there with bells and whistles."

"Me, too," Aunt Kay added, letting a small shot of sunshine into her otherwise dark moment of grief.

"And watch out, because I might do one of those new dances the young people are doing."

"Aunt Ida," is all Angela could get out before the women erupted into merriment.

"Never know."

"Now, Aunt Ida Mae, you're too old to be doing those new dances."

"Nothing gets old with me but clothes," Aunt Ida said, picking up a few grapes from the bowl of fruit sitting in the center of the table.

Angela sat back with a veil of her own heaviness falling. Only Aunt Ida Mae had the calming ability to take the remnants of a funeral, a family-fight scene and turn the time into one of unity and laughter. The Reynolds family needed her for as long as God would allow, which with the amount of chaos swirling, could be a considerably long time.

Chapter 29

On her home turf, in her environment, the one where she was in charge of her emotions and feelings, is where Sylvia planned to spend the next month, away from Delaware, away from her functioning dysfunctional family. A nice quiet dinner with friends was the therapy she craved. A few Sundays at church wouldn't hurt, either, might not help, but couldn't do any more damage to her psychological stability than the Reynoldses.

"I can't believe you broke up with that fine Mike," Karen said, perusing the menu.

"What? The relationship didn't work out. It's no big deal," Sylvia said, peering into the menu, avoiding direct eye contact and further scrutiny from Karen, who could be relentless at times in her search for information.

"'No big deal.' You say that now, but when he ends up with somebody else you're going to be singing a different tune."

"I don't think so. Once the relationship is over, I don't look back."

"True, we have to give you that," Beth concurred, sipping on water the waiter had placed on the table earlier. "When you break up with someone, we never hear about him again."

"That's really the way it should be," Karen said, joining in. "Why go back and forth? If the relationship didn't work the first and second time around, why waste time going back like men are going to change, because you know us ladies aren't," Karen said, giving Beth and Sylvia low high-fives, punctuated with a burst of laughter circling the table.

This was her therapy. Her counselor would get her time and money, but the more natural approach, talking with sisters that knew her, understood her temperament, and cared, was sufficient, more than sufficient, necessary. Otherwise the feeling of unrest would continue to grow, claiming more and more of her sleep each night, worse since Daddy was arrested and Deon died. Dismiss the thoughts, she demanded, determined to have a good time and get rejuvenated in Jersey, away from the people who possessed the ability to drain peace from her like the frigid cold drains juice from a battery.

"Forget about Mike. One of my coworkers wants to meet you."

"Oh, Karen, not a blind date right now. I just broke up with Mike. I need a break. This is a rough time for me dealing with my father's situation."

"That's right, what's going on with that?"

"Remember, I told you he's out on bail."

"Yes."

"Well, we're preparing for his trial date in May."

"Three months, why so long?" Beth asked.

"Actually, that's pretty fast. We want to get this over."

"I can't imagine my father being charged with a crime. I would just die."

Sylvia wasn't drinking but kept the straw to her mouth as if she was.

"Oops, I'm sorry. That was silly of me. I didn't mean to be so thoughtless."

"It's okay, not your fault."

"Well at least your father's innocent," Beth said.

Sylvia's natural instinct was to respond with an emphatic yes, but the words wouldn't come forward. They felt trapped behind a wall of confusion and flashbacks coming more frequently. No way could Herbert Reynolds, the best father in the world, have molested Latoya Scott, consensual or not. Worse, no way could he have molested his favorite daughter, wasn't possible, or was it?

The waiter appeared ready to take the orders. Beth and Karen ordered first.

"And what will you have?" the waiter asked Sylvia.

"I'm not very hungry after all. A bowl of your minestrone soup will be fine, thank you." It wasn't the appetite she'd just lost. It was her security in Herbert Reynolds's innocence. She was a clinically trained psychologist who knew her craft. She knew the signs of abuse and had known for some time, but the pieces didn't fit together, they couldn't. She hadn't allowed the obvious to have any leeway into her already crumbling world of mistrust and disillusion. She had chalked up the to diagnosis from her past therapists as lazy and off the mark when they'd hinted at possible sexual abuse in her childhood, but today, the feeling and the reality had finally burst forward, sending suppression, denial and any other barrier to the back of her consciousness. Who would she tell? Who would believe her? What if she was wrong and raised a flag in error like Latoya may or may not have done?

"You were the main one who wanted to bring Beth out to dinner for her birthday and now you're not hungry."

"Are you okay?" Beth asked, unaware of the agony swirling inside Sylvia.

At this moment, Sylvia wasn't sure if crying, screaming or lying was best and chose to take the latter, a conquest she was somewhat familiar with.

"Let's make a toast to Beth's thirtieth birthday," Karen said, lifting her glass.

"And to wonderful friends. I don't know anyone more kind, generous and more loyal than you are, Sylvia, and anyone more truthful than you, Karen. I love you both."

"That's me, Ms. Truth, telling it like it is. I don't believe in keeping skeletons in the closet. If it's to be told, I tell it. If nothing else, you can always say that I'm honest."

Sylvia participated in the toast and nodded in agreement, wondering what her truth was.

Chapter 30

Reese slid his credit card into the automatic reader and began pumping gas into the SUV. He was off work but had no real plans, same routine. Get off, grab a bite to eat, go home, relax in front of the TV, wait for Angela to arrive and determine what mood she was in, and then watch her escape to a different room in the house, away from him. Two out of seven nights, she was in a fairly decent mood, wanting to eat and spend time together in the same room. As he pumped the gas, his mind wandered to home, wondering what tonight would bring.

Could his situation get any worse? A black Honda Accord made a beeline for the pump in front of him. Of the ten pumps at the station and the thirty stations around Wilmington, why did Felicia have to find herself at this one, directly in front of him? Too late for him to run away, she'd locked in on him and wasted no time hopping out of her car.

Reese stuffed his hands in his coat pocket and tried to present a staunch demeanor. Better yet, leave with whatever gas he had. There were other stations on the way home. He could finish his fill-up on the run.

"Reese Jones, well, well, well, imagine running into you," she said, grinning from ear to ear.

"Felicia," he said, hurriedly pulling the nozzle from his gas tank, spilling some in the process.

"Did your wife tell you about me and Junior running into her at the store last month?"

Reese wanted to remain in control, but his hands and feet couldn't seem to move as quickly as he wanted. No way could Angela or anyone close to her see him at the station with Felicia. If any of the Reynoldses popped in for gas, he might as well kiss his marriage goodbye. Angela wasn't going to buy the chance-meeting explanation. He'd already slipped up too much for that lame excuse to work, although it happened to be the truth. Truth wasn't Angela's reality; perception was.

He gave the gas cap a few turns, not completely sure it was on tight. He'd fix the cap down the road at the next gas station. He had one goal in mind, get out of there, fast. Felicia stood between him and his car door.

"I'm on my way to get Junior from daycare. Would you like to follow me over and see your namesake?"

Reese eased gingerly toward his door, with her taking tiny steps back but not clearing the path. He was within a breath-length of her, another step and they would be in kissing-length. "No, thanks. I have to get home to my wife."

"You sure?" she asked, letting her body and eyes do most of the talking.

"Positive," he belted out, and pushed into her body just long enough to get his hands on the door of the SUV. With a quick motion he had the door open, creating a divide between him and her. She was on one side and he was on the other, where he needed to be. Secure in the driver's seat, he started the engine with Felicia standing next to the door of the truck.

"My number's the same," she said, mouthing the words through the glass because he wasn't about to let the window down and prolong the dangerous unsolicited rendezvous. "Call me," she mouthed, with her thumb and baby finger positioned near her mouth like a phone handset.

He gave her a nod as his tires squealed off. He took a deep breath and released a sigh when he reached the street. Close call. Wilmington was small. Would he forever be plagued with avoiding Felicia and her son? If only he'd understood the full brunt of consequences resulting from their one encounter. How could he have known? The moment caught him weak, and bam, there he was, a full-fledged member of the adultery club—him, the man who couldn't wait to get married and raise a family. He understood Angela's hurt and dismay; it was hard for him to believe, too. But what was done was done. He couldn't take back the time he'd slipped. He had to concentrate on being the best husband he could to Angela and hope that one day she would agree to have his children.

He turned off the road into another gas station. Ironic, he thought, the woman he loved didn't want his child, but Felicia, the woman he was going out of his way to avoid, wanted nothing more than to have his child. He had to chuckle. Life was funny, and most of the time, out of his complete control. He wanted counseling, they needed counseling. Angela wasn't going anytime soon. Next best thing, he'd call Sylvia and see if she was home. He couldn't talk to Angela, especially about Felicia, but Sylvia was levelheaded and a good listener. That's what he would do. He hopped out of the SUV again, hoping to complete the simple task of filling up without being chased down by the very person he had to avoid at all costs. Hurry, hurry, hurry, he was thinking, fixing his gaze on the street and taking note of every car passing, hoping they weren't black Honda Accords. Sylvia could help him, provide some counseling, and Angela wouldn't have to know. Besides, Sylvia was her sister, nothing to worry about there.

Chapter 31

Making the trip across the bridge into downtown Wilmington was becoming routine. Between conference calls and frequent trips from New York, Attorney Jackson was progressing with Daddy's defense as expected. The impromptu meeting today was alarming, but no reason to panic prior to the meeting.

Last time she'd parked in the garage and was prepared to stay all day if necessary. Today Sylvia parked at a two-hour meter. She didn't want to dwell on the case. She had her own problems to deal with. Her nights were restless as it was without piling on more details of Daddy's alleged crime. Sylvia entered the office building and met the rest of the family at the elevator.

Greetings were exchanged.

"I hate you had to come down here in the middle of the day," Daddy said.

Sylvia intentionally stood in the back of the elevator out of his arms' reach.

She didn't have much to say. She couldn't get Latoya Scott off her mind.

"I'm not sure what this new revelation is, but it must be important to have us get off work and come down here," Angela said.

"We'll soon see," Sylvia said, sliding past her parents and entering the room where Attorney Jackson was waiting.

Greetings were quick. Formalities were no longer required.

"I'm glad you could make it on such short notice."

"We're eager to find out what's going on, Mr. Jackson," Mom said in a very calm tone, considering.

"I'd like to meet with Herbert alone for a few minutes."

Sylvia could sense stares from around the room, most likely expecting her to protest, but she didn't have the fight in her.

"Okay, we'll go to the reception area," Mom told Attorney Jackson.

"This should be brief," he assured her.

"Then we'll wait in the hallway," Mom responded.

Ten minutes passed, seeming more like an hour. Attorney Jackson emerged from the office, extending an invitation into the room as he exited. "He's all yours."

Mom entered the room, taking gingerly steps, and took a seat. "Herbert, what is it?" she asked, holding Daddy's hand.

"Another student has come forward."

"What?" Mom and Angela said in unison. Daddy reared back in the metal chair. The room and accommodations were meant to be comfortable, efficient and convenient.

Most of the rooms on the fifth floor were frequented by criminals and their attorneys working out ways to escape their crimes, like Daddy. Her nightmares were becoming clearer and clearer each night, the closet, the man, her. How could she believe he could do such a thing? No, block out the mere thought. Focus on truth. Do what she had to do and get out, back to the bridge, away from Delaware, away from the closet of her torment.

Conversations were happening in the office, but she didn't hear the words. Latoya Scott, that's where her mind was.

"A second student makes the case harder," Angela stated.

"Who is it?" Mom asked.

"Rosaria Kimble."

Daddy winced and leaned onto the table. "She and Latoya are friends."

"So now Latoya has her friends creating lies, too. Oh, this girl is a trip. She has no dignity obviously," Angela said.

"You don't know that," Sylvia said, unable to catch her words and drawing the attention of every person in the room. The quiet was deafening.

"You act like you're defending her," Angela said.

"I'm not defending her, but I'm not going to talk about a teenager as if she's a monster."

"To tell a pack of lies on your principal, somebody who has tried to help her, makes her a monster."

"We don't really know Latoya. We don't know why she's done this. Maybe she's reaching out for help. Have you thought about that?"

"Fine, get help if she needs it. You can give her counseling if you think that will encourage her to tell the truth about Dad. In my book, sending a man to prison is a funny way to reach out for help."

Mom placed her folded hands on top of the table and fidgeted in her seat.

"You know, for someone so wrapped up in the church, you are very judgmental," Sylvia lashed out at her sister. "Not everybody has a perfect life like yours. Of all people, I'd expect you to be more compassionate."

"Girls, stop right now. I'm sorry, Herbert," Mom said.

"No need for apology. We're managing the best we can with a tough situation. I'm just glad to have you here even though I'm sick about putting all of you through this. But don't worry. Mr. Jackson said the new accusation wouldn't derail our defense."

How many Latoya Scotts would have to come forward before Attorney Jackson's defense strategy was derailed? The attorney hadn't bothered asking Daddy if he was guilty. They never asked, didn't want or need to know supposedly. She'd expect him to say no, he wasn't guilty, but the gravity of the charge at least warranted someone asking the question. No one in the room seemed to care about a fourteen-year-old girl who was somewhere living out the shame of this case, too. Daddy wasn't the only victim. Maybe he wasn't a victim at all. She couldn't bear the thought, but what if, by some remote stretch of the imagination, what if he did do it, not once but three times, to both students, and a third time, to her? She couldn't sit. What if he was the guy haunting her dreams for twenty years?

"Well, Sylvia, looks like you'll be doing a lot of psychological profiling for Mr. Jackson," Mom said.

"You can count on my Sylvia, right, baby girl?" Daddy asked, patting her hand.

His touch felt familiar. She wanted to leap out of her skin, but resisted, fighting for clarity and answers.

"I'm not sure what I could say or do that would help the case," she said, excusing herself and rushing from the room, hungry for fresh air, away from the stifling closet of an office. She was spending most of her nights in the closet and couldn't stand spending her days there, too. Mom and Daddy wouldn't understand, but this wasn't about them. This was about a little girl standing up to her alleged abuser. Latoya had stood up, and who was Sylvia to take that away from her? If Daddy was innocent, the truth was going to surface, without input from his baby daughter.

She had to get out. She had to breathe. Sylvia darted down the hallway, bypassing the elevator and dashing down the five flights of stairs in her escape.

Chapter 32

They were close, so when Denise said she was coming by for a visit, Sylvia wasn't surprised.

"I'm glad you stopped by, because I was heading over your way," Sylvia told her cousin.

"It's hard to catch me at home these days. I'm trying to spend as little time at the town house as I can, too many memories."

"Where are you staying, at your mom's?"

"Most of the time. It's been three weeks since he passed and she's starting to take it hard. Having Dad staying over there with his other woman isn't helping at all."

"I thought she was doing okay."

"At first, she was. She was very strong during the funeral and right after, but you know how it is. After that second week passes, true grief kicks in. My mother is so mad right now. I can't tell if she's mad at Deon for taking those pills or Dad for leaving her."

"Could be both."

"I don't know what my father is thinking staying over there with all those kids. He and Mom have problems, but what he's doing is wrong, moving in with another woman barely older than I am."

"How old is she?"

"Thirty, I think."

"You're kidding me. Oooh, Uncle Arthur has a woman that young, wow, that must be awful for you and for Aunt Kay. If my father did that…" she said, before catching her words and thinking about what she really wanted to say or not say.

"I'm sorry about Uncle Herbert, really I am. He's the only decent man in the family. I'm so sick of the Reynolds men— uncles and cousins—all of them. They're basically no good."

"Somebody has made you mad today."

"Not just today, every day. I can't believe my brother is gone. He was the only decent man out of our generation and they helped kill him."

"Why do you say that?"

"Tony molested Deon when he was a child."

The topic was already making Sylvia uneasy, but she couldn't run and hide. Denise needed to talk. Sylvia was family, but for now, she was a trained professional providing the forum her cousin needed to find peace.

"Nobody wants to hear it, but it's true. He did and Aunt Mabel probably knew about it. She knows everything else about everybody else's business, but she tries to keep her family business secret, like we don't know what's going on over there with her and Uncle Sam."

"You might be surprised, but I don't know anything about what's going on with them. According to Aunt Mabel, they're the perfect couple and have been for thirty-eight years," she said, with Denise simultaneously chiming off the years.

"Everybody knows the number of years they've been together. She might as well put her speech on CDs and pass them out on the streets."

Sylvia couldn't help but giggle at the image of Aunt Mabel handing out CDs on the street.

"Seriously, she has nerve talking about Deon with sons like Lee and Tony." Denise groaned, loud, deep, concluding with a sigh. "I'm getting mad just thinking about her talking about my brother. She really does have some nerve, living in her glass house with her trifling men."

"Are you talking about Tony?"

"No, forget him. He's going to get his. I'll make sure of that."

"Please don't tell me that Lee is a predator, too? Please don't. He's uncouth, but I like Lee. He always looked out for me in school and he's been like a big brother to me, in a way. I would be hurt if he was sick, too."

"No, Lee's cool, I mean as cool as you can reasonably be coming out of Aunt Mabel's house. No, I'm talking about Uncle Sam."

"What?" Sylvia asked with a taste of humor and anticipation in her question.

"You know he has another family."

"Get out of here, no way," Sylvia said, maintaining the taste of humor, unable to truly accept what Denise was saying.

"Uh-huh, he does," she reiterated.

"No way, we would have heard about this."

"Maybe, maybe not. Our family keeps a lot of secrets. See, you've been gone for a long time. You don't hear what I hear."

"I'm not that far away. I'm right across the bridge."

"I know, but you've really been gone ever since you left for college. You haven't really been knee-deep into the family business like the rest of us living in Delaware. You got out."

"But Angela and Mom and Daddy are there. I wonder if they know."

"Oh, I doubt if Angela and your dad know this, but your mom might."

"Why would she know and not Dad?"

Denise's eyes widened and her neck slowly turned away.

"You might not want to know what I know. Not right now, not while your father's case is going on."

Sylvia stepped to the sofa where Denise was sitting and plopped down next to her cousin, heart racing, thoughts flying around, out of control. "Please," she said, grabbing her cousin's hand, "tell me, before I go crazy."

"Are you sure you want to hear this?"

"Yes."

"Your mom and Uncle Sam had an affair."

Sylvia jumped up, almost knocking the lamp sitting next to the sofa onto the floor. "You're lying."

"No, I'm not," Denise said, shaking her head. "It's true. I don't know who all knows about it, but it's true."

"When?"

"This was before you were born."

"Were Daddy and my mother married at the time?"

"Oh, yes, they were married, and Uncle Sam was married to Aunt Mabel, too."

"Does Daddy know?"

"I doubt that he knows. I think he was away at war when it happened."

"How do you know so much about it? You're younger than I am. So you weren't born at the time, either."

"My mother told me. We talk about all kinds of stuff."

"I wish Mom and I could talk like you and Aunt Kay. I can't believe she told you this when I didn't even know. At least it was a long time ago, before any of us kids were born. Doesn't make what they did right, but at least it's over and done."

"Actually, Donny was already born at the time. Angela definitely wasn't born, not before Uncle Sam got involved with your mom," Denise said, letting her gaze slowly shift away.

It took a minute to digest what Denise wasn't saying. "You're not trying to say what I think you're saying. No, no way, that's not possible."

"It is. I'm not lying to you, for real."

"I would have heard about this before now. As much as Aunt Mabel talks, come on."

"Think about it, why would she tell something like that? She has the perfect husband, perfect marriage, perfect sons and perfect life. She'd rather die than to let someone know her husband cheated, and Angela isn't his only child born outside their marriage. Uncle Sam has another set of children in Baltimore. I've never met them."

"How do you get this information?"

"My mother happens to know the mother of his other children. They went to high school together."

"I need to sit down. This is too much to process. I know you wouldn't lie to me, but I can't believe this is true. Angela is Uncle Sam's daughter? That's crazy. That's impossible."

"It's true, and the only reason I'm telling you is because this family needs to stop hiding all of these lies and get to the truth. I'm tired of carrying these secrets. It's time to come clean. If we had dealt with the truth, my brother would still be alive today. What Tony did to him bothered Deon for a long time. He was constantly battling depression and Tony is living it up with his child-molesting self."

"I don't know what to say."

"I hate to ask you this, but since it's confession time, we need to get the facts on the table. I love Uncle Herbert. I believe he's one of the few good men in this family, but do you think there's any truth to his charges? Uncle Herbert is a Reynolds and those men have problems."

"No, you didn't ask me that."

"No, wait, wait, I'm not trying to hurt you or to get you mad at me, but I'm trying to be honest about everything in my life now. If he's innocent, fine. I love Uncle Herbert and wish him the best. He's your father and I understand, but when I think about the fact that nobody stood up for Deon when he was being abused, I have to speak my mind. What if the student is telling the truth? What if your father did touch her? Shouldn't she be protected and taken seriously?"

"Denise, I thought you were coming over for counseling. Now that you've dropped this load of toxic information on me, I'm the one who needs counseling."

"I hope you're not mad at me," Denise said, embracing her.

"I can't be mad at you for telling me the truth, even if the truth isn't what I want to hear."

"Well, I'm sorry if I've hurt you. You know I didn't mean to. I love you."

"I know."

"Let me get out of here and go put on my boxing gloves."

"For what?"

"Apparently Deon had a few of his own little secrets, can you believe it? As close as we were, I thought I knew everything there was to know about my brother, but apparently not."

After dropping the twenty-ton load of revelations, what else could Denise have excluded?

"Deon didn't have a will, and it looks like he had about one hundred and twenty thousand dollars invested in a couple of mutual funds, plus his house and car are paid for. Can you believe it? Paid for. Now Mom refuses to let Dad get any of the money. She's afraid he's going to spend his portion on his woman and Mom won't stand for it. I have a feeling this is going to get ugly. I wish a thousand times Deon had left a will or note, kind of showing how he wanted his belongings to be divided. My parents are already fighting as it is, and a little bit of money might drive them apart for ever."

"You lived with him. Don't you have some idea of what Deon would have wanted?"

"We never really talked about money. I constantly offered to pay rent. He would never take my money. So, I bought the groceries, supplies, you know, little things like that. I also paid the utilities and the phone."

"Hmm, odd, not a clue, huh?"

"No, and we were living under the same roof. I hate to say this, but that's why you have to give consideration to Latoya Scott. You just never know all there is to know about a person even when they're sleeping under the same roof. I've learned the hard way. Don't you make the same mistake."

Chapter 33

Sylvia wasn't expecting company when the doorbell rang. She crept into the guest bedroom and peeked from behind the blinds to see if there was a recognizable car in her driveway. From her angle, she could see the back of a black SUV, Reese's vehicle. She hustled into the hallway and down the stairs in her tank top and loungewear pants. Weren't too many people she was interested in seeing. Reese was one of the few. She opened the door.

"Well, well, well, did my sister kick you out again?" she said, standing to the side for him to enter.

"Not yet, but might be any day now," he laughed, and handed over his coat.

"What brings you all the way over here to New Jersey?"

She directed him to the living room. He took a seat on the sofa and looked fairly relaxed. She took a seat at the other end of the sofa.

"I was out driving around."

"And you ended up here? Right. What's going on?"

"Okay, okay, it's your sister."

"It's always my sister. That's why you came over here last week, to talk about Felicia and my sister?"

"Well, guess what, it's the same subject this week and probably next week and the week after that. This thing with Felicia is never going away. I've apologized and I'm trying to be what Angela needs."

"Does my sister know what she needs?"

"I don't know, but whatever it is, I don't think I'm it. We need counseling."

"She still won't go?"

"Nope, and now with your Dad's case, she doesn't want to talk about our issues. She acts like we're okay, but she knows and I know we're not."

"That's the way my family is. They live in denial," she said, exhibiting more emotion than she'd planned, to the point of choking up.

"Hey, what's wrong?"

"Nothing," she said, pulling the throw pillow to her chest and resting her chin, with tears pressing forward but without adequate gumption to surface, much like her secret. No one could know what she suspected. Verbalizing her fear, giving the nightmare a voice, made the violation real, unavoidable, and would force her to deal with the issue that had nagged and gnawed at her soul during the day and her rest during the night for more than twenty years. No one needed to know, but she couldn't contain the bubbling explosion. Therapy was the key, and who better than Reese, her brother-in-law, someone who confided in her, one of the few men she trusted. "Reese," she said, extracting a tissue from the end table, "I have something to tell you, and I haven't told anyone else."

He sat up on the end of the sofa and faced her. "What? You can tell me anything."

"You can't tell anyone."

"Sylvia, you can trust me, you know that."

"Not even my sister. You can't tell her, nobody."

"I promise, not even Angela."

She tried to say the words, but they were lodged behind her love, stuck, clamoring to escape, to bypass the road-blocks. Each attempt to speak was blocked. Reese didn't rush her or pressure her into speaking. He was kind, compassionate and patient, what she needed. Finally, the truth would not be diverted any longer, pushing past her emotions, fears, shame, confusion and devotion to Herbert Reynolds. "I think my father might be guilty."

Reese didn't pounce on her words. Time passed as if the words were talking during the silence.

"What makes you think he might be? Do you know the girl or her family?"

"No, I don't know Latoya Scott or her family, but I know me."

"I don't understand."

She tightened her grip on the throw pillow and spit the words out like puzzle pieces, letting them fall at will. "He might have molested her because I think he molested me." There, she'd released her demon, the one of denial and secrecy. For a tick of a moment, she felt relieved.

Reese's eyebrow arched and eyes widened. "Are you sure?"

"I'm pretty sure."

"Wow, that's deep." They were both quiet and finally he broke the silence and said, "I don't know what to say."

"Imagine how I feel," she said, having forgotten about the dormant tears that were beginning to resurface. She plucked a few more tissues from the box and put them to immediate use.

Reese slid across the sofa and wrapped his arms around her. She didn't want to be helpless or solicit his pity. She was an intelligent woman who'd counseled many children and adults during crisis times in their lives. She was the giver, not the receiver. She should have been repulsed by the embrace of a man, as she had been for so long, but Reese felt different, comforting, secure and real. Sylvia allowed her body to relax in his embrace while her soul poured out a thunderstorm of tears. There weren't many times, but every now and then she wished her big brother was around for such moments. He wasn't, Reese was. She cried until her bucket of tears was empty.

"There's more," she said, pulling away from Reese and wiping her eyes with the soaked ball of tissues. "Mom and Uncle Sam had an affair and," she shared before stopping to blow her nose, "Angela is Uncle Sam's daughter."

"What? No," he said flopping back on the sofa. She could see he was struggling to get his words together. "Why hasn't Angela told me about your uncle?"

"Probably because she doesn't know."

"Get out of here. Your parents never told her?"

Sylvia's head titled. "Not once. I just found out myself. As a matter of fact, I'm not sure my father knows."

"Are you going to tell him?"

"Hadn't planned on it." She hadn't spoken to Angela or her parents in ten days, since the last meeting downtown with Attorney Jackson. She wanted time and distance to sort out her feelings and to deal with her issues surrounding Daddy.

"Oh, man, if you do she will be crushed. She loves her family and your mother in particular. If she found out, I'm not sure what Angela would do. Oh, my goodness, she would freak out. Oh, your mother, cheating on your father with his brother, oh man. And Angela is mad at me? Whew. You better hope she never finds out. She will trip, for real. She will trip."

"I'm not sure if the rumor about Uncle Sam and Mom is true, that's why I'm not saying anything. I told you, but you're different. I can be honest with you."

"As much as I've told you about Angela and Felicia, we're stuck together. But I do think you should at least talk with your mom. I can tell this is bothering you."

"The issue with my father is bothering me more," she said, retreating back into the foyer of her despair.

"Right, right, that's heavy," he said, releasing a sigh. "How can I help you?"

She let her head rest on his shoulder. "You're already doing it, just being here and listening. I couldn't ask for any more." God was probably somewhere around, but Reese was here now, a friend, a good friend, maybe her only true friend.

Chapter 34

Reese was right. Talking to Mom might help, no other therapy had. Besides, she was entitled to hear the truth from her mother instead of the rumor mill. Sylvia entered the house with a fast-forwarded image of leaving. She found Angela and Mom seated at the dining room table guarding hundreds of photos and memories in front of them.

"What a surprise," Mom said, with a warm expression. "Your father just left. He'll be glad to see you when he gets back."

"I don't plan to be here too long."

Mom shuffled around a few photos. "We miss you."

"Wouldn't hurt to stop by and check on Mom and Dad every now and then, Sylvia. I can't do everything." Angela covered her mouth as Mom gazed at her. "I'm sorry, Mom," Angela said touching her hand, "I didn't mean that the way it sounded," she added with a soft voice. Her tone deepened when she said, "What I meant is that they need us now more than ever, Sylvia."

She didn't make the trip to encounter an argument with her sister. What Angela was harping about was right, but of no consequence today. Sylvia had to accomplish what she came to do. "Mom, I need to talk with you about something," she blurted out before taking a seat on the solid wood king-size chairs her mother had kept for three decades, unwilling to swap them out for another set, afraid a new set might not be as sturdy.

"Let's pick out the slide show photos first. I can go home and you can visit with Mom, something you don't do too often, right, Mom?"

Mom didn't respond. She pretty much stayed neutral when her daughters were feuding, until the battle became too heated and she jumped to Angela's defense nine times out of ten.

"This is important."

Angela griped but Mom didn't get sucked into the tiff. "What is it, Sylvia?"

"Is Daddy coming right back?"

"Not right back. He's taking care of some business at the bank," she said, fumbling with more photos. "Why?"

"Is Daddy the only person you came to see? Mom needs you, too."

Sylvia ignored Angela and kept her focus on Mom. "Good, because I need to talk about the case." Mom sat tall in her seat, with full attention directed Sylvia's way. "I'm not sure if Daddy is innocent." There, she'd given a voice to her deep-seated anguish, but the words still hurt, more than she could explain.

"What?" Angela belted out.

"What are you talking about?" Mom said in a tone so serious Sylvia was intimidated and unsure if she'd be able to continue with her suspicions.

"Is there any possibility that Daddy could have done what Latoya is alleging he did?"

"I can't believe you, Sylvia. I don't care how much psychobabble you do for other people, this is our father."

"I know exactly whose father he is, do you?" Mom didn't appear to be any wiser about the knowledge Sylvia was armed with, which was fine because the purpose of the chat was to talk about Daddy and not Angela's paternity.

"Is that supposed to mean something?" Angela asked, unaware of what she was really asking.

Control, control, control, she couldn't let her rivalry with Angela derail her primary purpose for showing up today. Sylvia needed to purge the notions, concerns and fears living within her consciousness, refusing to let her have a restful night. She wouldn't live like Deon, harboring the anguish of his abuse, letting denial and an inability to expose his demons claim precious years of living. She wouldn't end up using sleeping pills to handle the torment. ACE, her proven method of therapy (acknowledge the issue, confront the source and embrace the future) worked for her patients and would have to do her justice, as well.

"How do we know Latoya Scott is lying?"

"Because I know my husband."

"How well can we really know anybody? I'm finding out more and more secrets about this family. I don't know who or what is true."

"Do you have evidence?" Mom asked.

"No, but," was the extent of her answer prior to Angela cutting in.

"Why would you say something like that if you're not sure? What are you trying to do to us, Sylvia? You should be ashamed of what you're saying and what you're doing to Mom. You are so selfish. All you're thinking about is yourself. How dare you stand in our parents' house and accuse our father of something so sinful. I can't believe you. I thought you knew our father better than anyone next to Mom. He always treats you like a princess. No matter what I do, it's never as good as what Sylvia is doing."

"Your father has never said that to you, Angela," Mom said emphatically.

"Maybe not in those words, Mom, but his actions say that Sylvia is his favorite. I wonder how he would feel knowing his princess thinks he's a molester."

"You don't know what I think. Why would I raise the question without a good reason?"

"I don't know what you're capable of."

"Stop it, both of you," Mom said, slamming the album photos onto the table. "I'm tired of the two of you fussing and fighting when my husband is trying to stay out of jail. Grow up, you two. I didn't raise you to be so hateful to each other. You're sisters, for goodness' sake. It's time to put your petty differences aside and act like you have some sense. Of all times, we need to come together for your father's sake if for no other reason."

"But, Mom, I have to get what I'm feeling about Latoya and Daddy off my chest."

"Not right now," Mom shouted, causing both of her daughters to sit up straight and offer a brief truce.

"You're a psychologist. Can't you talk to one of your friends and spare Mom your psychoanalysis?"

"I don't need a psychologist. What I need is to be heard by my mother."

"Unless you're talking about your father's innocence, there's no room in my heart right now for any other conversation pertaining to Latoya Scott and her mother."

"So if you don't want to hear the truth about Daddy and Latoya, then I know you don't want to hear about what Daddy did to me," Sylvia said, grabbing her purse and coat but not exiting fast enough to bypass Mom's retort.

"What did your father do to you?" she said, making it difficult to differentiate the look in her eyes from anger or fear.

"Nothing, forget it," Sylvia said, gently ushering around her mother, who was still seated but rising.

"You're not going to make a comment like that and then walk out of this house. What did your father do to you?"

"What does it matter, you wouldn't believe me, anyway."

"Don't beat around the bush with me, Sylvia. Say what you came here to say. Herbert is my husband and you're my daughter. Say what you have to say," Mom said, standing solidly on her feet.

"What if I said Daddy abused me, would you believe me?"

Mom should have lost faith with such a revelation, but she didn't budge, holding her ground, unlike Angela's ranting and raving in the background.

"You mean abuse, like whopping you with a belt, because I'm the one who lit your behind, yours and your sister's. Your father has never so much as raised a hand to you."

"No, Mom. Forget what I said. I doubt if you'll believe me, anyway."

"You're not making any sense."

"Yes, she is, Mom. She thinks Dad is guilty and wants us to believe he is, too. Even if you have evidence, I don't believe you," she said, resuming her photo selection. "What else is there to say? Sylvia, why don't you go back to New Jersey and let me and Mom get back to our anniversary planning. You'd done enough damage here today."

"Angela, that's enough. I won't have you telling your sister to leave my house."

"That's okay, Mom. Fine, Angela, if this is the way you want it," she said, collecting her belongings and springing to her feet. "See, there's one of our problems. I just told you I have issues with Daddy's innocence and all you can talk about is an anniversary celebration? What a joke. Daddy's been charged with molesting a student. Deon just died and we find out his own cousin molested him, and all you can talk about is putting together a party. You have to be kidding me."

"You don't have any right to tell me and Mom what we can and can't do, Sylvia. Mom's not your daughter."

"Look who's talking. Daddy's not even your real father." Oh no, she didn't mean to let the words escape, although they'd been raging to be released for some time.

Both Mom and Angela turned pinkish red with the rush of blood mixing with their skin color. She felt awful letting her emotions get the best of her and hurling a life-altering truth at her sister. Sylvia darted out the house, amid pleas for her to come back. The next stop she made would be her driveway in New Jersey, the sooner the better.

Chapter 35

Sylvia scrubbed and scrubbed in the shower, trying to cleanse, to purge and to wash away the images of him touching her in a way that felt disgusting. Deon, Tony, Mom, Uncle Sam, Daddy's little girl, Latoya Scott, the therapist meshed in her mind, with Mike's words about her inability to show affection wrapped around those dancing in her head, strangling, blinding, crippling. The warm water soothed her brown skin, but no matter how hot she got the water, it didn't reach the dirtiness dwelling in the dark caverns of her soul. She'd hoped to feel better by coughing up a bit of the unrest encountered this afternoon with Mom and Angela. Maybe there was a tad of relief, but the amount was so insignificant she didn't count much change. She had to deal with her demons. Did Daddy? Could he? She'd been counseling long enough to know the answer, but denial had worked for years, why drag the truth to light, particularly when she wasn't exactly sure of what the truth was.

She could hear the faint ring of the phone and suspected her mother was calling, as Mom had done since she left their house earlier. Sylvia continued letting the water stream down, from the top of her head, drenching her twisty braids, continuing down her long, lean body, water drops finding their way to the drain, where she wanted to send the rest of her tormentors. Everyone had looked out for everyone in the family. No one was looking out for her. Time to take charge of her life and a warm bath wasn't the solution. Basic therapy was effective, her own. She had completed the "A" in ACE, with acknowledging her potential abuser. She was at the "C," confront the source.

Crying and hoping wasn't her style. She'd gotten absorbed in the moment, but the survival instinct and sassy fire she harbored in her personality was rekindling and Sylvia was ready to take action. She'd tried accumulating psychology degrees, intense therapy, accepting Christ last year, actually more like joining the church because she hadn't really approached Christ with her issue. What would she ask Him? Better to stick with what she knew: ACE, Sylvia style. No need getting Christ involved when she was well equipped to handle her problem—her degrees, training and awards said so. She could resume her newfound church life once her troubles were rectified and she was back on track to a fulfilling future. Besides, the people at church were so busy with their religious world, they hadn't noticed her absence.

Chapter 36

Angela didn't want to make the trip across the Delaware Memorial Bridge into New Jersey. Why go looking for trouble when a ton had already been deposited at their doorsteps in Delaware? But Mom was adamant about going to Sylvia's. She'd called every number she had for Sylvia, incessantly, work, home and cell. She would have called Mike, too, but Sylvia wasn't in the habit of sharing her friends' numbers with the family. Angela slowed the Nissan as she approached the last curve leading to Sylvia's luxury town house development and turned onto Marigold Circle. Angela admired the setting, plenty of trees, quiet neighborhood, attached garages and full clubhouse amenities. She and Reese did okay with two modest incomes, but Sylvia was doing better on one. Angela glided into Sylvia's two-car driveway. Angela peered along the street in search of her sister's 5 series BMW as they negotiated the walkway, Mom following at a rapid pace.

"Mom, she might not be home," Angela commented, ringing the bell again.

"I don't care. I'm not leaving until I talk to my child," Mom said, knocking firmly.

"But she might not want to talk. She left with such an attitude earlier, I'm not sure what's going on in her head. Why don't we go home, let everyone clear their heads and come back."

"Angela, I told you, I'm not going anywhere. I will sit on this ground and wait all night if I have to, but I plan to see Sylvia this evening. Now, I don't mean to hold you up. You go on home if you want."

"Mom, I can't leave you here."

"Don't worry about me. Your dad will come and get me or I can take a cab. Either way, I'm staying here. That's all there is to this conversation."

Angela wanted to scream. Sylvia had Dad groveling and now Mom. What was left for her? She was the good daughter, the one who followed the rules, showed no disrespect and stayed close to home. Yet Sylvia, the free spirit, who had to do what she wanted without consequences, ended up with the attention of both parents. Angela had her own trauma and could use unlimited support. Trying to hold the marriage with Reese together was taking more than she had to offer, and now with Dad, Sylvia, Mom, Deon, Denise and Aunt Mabel, what else could she handle?

"I can't leave you waiting out here. I'll stay with you, Mom," she said lacking enthusiasm. "Let me give her a call in case she's home and doesn't hear the bell," she said, fumbling in her coat pocket for the cell phone. "I can't imagine why she can't hear the bell. Her place is big, but not that big."

* * *

Sylvia heard the doorbell ringing, first repeatedly, then less frequent with the phone calls trailing off, too. She could see the tail of Angela's Nissan parked in her driveway. She wanted to reach out to her mother but couldn't find the words. What was there to say? Mom was Herbert Reynolds's biggest fan, unconditionally. She would never be able to objectively hear her daughter's plea or acknowledge the implications of the flashbacks, which were coming more frequently, no longer relegated to Sylvia's dreams at night, but spilling into her days. She was sorry to have blurted out the part about Uncle Sam and Mom, especially in front of Angela, but there was nothing she could do about the slip now. Besides, too much had been concealed and left to chance. As disheartening as the revelation to Angela was, she'd be better off later knowing, or at least Sylvia had to believe her words did some good.

Angela glanced at her watch. Almost an hour had passed, twenty minutes of waiting at the door with the loss of daylight forcing them into the car. "Mom, she's either gone or home and not willing to answer the phone," Angela said, raising the heat level in the car.

"I don't want to leave her alone like this."

"She's tough. She'll be just fine."

"She's not as tough as you think. She's my daughter, my baby. Unless you're a mother, it's hard to understand the pain I'm feeling knowing my daughter resents me, and worse that she truly thinks her father could hurt a child like Latoya. I'm crushed," Mom said, choked up. "Lord, You're going to have to give me strength. I need You now like I've never needed You before."

"Mom, I don't want to ask this, but what did Sylvia mean about me not being Dad's daughter? I think we might have to get her some help, real help, not another one of her psychology friends, but a real psychiatrist."

"There's nothing wrong with your sister."

"Then she's just being mean, hateful and disrespectful, which she can be at times."

"Not this time."

"Then what did she mean? I don't understand."

"I don't know who told her or how she found out, but she knows something that has been kept away from you girls and from your father your whole life. I don't know why it's coming up now, but I can't stop what is."

"What are you talking about, Mom?" Angela said, turning down the flow of heat coming from the vents.

"I was hoping to never have this conversation with you, your sister or your father, but looks like I have no choice."

Angela's body tensed; her palms became moist and her heartbeat trotted.

"I love you. Your father loves you."

"Mom, you're scaring me. What is it? Just say it. You don't have to beat around the bush with me. Tell me. What is it?" she asked gripping the wheel but keeping her gaze locked in sync with her mother's.

"I made a mistake thirty years ago."

"What kind of mistake and what does that have to do with what Sylvia said?"

"When your father was in Vietnam, I made a mistake."

"What kind of mistake?" Angela said with her voice elevating.

"I was with your uncle Sam."

"What do you mean 'with Uncle Sam'?" she asked, as if she didn't have a clear idea of what her mother was struggling to say.

"I had a brief affair with your uncle. It was a mistake."

"How could that happen? You and Dad have always been a happy couple to me. I never knew you had problems." The last stable couple she knew on earth was crumbling before her eyes. There was no hope for her and Reese. "I've always thought you loved Dad. I didn't know you were unhappy. All these years, I never knew. Where was I?"

"I do love your father. We're happy, truly happy, couldn't be happier together."

Reese supposedly loved her, too, but that didn't stop his indiscretion. Didn't love have any power over adultery? "If you love Dad, how could you do this to him? Mom, I look up to you as a strong Christian woman. How could you commit adultery?"

"Angela, that was a long time ago. I was young then. I hadn't committed my life to the Lord. I was scared and lonely when your father was gone. Your uncle was kind to me at a time when I was vulnerable and weak-minded. There was never any love between us, not like what I have with your father. My time with your uncle was just a mistake. One time, that was it."

"One time was enough."

"What happened is in the past, where it should stay."

"How can you say that? Uncle Sam is my father, not Dad. How am I supposed to live with that? How is Dad going to feel?"

"Your father doesn't need to know this. This is an old mistake, buried, done with."

"You don't think Dad should be told? When Reese cheated on me I wanted to know."

"And what good has knowing done for your marriage? Sometimes, not all the time, but sometimes we have to let sleeping dogs lie. We have to accept the past for what it was, seek forgiveness, learn the lessons and grow in wisdom, making better decisions the next time around."

"Mom, I don't know what to say. I'm so hurt and confused."

"You and Sylvia are going to have to find your peace, which I've found can only come from the Lord. After the hurt and shock subsides, then you have to let this heal. Then you can move on, like I've done."

"Doesn't the secret bother you?"

"No."

"Not even a little? I've only known for a few minutes and it bothers me. To be honest, I wished I'd never found out, instead of having to pretend from now on that I don't know. This is terrible."

"Angela, I wasn't saved back then. When I accepted Christ as my Savior, the Son of God, I confessed my sins to Him and I was forgiven. He forgave me for my sins, all of them. That I know, no matter what, and I became a new person in Jesus. Took me a while, but I learned how to forgive myself, too. I let my mistake go. I probably should have told your father a long time ago, but the time never seemed right, and as the years passed, the need to tell him felt more harmful than good. I'm not proud of what I did, but I'm happy with who I've become and where I am in my marriage and in my walk with the Lord."

"That's easy to say, Mom, but I have to deal with the fact that my father is my uncle and my uncle is my father. What sense does that make? What a disaster. I wish I'd never found out," she said, clutching the steering wheel and resting her forehead on the wheel, too.

"Exactly my reason for not telling your father, especially now when he's already under attack. Besides, I don't honestly know the truth. Your father came home for a leave around the time you were conceived. So, I just don't know. Back then, asking for a paternity test was a big deal and it didn't make sense. Sam was married to Mabel with a child at the time and I was married to your father with Donny. Letting the family know wasn't the best decision at the time, so I didn't tell your father, Sam or Mabel."

"How did Sylvia find out?"

"The only person I confided in was Kay. Whatever happens, your father can't know. No good can come from his knowing, too many years have passed. He needs our full support and we owe him that much, Angela. Don't penalize him for my thirty-year-old mistake. Look at me, remember how you felt when you found out about Reese's indiscretion?"

"I felt like dying."

"Your father has been nothing but good to me through-out our entire marriage, to me and to you children."

"That's all the more reason you should tell him. Married people can't hide secrets and expect to keep a marriage together. The truth is better any day, even if it hurts."

"You're right about truth and secrets, but your father doesn't deserve more hurt piled on, not now. He's already going to be crushed by Sylvia's doubting his innocence, more than you'll ever know. He loves you girls, and having Sylvia suspect him of violating his student will kill him."

"Because she is Dad's princess, she always has been. Now their relationship makes sense. She's his only real daughter," she said, unable to hold back the flow of tears.

"Stop that kind of talk. Your father loves you as much as he does Sylvia. Just so happens that she has his temperament and you're more like me. Seems like we each have our favorites, but that's not true. We both love you girls equally. Sylvia is upset now, but she's my daughter and you're your dad's daughter. Nothing has changed for us. We're the same family, no matter who your biological father is."

"Easy for you to say, Mom, but you don't know how it feels."

"Stop," Mom bellowed three levels above her normal voice. "You can't allow your soul to be beaten down by circumstances, especially those that you have no control over. I've taught you better than this, Angela."

"I can't help how I feel," she said, pushing back her emotions.

"Yes, you can. If you're ever going to get through this life, you have to realize that people are not perfect. Those that believe in Christ Jesus are redeemed from their mistakes and imperfections, but they aren't perfect. I'm not, you're not, your Dad isn't, and your husband isn't. The reality is that people will fail you, including those who love you, but love covers a multitude of sins and shortcomings."

The tears were flowing, not in a gushing way, but soft, warm, almost soothing, cleansing.

"You have to get past yourself, and I don't want to sound hard on you, but I don't want you to lose hope every time a crisis hits your life, my dear. Challenges are going to come. In this world you will have trouble—"

"Mom, you've quoted that scripture for years. I know it well, John 16:33."

"Do you, do you really know it? I'm not talking about memorizing the words. I'm wondering if you've let it saturate your spirit or if the words are just parked in your head. I'm your mother. I will always love you, no matter what. So don't let my age-old sin rob you of the peace and joy God has for you. Most of all, don't lose your hope, no matter what. Don't ever give up on God."

Angela didn't respond, but the words were seeping in.

Mom rubbed her thumb gently across Angela's cheek. "Do me one favor."

"What?" Angela whispered.

"Read Romans 5:3 for me, will you do that when you get home?"

Angela hesitated, but even now couldn't refuse her mother. "Yes."

"You promise me."

"Yes, Mom, I promise."

"Okay," she said, allowing her mother to draw her into a makeshift embrace in the tight quarters of the car.

Chapter 37

Home wasn't stable, but for Angela, home was the only place where she could hide from the darts and daggers being hurled her way. First Reese, then Dad's arrest, now Mom and Uncle Sam on top of Sylvia betraying Dad's loyalty. How many more people could betray her? How much more was God going to allow her to bear? She wasn't going to cry. She was beyond tears. She was mad, downright mad. Mad at Mom for betraying her father's trust and mad at Dad for not knowing. Reese cheated, but at least there wasn't a child popping up thirty years later. She opened the kitchen door and didn't stop until she was sitting next to Reese in the family room.

"You're back," he said, watching the TV.

"I can't take much more."

"What's wrong?" he asked, putting the TV on mute.

"My mother, Uncle Sam and Sylvia, they're what's wrong."

"What happened?"

"Sylvia doesn't believe my father is innocent."

"Wow."

"You think that's bad, wait until you hear this. Sylvia claims Uncle Sam is my father."

Reese looked away, scratched his earlobe and kept quiet.

"Of course I didn't believe her. That's crazy, you would think, but I asked Mom point blank and she confessed."

"Really?"

"Can you believe that? What else can go wrong in my family? How can Uncle Sam possibly be my father? That's crazy."

"Does your father know?"

"No, and Mom begged me not to tell him."

"Are you going to?"

"I don't know what to do. I'm in shock. Even if I don't tell him, Sylvia might. She's really out there right now. I don't know where her head is, thinking our father is capable of sexually violating a child. I mean let's call it what it is. Dad's case has sent her over the edge. She's my sister, and I love her, but I can't afford to worry about anyone but me right now. I have to figure out how to deal with this. I am so mad at my mother. I can't talk to her. I don't want to see her. I feel like she's such a hypocrite. She's the one who has always taught us about the Lord and how important honesty and integrity is, and then she does something like this."

"She made a mistake, Angela."

"One you would understand."

"This isn't about me. This is about your mom. You have a great relationship with her. Don't let it get ruined."

"She's lied for years to me, to my father and to our family. I can't trust her."

"Your mom and your uncle happened a long time ago. Maybe she's a different person today than she was then."

"So what, am I supposed to forgive and forget?"

Reese hunched his shoulders.

"How can I forget? My father isn't my father. All my life I've been Angela Reynolds, the oldest daughter of Louise and Herbert Reynolds. Today, after thirty-one years, I find out I'm not that person."

"You're still the same person, regardless of who your father is."

"You sound like Mom. Where do you guys get this stuff? Is there a handbook for cheaters that you all use?"

"If you want to keep digging at me, fine, but I was only trying to help. If you can't see that, then that's your problem," he said, taking the TV off Mute and raising the volume several notches. "Deal with your own family problems. You have all the answers, Angela. You always do. You don't need me."

On second thought, he turned the TV off. Sitting under her scrutiny didn't feel like a viable option tonight. Besides, if Angela was upset about the blowup with Sylvia and her mother, then Sylvia most likely was, too. Sylvia was the bearer of bad news but didn't deserve to be alone.

Reese called Sylvia from the garage. She was home and welcomed his company. He fired up the SUV and backed into the street. Angela would be okay. She always was. Sylvia was the sister who needed his help and compassion and that's what she would get. He sailed down the road, taking pride in the notion of spending an evening with someone with whom he shared mutual respect.

Chapter 38

Cherry Hill Mall was convenient; typical anchor stores chocked with the regular outlets in between, no fanfare or danger of running into family members, those populating her other world, the damaged one. Sylvia was thrilled when Beth called with the invitation to meet her and Karen, although the only mall Sylvia frequented on a regular basis was the one in King of Prussia. Since it had a collection of her favorite stores in the same location—Neiman Marcus, Nordstrom, Tiffany, Versace, Cartier and Bloomingdale's—the forty-minute ride into Pennsylvania was worth every drop of gas. But given the choice, boutiques were her preference. She didn't mind taking the hour-and-a-half ride to New York or two-and-a-half-hour ride down to the Chevy Chase section of D.C.

Today wasn't about shopping, not really. She was content with a meal, a laugh, an oasis from her dreadful, self-inflicted lonely existence. She wouldn't have cared if Beth's invitation was to sit on the side of the road and watch cars pass by in the company of her friends. She needed them more than they dared realize.

"I have got to get a new pocketbook," Beth stated.

"Didn't you just buy one a few weeks ago?" Karen asked.

"So what, you can never have too many pocketbooks."

"What about you? Any store you want to go into?" Karen asked.

"Not really. I'm just here to hang out with the two of you," Sylvia responded. "Plus, I can't afford to spend a lot of cash right now."

"Money is never a problem with you," Karen said. "What's up?"

Sylvia felt as if there was a bag of turmoil flopping around in her mind. She wanted to share the woes with her friends, her sisters, but was afraid to let the bag open even a little, fearing she wouldn't be able to stop the outpouring. Better to keep the bag shut, except for the incidental information.

"I'm helping to pay for my father's legal defense."

"Wow, how wonderful are you. You're really a good daughter. That's really great," Beth said, giving her a quick, loose hug. "You are such a generous person Sylvia."

Karen walked into Strawbridge's cosmetic section. "My father better stay out of jail, because I won't have any extra money after today, either," Karen said, which lightened the mood. "Seriously, how is the case going?"

To be honest, she'd have to respond by saying she didn't know, that she hadn't spoken to her father in almost a month, that she didn't know if he was guilty, that she didn't know if he was capable of molesting Latoya or her. Revealing the truth to Beth and Karen in the middle of the Cherry Hill Mall required more energy than she could expend. Truth was draining. Like food to a starving person, one bite led to the need for more and more and more and before Sylvia knew what was happening, she'd be spilling out her life history, parts she wasn't certain of and didn't want to rehash. "The trial is in May."

"Only two months away, already? I can't believe your father was charged with a crime. I don't know what I'd do if my father was arrested and had to go to trial," Beth said, in the most sympathetic tone possible given the subject.

"I can't believe this is real, either. I guess everything happens for a reason and that something good has to come out of this, otherwise we will have dealt with this nightmare for nothing."

"I don't know the Bible well, but doesn't one of the scriptures talk about every bad situation can lead to good?" Beth said.

"Girl, you didn't read that in the Bible. You heard it in philosophy," Karen clarified.

"I wouldn't know, Beth. I don't know much about the Bible," Sylvia answered.

"You've been going to church for a little while now," Beth said.

"Doesn't look like church is for me. I'm definitely no better off, maybe worse. I've decided to stick to psychology, which works for me." She hadn't decided if knowing the truth about her childhood delivered more freedom in her spirit than her twenty years of ignorance had. Whoever said the truth shall set you free wasn't a Reynolds.

* * *

The afternoon passed gently, without fanfare. Before long she was back home and feeling better. Just the break she needed. Getting out was good medicine. Sylvia sat in her den, skipping through her voice messages. One she listened to in its totality. "Sylvia, this is Dr. Jan. I'm calling because you've missed your last two appointments. Are you all right? Please call the office and let me know how you're doing and if you feel comfortable proceeding with your sessions. I look forward to hearing from you."

Chapter 39

"New Allegations in Local Molestation Case" was on the cover page of the *News Journal*. Weren't other crimes being committed in Wilmington? Every week there was another story, another headline, pouring bleach into the tender areas of Dad's integrity. He didn't speak about the case often. At a time when his concentration should have been on developing a solid defense and beating the ridiculous charges, he was pining over his daughter's absence. Didn't he see her there, Angela, his other daughter, the one who cared to give him the benefit of the doubt?

"Herbert, don't worry about the article," Mom reassured.

"We have a solid case," Attorney Jackson said, "and I have reason to believe the charges leveled by Miss Kimble will be dropped before the week is over. It seems that she will be recanting her story. That's all I can say."

"Praise God," Mom bellowed. "I don't know why she lied in the first place, but that doesn't matter. It's good news."

"Of course we won't adjust our strategy until we get confirmation, but my source is quite reliable. This is indeed good news for our case. Whatever attack the D.A.'s office is waging, we'll be ready."

A warm sensation covered Angela, but Dad wasn't as jubilant. She knew what was bothering him. The fight seemed to have drained from his body when Mom finally had to tell him a few days ago that Sylvia was dealing with personal challenges regarding his innocence. Guess she didn't have the heart to tell him the full story, not the part about Sylvia babbling about abuse or the piece about Uncle Sam. One major accusation or revelation per month was probably the most Dad could take. It was definitely all she could handle.

"Thank you for coming to our house today, Mr. Jackson," Mom said. "We certainly appreciate you making the trip from the train station out here."

"Yes, thank you," Dad said, not in his voice of distinction, but in a low almost muffled tone.

"No problem, at all. You just take care of yourself, Herbert. We want you healthy by trial time."

"I'll make sure of it," Mom said. "Mr. Jackson, can I get you a cup of coffee?"

"No, thank you, Louise, and please call me Lloyd. After two months, I feel like I've gotten to know you. I will be honored to have you call me by my first name."

"All right, Mr. Lloyd, would you like water, soda?"

"Water would be fine. Thanks," he said, directing his attention back to Dad when Mom left the room. "You have a stellar reputation in the education system and a decorated service record in the military."

"I was in the service a long time ago."

"Yes, but being a military officer can't hurt. You never know what sways the opinion of a jury, particularly in this case where it's your word against a minor's."

"What happened to the physical evidence the prosecutor has been talking about for the past two months?" Angela asked as Mom reentered the dining room, which was doubling as an office.

"There probably isn't any," Mom stated.

"But why would the attorney say there was evidence in court in front of the judge?"

"I can't speak about this case specifically, but in general, it would be considered posturing for the dramatic effect."

"Posturing sounds a lot like lying to me," Dad said.

"I wouldn't use the term *lying*, because as legal representation, we're bound by the law as well as a code of ethics. However, I do have colleagues who push the envelope."

"Still sounds like lying or right close to it."

"Let's face it. As your legal counsel, my job is to prove our case using every legal means at our discretion. Some of my colleagues will push the envelope. Sometimes the gesture works and sometimes it doesn't."

"Sounds awfully random to me."

"I have to admit, you're right, but when it comes to justice, we want to win our respective cases, but we are sworn to a code of ethics, which I intend to uphold. You can rest assured, Louise and Herbert. I will do everything within my legal and ethical right to garner a victory for you," he said, obtaining a long legal pad from his portfolio. "Any decision on Sylvia's assisting with the psychological profiling?"

"Not sure yet."

"With her prominent psychological background, she will be an asset behind the scenes."

"We'll see. I'm not sure if I want my family involved."

"We *are* involved, Herbert. Mr. Lloyd, we're willing to do whatever you need in order for the jury to find my husband innocent."

"Louise, I can't—"

"I know, I know, you can't discuss the case with us. I understand, but I want you to know that Herbert has our unconditional support. Whatever you need from his family, just say the word, and I'll make sure you get it."

"Thank you, Louise, your support is exactly what we need."

"That's right," Dad chimed in with his gaze locked on Mom, evidenced by a full smile from them both.

Mr. Jackson stayed two hours and left in time to catch the five-thirty Amtrak back to New York. Setting bail was one expense, but paying Mr. Jackson would require a small fortune. With Sylvia chipping in, the cost was manageable. It remained to be seen if she was going to continue contributing. Angela was willing to donate her savings, which wasn't much after the six months of she and Reese running two separate households. They had a few thousand, but nowhere near the amount Mr. Jackson charged. Mom and Dad hadn't asked for any help, but then they shouldn't have to. Sylvia always wanted the best: best car, best house and best clothes. Well, she wanted the best attorney. Hopefully she'd continue paying for him.

Defending his innocence and paying the legal tab was the furthest from Dad's mind. "I have to keep reaching out to her, Louise. She has to know I would never commit a crime."

The first and only time Angela saw her father cry was when Donny died. This made the second. Dad's crying ignited an automatic boohoo session for Mom. Angela stood with the intent of walking out of the room, not being able to sit there and watch her parents fall apart. Latoya was bad enough. How could Sylvia do this, too?

"She'll come around, Herbert, she has to. She knows how much you love her. We all do." She took his hand and sandwiched it between her soft, tiny hand and her cheek. "I don't know how, but I know God is going to fix this predicament. He has to. We have to keep the faith and not get caught up in what we see in the natural. God is able and His grace is sufficient for us to overcome this bump in the road," she said, with the kind of confidence Angela dreamed of possessing one day for her and for the marriage she shared with Reese. But for now, she felt like the family she'd poured her love, faith and hope into had let her down, every one of them. For a second Angela tried recalling the scripture she'd promised Mom that she'd read several weeks ago. Good thing she had it written down at home. She hadn't read it yet, didn't know when. She wasn't ready.

Chapter 40

Angela sat at the table, picking at the plate of food in front of her. "This is so hard. Every time I think about the possibility that my father might go to prison, I'm terrified."

"I thought the case was moving along in his favor."

"It was," she told Reese, setting her fork down, "but we don't know what's going on with Sylvia."

"What do you mean?" he asked.

"She didn't show up for our meeting with the attorney today. He's counting on Sylvia to do some kind of psychology stuff for him, not in court, but behind the scenes."

"It's not like her to miss an important meeting, is it? She must have a good reason."

"What reason could she possibly have for missing her father's trial meeting? This is the second meeting she's missed without so much as a phone call. If she's not going to show, Sylvia should let the attorney know so that he can get someone else to do what she had volunteered to do for free. I don't know why she's doing this to Dad."

"Have you asked her?"

"No, and I'm tired of running back and forth to Jersey tracking her down when she doesn't want to see us. My mother wanted me to go over there after the meeting today and I wouldn't. Why should I? We haven't been able to get in touch with her for more than two weeks. You can't find someone who doesn't want to be found."

"She must be going through something. Otherwise, I think she'd be there. You know how close she is to your father."

"Don't remind me," she said, taking a small bite of potatoes. "My family is so messed up. There I was sitting in a room worried about a man who's not my father. Isn't it ironic? He's probably the most honest man in the room. Yet he's the one facing criminal charges. My mother has lied to him all these years, yet she's upset with Latoya for lying. And then there's my award-winning sister whom my dad worships. She hires this expensive attorney that none of us can afford without her help. Then in midstream she decides Dad's guilty without any evidence and then goes into hiding. This is her father. He's not even my father," she said, sobbing.

"Doesn't make sense for her to intentionally avoid the family. There's no doubt in my mind that she has a legitimate explanation." If she missed the meeting, he suspected Sylvia was feeling awful. She couldn't continue torturing herself about her father. She needed to get the truth on the table and deal with the consequences. He'd been down the road she was traveling, not molestation, but the affair with Felicia. What if he'd approached Angela in the beginning, when there was time to work out their issues? Instead, he let the problem persist, and as a result, one year later the situation was ten times worse. He would convince Sylvia to at least talk with her mother and let her know what was going on.

"There is no excuse. She's being her usual Sylvia self," she said with lips contorting and each word spoken with a sharp cutting edge.

"I don't buy that. She's very responsible. This is not like her."

"You almost sound like you're defending her."

"Just trying to be helpful."

"Well, defending my trifling sister isn't the best way to be helpful," she said, standing. "I'm tired of always talking about Sylvia. I'm going to Denise's sorority event in Philadelphia tonight. So I'll be out late."

"You didn't ask me if I wanted to go."

"Didn't think you'd be interested." She laid her paper napkin across the partially eaten plate of food.

Reese wanted to chime in and enlighten his wife about two subjects she didn't seem to have much interest in: what he wanted and what her sister was dealing with. Angela didn't have a clue about what Sylvia was enduring on her own, without the support from her family. After dinner, he would take what was becoming a familiar drive across the bridge and check on his sister-in-law—no one else was. Besides, spending time at her place was a nice break away from the constant tension under his roof—the put-downs and disagreements. Sylvia talked and listened. She respected him, understood him and valued his opinions. He wolfed down the next few bites of dinner. If he hurried, he could catch the tip-off of the 76ers game at Sylvia's and be able to enjoy the game without fear of a random tongue-lashing. He was sure the impromptu visit was okay with Sylvia, but he'd call her en route to be sure.

Chapter 41

"In this world you will have trouble…" It was a scripture she'd committed to memory when Donny died. John 16:33. Reflecting on the second half of the verse—"But take heart! I have overcome the world"—gave her courage and renewed her faith. Every fiber in her flesh wanted to take on the spirit of hopelessness, or total calamity, mired in guilt and shame. But her faith was in charge, commanding that her emotions and fears, and even her buckling knees, bow down to the Word of God she'd implanted in her spirit. She wasn't a victim. Her family wasn't defeated. If only her daughters could have that assurance in their spirits, regardless of the problems crossing their paths. Her constant prayer was that Sylvia and Angela would grow in their faith and hope and not be boggled by challenges. She'd made her mistakes, but by the blood of the Lamb they were behind her and she knew it. Didn't matter how much confusion and pain was piled on top of the Reynolds household, she was determined to stand steadfast on the Word of God and not be moved by what she was seeing in the natural, in the mounting issues surrounding the Reynoldses. Her daughters loved her, both of them. Her daughters loved and needed their father, both of them.

"You need me to get you anything else?" she asked her husband, who had gone to bed a half hour earlier.

"No thank you, hon, I'm fine. I'm going to lie here and take a nap."

"It's six-thirty. You don't go to bed this early," she said, walking the delicate line between disruptive worry and healthy concern.

"I guess today wore me out. I'll take a little nap and get up later. Then I can drive you to Sylvia's."

She kissed him on the forehead and pulled the covers up to his neck. "I love you, Herbert. There is no man in this world more phenomenal than you."

He was troubled. His responses had been labored for the past week.

"Thank you, Louise, for being my wife. I don't deserve you and the girls."

"Shh," she whispered, tapping her index finger against her lips.

"No, let me say this. I'm so sorry to put you, Angela and Sylvia through this. I never wanted to cause you any pain or embarrassment. I've worked my whole life to make sure my family was safe and protected. I don't know how I allowed this to happen. I'm sorry for getting us into this trouble."

"Herbert, you don't owe me or the girls an apology. You didn't do anything wrong," she said, sitting on the side of the bed as he made room. She stroked his forehead. "We're going to get through this. All you have to do is hang in there with me. It's going to be all right."

"You'll never know how much you mean to me. You're the one who has kept our family together. No matter what happens, you're always positive."

"God is with us, no matter what. He'll never leave or forsake us. I believe it in my heart."

"Louise," he said, sitting up, "I have done some things in my past I'm not proud of, terrible things. I've never told you, because I was too ashamed."

"It doesn't matter what you've done," she told him.

"But I need to tell you. I've let this secret nag at me for more than twenty years."

She was in total sync with the man sitting before her. He was her husband before God and man, until death did they part. Whatever he had done twenty years ago wasn't beyond her unconditional heart of forgiveness and God's abiding love and forgiveness. Sylvia flooded her thoughts.

"You don't have to tell me. Whatever you did doesn't matter, not at all, doesn't change who you are or my love and respect for you."

"I have to tell you. I've never kept anything from you. You deserve to know."

"Herbert, let the past stay in the past. I don't need to know."

He pursed his lips and wrenched his hands, but acquiesced to her request. Present troubles they had. She saw no gain in inviting more heartache and turmoil into their family. She glimpsed a twinkle in his eyes.

"I'm feeling better. Why don't we head over to Sylvia's," he said, tossing the covers back.

"No, you have to rest."

"But we need to check on Sylvia. This case hasn't been easy on her and I realize it," he said, dropping his glance.

She refused to let the melancholy in the air attach to her husband. "Don't you worry, Sylvia is tough. She's so much like you that it drives me crazy half the time, but she has your drive and your heart."

"Huh," he chuckled, "my heart for Latoya is what got me in this situation."

She stood to her feet. "We're not going there," she said, covering his legs with the blanket. "Don't change who you are. Rosaria Kimble finally admitted to lying about you. One day Latoya will realize her mistake, too, and may the Lord show her the same grace He's given to me and to you."

"Amen."

"In the meantime, I'm going to call Denise and see if she can run by and check on Sylvia since she won't answer my calls."

She left the room and thumbed through the phone directory in the kitchen. A few minutes elapsed before she dialed the phone and Kay answered. After greetings were exchanged, she asked Kay, "What is Denise's phone number? There're too many numbers to remember nowadays."

Kay rattled off the number. "But you won't be able to reach her tonight. She went to one of her sorority programs with Angela. I don't expect her home until late."

"Oh," she said, unable to avoid letting out a sigh.

"What's wrong?"

"We haven't heard or seen Sylvia in two and a half weeks. She's missed our last two meetings with the attorney, the one today and the one two weeks ago. Not like her to miss an appointment, not twice. She's not herself. This case has torn her apart. You know how close she is to her father."

"Do you think there's something wrong? Should we call the police?"

"I don't think so. I've called her job every day and her secretary says she's in but busy."

"You haven't gone to her job?"

"I've thought about it two or three times, but you know I don't like driving in New Jersey by myself. Herbert hasn't been feeling the best and Angela has her own life."

"My car's in the shop, but I have a rental car. Why don't I drive over for you?"

"Would you?"

"Sure, I'm not doing anything. The drive will get me out of this empty house and help to get my mind off Deon."

"I'm sorry, Kay. I know you're fighting your own battles right now. I've intended to come by your house for the past two weekends, but like I said, Herbert hasn't been feeling the best. But know that you are in my thoughts and prayers daily."

"Don't worry about me, Louise. I know where your heart is and I appreciate your prayers. Running over to New Jersey will do me good."

"Kay, thank you so much. You're a godsend."

"But I've only been there a few times and each time was during the day. Let me get a piece of paper and write down the directions."

Chapter 42

Kay maneuvered her Buick across six lanes to the side of the road after paying the toll attendant. She reread her directions and crawled along I-295 in search of the Woodcrest exit, successfully navigating the automobile until finally, the sign read Cherry Hill. What should have been a fifty-minute drive had stretched into nearly two hours. Finally, Balboa, and two blocks later she was turning onto Marigold Circle.

Deon would have made the trip and returned home to Delaware by now. She missed her son. Emotions got the best of her, and she prayed there was no truth in Denise's claims about Tony and Deon. Had she been so blind to the truth that it had cost her son's life? Too many secrets, too many lies, too many lives affected. Even if it were true, there was nothing she could do for Deon. Her baby was gone. Going forward, she wouldn't carry the weight of any more secrets, not her own, not anyone else's.

She kept her eyes peeled, creeping along the road reading the addresses on the town house buildings, which weren't prominently displayed on the doors and not as visible at night as she would have liked. She eased around the cul-de-sac, getting close to the curb and seeing the truck lights approaching from behind. Good, the truck turned in the driveway, eliminating the pressure for her to move along faster. There was 1137, oops, she'd missed the house. She applied the brakes. Eleven twenty-nine, there, she'd found Sylvia's house and claimed a glimmer of satisfaction, proud of her accomplishment. Instead of backing up, she glided close to the curb. She removed the cellular phone from her purse, preparing to call Louise with the good news, then decided to wait and call once inside the house with Sylvia. She gathered her belongings, peering periodically out the rear window, elated at her success.

Her reassurance increased. There was Reese hustling up the walkway. Instead of wasting time yelling from the window to get his attention, seeing her car was parked four houses away, she'd hurry with the intent of catching him at the door. Why didn't Louise tell her Reese was coming over? Oh, well, she'd go in, lay eyes on her niece, report back to her parents and maneuver back to Delaware in a trip that would probably take until midnight. Kay opened the car door and got out, adrenaline flowing, keeping Reese in eyesight as he reached the doorstep. She caught the door right before it slammed and hurried toward the town house with excitement in her steps. She'd crossed two of the three driveways separating her from Sylvia's town house and froze in front of unit 1133, unable to process the image of her niece

standing in the doorway with such a big grin for her sister's
husband. They didn't do anything inappropriate on the
doorstep, but something didn't feel right. She raced back
to the car. Thank goodness she was in a rental car and not
her own. She hopped in the car, spying through the rear
window, hoping they hadn't recognized her. What in the
world was going on? Why was it taking him so long to go in?
Reese was hugging Sylvia at the door, then they went inside.
Her heart was pounding. She discounted the notion and
made another attempt to exit the car and then stopped.
Should she go in or not? She really didn't know what to do.
Couldn't possibly be what she was thinking, no way. Sylvia,
Reese, no.

   She started the engine, still not sure if she should go to
the door. If there was anything going on, perhaps she could
stop it. On the other hand, maybe she should mind her own
business and not jump to conclusions. She drove around the
cul-de-sac, headed to the exit. What if Tony had abused
Deon, or what if Deon was suicidal, just what if? Would she
have wanted anyone who had knowledge of his situation to
mind their own business? The answer was clear. She realized
what had to be done, only not how to do it.

Chapter 43

Dad had Mom, Sylvia had her friends, and who did she have? A bad marriage, another woman's baby, the case, Sylvia and, of all people, her mom and Uncle Sam… How much more could she take? Her head was pounding as she sat at the dining room table.

"You're putting too much on yourself, Angela," Aunt Kay said.

She didn't want to talk to her pastor and his wife or a strange counselor. With the problems in her life, she needed a month to get the counselor up to speed on her boatload of issues. Aunt Kay and Aunt Ida were her rays of hope. They knew her. They cared. They didn't love her the way Mom and Dad did, they couldn't, but the love they offered was more than sufficient to survive the overwhelming feeling of defeat and hopelessness drowning her.

She rubbed her cheeks with open palms. The news about

Mom and Uncle Sam was an endless stomachache. If she could regurgitate the vial stench of their infidelity, maybe there was a chance for her and Mom to restore their relationship. She missed being able to talk to her mom about any and everything. She loved Mom. Her feelings hadn't changed, but her perspective and image had.

"You're worried about your father, aren't you," Aunt Kay asked.

"I am worried about Dad," she said, gazing at the table, sorting her thoughts, "but that's not what's bothering me. I came here because of Mom."

"I know Louise is having a hard time. She loves her Herbert Reynolds," Aunt Kay said.

"She's a woman of faith. She knows the Lord. You don't have to worry about her. The truth will come out and your parents will be sharing their testimony," Aunt Ida echoed.

"Keep hanging in there with them. They need you now more than ever."

"That's my problem. I found out something about my mother three weeks ago and ever since then it has been awkward around my parents."

"What is so bad that it has you this shaken up?" Aunt Ida asked.

Angela suspected Sylvia had found out about the affair from Denise and Denise from Aunt Kay. If Aunt Ida wasn't there she might have been able to talk openly to Aunt Kay, but exposing such a deep secret with far-reaching ramifications to the entire family wasn't feasible. She wanted, needed, to discuss the tragedy but was afraid revealing the information would be too costly and cause more problems.

She was fuming. Why did she have to bear the brunt of somebody else's lie? Were they suffering to the same extent? She couldn't hold back any longer. Aunt Kay most likely already knew and Aunt Ida was a saint.

"I found out about Mom and Uncle Sam."

Aunt Kay sat down in the chair. Aunt Ida's expression didn't change, no sign of shock, dismay or confusion.

"How did you find out?" Aunt Ida asked.

"Mom told me."

"She did? What made her do that?"

"Actually, Sylvia found out and confronted Mom, then Mom confessed to me later. Even though she told me it was true, I can't believe it."

"Did she tell Herbert?"

"No, and she asked me not to tell him, either."

"Good," Aunt Ida said, "no sense stirring the pot with old news."

"You're right, what they did happened a long time ago. Your mother was a different person then. She's changed a whole lot."

"So you both know?"

"Some things you know and it's best to keep to yourself," Aunt Ida encouraged.

"Aunt Ida knows everything there is to know about this family. Not a thing gets past her."

"Once in a while a person needs someone to talk to, to get troubles off their chest," Aunt Ida said.

"And everybody comes to you."

"Probably because they know whatever they tell me won't go any further."

"Does Aunt Mabel know about Mom and Uncle Sam or about me?"

"I doubt it," Aunt Kay said. "You know how your aunt is. She's very secretive when it comes to her husband and children. If she does know, we'd never know. Like Aunt Ida Mae said, no sense stirring the pot. If she doesn't know, no sense telling her and starting a whole world of mess in this family. We have plenty to deal with as it is without going out looking for more trouble."

"But it's really not old news. If Uncle Sam is my father, that's not old news. I'll have to live with this information for the rest of my life. I feel awkward around him now. I don't know what to say or how to act."

"You act the same way you always have. He's your uncle, that's all there is to it," Aunt Ida declared.

"No, he might be my father, not my uncle."

"Herbert Reynolds is your father. This hoopla with Sam and your mother doesn't mean a hill of beans. Herbert believes you are his daughter. He's raised you from birth. You can't ask for a better father. Sometimes it's best to leave a situation alone," Aunt Ida preached.

"So you don't think he deserves to know?"

"Sometimes you have to let sleeping dogs lie. There is not one bit of fruit that can come from bringing up old dirt, especially in a family that's seen its share of challenges this year."

"But I'm living a lie."

"Angela, you've been saved long enough to know what you need to do. You need to forgive your mother and your uncle, release them and what you're feeling to the Lord and walk on past this. Don't let a thirty-year-old mistake bring you down. Get on your knees and stay there until you find your peace. You have to let this go for your sake. Won't be easy, but if you don't, the situation will nag at you like a sickness, and you deserve better," Aunt Ida said.

"It's hard. How can I forgive Mom and not forgive Reese? His mistake isn't any worse than hers. How can I forgive her and not him without being hypocritical?"

"Listen, young lady. You make peace with your husband. Take this advice from a woman who has lost her husband to another woman." Aunt Kay pointed her finger. "If you love your husband you better work it out. Don't wait or it might be too late," she advised in a tone of certainty.

"Why do you say it like that? Do you know something you're not telling me?"

"Just take my advice. Don't give your husband a reason to go hunting elsewhere."

Angela extended her hands to her aunts. "Thank you for listening to me. You're both special to me."

"We're family, no thanks needed," Aunt Ida said.

"And I won't tell Dad about Mom and Uncle Sam, but I can't speak for Sylvia. She's not talking to the family right now. So we'll have to see what she does. There's no telling how far she'll go. She's always lived by her own rules."

Chapter 44

March was dashing by, halfway gone and leaving room for April to deal with the Reynoldses' house of cards. Sylvia was able to successfully dodge her parents and her sister. She hadn't wiped her immediate family out of her life, not totally, not yet.

She needed time to sort through her feelings. Had she been violated as a child? Did she believe in Daddy's innocence? She just wasn't sure. She could tell by the sadness and heaviness in the messages Daddy and Mom left that they were devastated by her pulling away from the family, but until she could sort out her position, she couldn't be of help to anyone.

Venturing to Aunt Kay's was risky, but Denise pleaded with her to come. Her cousin needed her and she didn't want to let Denise down.

"I'm glad you came over," Denise said. "I can't deal with my parents on my own. This whole division of Deon's assets has become a flat-out disaster. Let this be a lesson, cousin, get a will. I don't care if you have to scratch your wishes out on the back of an envelope and get it notarized, because splitting money is the fastest way to destroy a family. So-called love flies right out the window when free money is involved," she said, flicking her wrist.

"Somehow I don't think the envelope version will stand up in court."

"Forget about court. With the way my parents are fighting, they won't make it that far. I'm praying I don't have to call someone to intervene."

"God or the police?"

"When you see them in action, you'll know the answer is both. This is absolutely ridiculous. This is our third attempt to split this money."

"After you told me about what was going on with your parents, I spoke with one of my legal colleagues in Jersey to see what you could do. She told me that laws pertaining to wills and estates vary by state. Delaware might be a little different, but overall in the absence of a will, Deon's estate would be split equally between his parents, since there is no wife or children involved. So there really shouldn't be a problem."

"Yeah, but the problem is that regardless of what the law says, Mom doesn't want Dad to have anything, basically, not as long as he's with that woman. She's not going to let him have a dime without a fight."

"And why did you want me here, because I certainly can't change her mind?"

"Moral support, sister, that's it in a nutshell, moral support."

Sylvia followed her cousin into the dining room, planning to maintain a closed lip. This battle wasn't hers and being present was the only support she could offer Denise. The entire time she'd be jittery, wondering if by some strange fluke of events, Angela or her parents were going to pop up. She wasn't ready to face them yet. She was dealing with the flashbacks and searching her soul for answers, slowly, in no hurry to uncover the truth.

"Sylvia, I wasn't expecting you."

"Denise asked me to come over, so I did."

"Excuse me for one minute," Aunt Kay said, and left, returning to her seat a few minutes later.

"Your mother has been trying to get in touch with you for weeks. You should give her a call before you leave."

Sylvia didn't want to lie to her aunt. She grinned without showing any teeth and took a seat, figuring the conversation with her aunt and uncle would heat up and no one would remember she was in the room. Not a second later, Uncle Arthur entered the room.

"Hello, hello, everybody. Hey, niece. You doing okay? Haven't seen you in about a month."

"I'm doing pretty good, Uncle."

"Good, good. I'm glad to hear Jersey is treating you okay." His glance darted to Aunt Kay and then away. "Kay."

Aunt Kay didn't say a word. Her body shifted in the chair and her neck stiffened. She was like a different woman when Uncle Arthur entered the room.

Denise sat at the head of the table with a parent on both sides. "After the funeral and burial expenses were paid, between Deon's insurance and savings, there's $160,000 left."

"Denise, you were the beneficiary of his $50,000 policy," Aunt Kay said. "That's your money. Deon wanted you to have it."

"I know he did, but I'm including all of the money together."

"No, the money is yours. It's the last gift you'll ever get from your brother, and I want you to have it," Aunt Kay said with her voice fading for a moment.

"Me, too," Uncle Arthur agreed.

"I want to split the money equally," Denise said, discounting her parent's input. She punched a few keys on her calculator and said, "We each get about $53,300 dollars each."

No arguments so far. Maybe the fourth attempt to divide the inheritance was the key.

"Now we have to figure out what to do with the town house and his car."

"Why don't you keep them both?" Uncle Arthur suggested. "He had your name on both the deed and the car title."

"I think he had my name on the house and car because we were staying together, but I feel like he would want the three of us to split everything equally."

"I believe he wanted you to have them."

"She might want the car, but Denise doesn't want to stay in that house. If you spent any time with your daughter you'd know she's hardly spent five nights there since Deon died. But then again, how would you know what's going on with your family?"

Uncle Arthur didn't respond to Aunt Kay. "Do you want the town house?" he asked Denise.

Sylvia wanted to leave. She had no business being in the

middle of their family matter. If she was up for a squabble, she could drive over to her parents' or Angela's place.

"Didn't you hear me?" Aunt Kay belted out in an elevated tone.

"I can't help but hear you, Kay. You keep yapping and yapping. Can't you let us work out this money and let me get out of here?"

"No, Dad, I don't want the town house."

"How much you think the place is worth?" he asked Denise.

"I don't know, maybe two hundred thousand. He owned the town house free and clear. So whatever we sell the place for is what we get, after closing costs."

"Wow, that's a bit steeper than I was thinking."

"Why? You sound like you want to buy the place," Aunt Kay said, smirking.

"The thought had crossed my mind."

"Who you buying the house for, your woman?"

"Let's see, what else do we have to look at here?" Denise eased in.

"How can you buy a house for another woman?"

"We could rent the house, but we would be in for a lot of work," Denise tossed in, with no takers.

"What I do outside this house is no concern of yours, Kay. You can't boss me around anymore. If I want to buy my son's house, I can. You can't stop me. You have this house. Denise looks like she doesn't want to stay in the place. So what's wrong with me living there? The town house belongs to Denise, and if she wants to sell the house to me, that doesn't concern you."

"How are you going to get the money, because you're not spending our savings. Half of what's in the bank is mine."

"Fine, I'll use the money I'm getting from Deon and put it down on the town house. I'll get a mortgage for the difference. How does that sound, Denise? Do you think that's fair?"

Aunt Kay didn't give Denise's brain cells time to process the question. "Oh, no, you're not buying a house for your woman with my baby's money. She had nerve bringing her behind to the funeral. I wasn't myself that day, but I'm feeling pretty good today, no weakness here."

"I should have known the woman on the steps of the church wouldn't last long. Back to your old self, huh, Kay?" Uncle Arthur looked at his watch as if time mattered. "Denise and Sylvia, I'm heading out. Denise, let me know if you need me to sign any paperwork. I am interested in buying the town house."

"I don't think so, not over my dead body."

"I didn't want to tell you like this, but you don't leave me too much choice."

"Now what? You've already moved out. What's left?"

"I'd like a divorce."

Aunt Kay was rarely at a loss for words. She didn't have the razor-sharp tongue Aunt Mabel brandished, but she could be quick-witted in her own right. Nothing came from her side of the table, nothing, not a peep. If there was a way to drill into the dining room floor and tunnel to her BMW on the street, Sylvia would have. Sitting in the midst of their family destruction was the last blow she planned to witness. How much more family could one person endure?

Chapter 45

Aunt Kay had to be the one who called her parents. Maybe the loss of Deon gave her an increased level of tenderness for hurting parents. Who knew what the reason was. Sylvia was convinced she had made a bad decision coming to the house with Denise. If she'd followed her instinct, none of this would be happening. She'd taken necessary precautions and been able to successfully avoid her mom for practically a month and Daddy longer. She had claimed her space away from the situation, from the problem. Feeling a bit betrayed by Aunt Kay, she decided to stay and hear what her parents had to say and then dart back across the bridge to Jersey. She would let them do the talking. The less retort from her end, the shorter the conversation and the faster she would be out of there.

Dad and Mom stood in the doorway. Mom looked well. In six weeks, Dad had aged ten years. His hair, which he kept short, covered his head like a sheet of freshly fallen snow, white all over. The puffiness around his eyes couldn't have been from crying? She'd only seen him cry once. The once tall, staunch man who walked with deliberate steps was moving one degree below shuffling. Herbert and Louise Reynolds, the community dignitary, the Christian warrior, had been reduced to a child molester and an adulterer. They were obviously going through a rough patch, but so was she. Everything had changed. Her frame of reference for what was right and wrong, for what was truth. The world she resided in on New Year's Eve, more than three and a half months ago, was forever gone. She was so angry at both of them, for different reasons, but seeing them standing in her presence began melting the chill on her heart. She was poised to move forward, to embrace her father, to bridge the gap between them, but her mind said no, reminding her of Mom's indiscretion and betrayal, and Dad's unfathomable abuse that she had to release before the cancerous images continued eating away at her soul, rendering her heartless.

"Come on in," Aunt Kay told Mom and Dad. "Make yourself at home. I'll be in the basement. I have some laundry to do, but like I said, make yourselves at home."

"Sylvia," Mom cried out, "we've been so worried about you. Thank God you're all right," she said, letting her words override her emotions.

Dad tried to embrace her but Sylvia stepped back.

"Sylvia, don't do that. Your father has been worried sick about you."

"This case is too much for you. Sylvia, I understand and I'm sorry. You have no idea how sorry I am," he sputtered.

She couldn't maintain her grip on her anger in his presence. She had to get out, away, fast. Being near them, the two people she loved and used to trust more than anyone in the world, was a crushing blow to her stability. She had to get out and get to the bridge, back to her buffer between the filthy stench of her family life in Delaware and the satisfying one she'd created in Jersey. "I need to go," she said, skirting around her parents and yearning to reach the door, freedom.

"Sylvia, wait," Mom called out, "don't run away. We're your family. No matter what, we're still your parents and we love you. We always will."

"That's right, baby girl, you will always be daddy's girl."

"Stop it, Daddy," she erupted before fully assessing the moment. Her words spewed out. Boiling, rumbling explosions were going off in her soul. She'd taken his nasty secret and left it in Jersey, but that wasn't good enough. Herbert and Louise couldn't let her be, clawing for more of her sanity. They had to keep pushing, gnawing, picking and picking until she couldn't take the irritating jabs at her heart anymore. They deserved to know what was going on. They were the architects in her monument of horror. They were entitled to share the pain plaguing her life, night and day for weeks, months, years. "Just stop," she said turning to them. "Daddy, when are you going to stop?" she fired at him. His look of confusion almost seemed authentic. "Don't you get it, I know the truth."

Mom let out a sigh. "Sylvia, don't do this. Please, honey, don't do this. I know you're upset with me and that's okay, but think about what you're about to do. You will change the course of an entire family. Be mad at me but don't hurt your father. Please, I beg of you, don't do this."

"Mom, this isn't about you. I'm not telling Dad about you," she screamed, absolutely determined not to break down. The adrenaline was pumping. This was it, her moment, the time when she'd counseled and prepared many patients for putting the "C" in ACE, the time to confront her abuser. "This is about Daddy and what he did to me."

"I've apologized to you about the case. I'm sorry this has hit you so hard and embarrassed you. I'm sorry, Sylvia. I truly am, but there's nothing I can do. Tell me how I can make this better for you. Tell me and I'll do it."

"You can start by telling the truth."

"I have been all along. I didn't touch Latoya."

"I'm not talking about Latoya. I'm talking about me. You touched me when I was five years old."

Dad fell into the chair closest to the door. The expression of bewilderment on Mom's face rendered her speechless.

"Sylvia, what are you saying?" Mom asked.

"I've had nightmares for at least twenty years, and finally I know why." The adrenaline was still pumping, at full throttle, keeping her focused and able to speak to her parents in a way she would never have dreamed of doing, but the demons inside had to be released if there was any chance of her acquiring a semblance of peace. "Daddy, it was you."

"Sylvia, I would never hurt you. Please, baby girl, you can't believe what you're saying."

"And stop calling me baby girl. I'm a grown woman and I'm not going to let you get away with what you've done to me and maybe to Latoya, too. You've hurt me, Daddy, more than you'll ever know. So please, stop lying and tell the truth. Tell the truth so I can have some peace, finally after twenty years. Can't you at least give me that?"

"But I didn't and couldn't violate my own daughter," he said, standing to his feet. "Don't you know I would freely give my life for you? Your entire life I've done everything in my power to protect you. I would never, never hurt you, never, and that's the God honest truth."

Mom took a seat, too. Maybe she was overcome with shock. Maybe she was praying like she often did in the middle of a crisis. People always relied on what they knew during overwhelming times and going to God was her place of security. If she was praying, there was so much broken in the Reynolds' family, she'd be busy for a long while.

"Fine, if you don't want to be honest, then there's nothing left to say," she said, opening the door. "And don't worry. I won't reveal your secret to the court. You have plenty to worry about with Latoya and her mother."

Aunt Kay entered the room. "Sylvia, are you leaving already? Why don't you stay awhile. If Herbert doesn't mind, the three of us ladies can talk about the anniversary plans. I don't have anything else to do."

Denise was gesturing for Aunt Kay to stop, but she didn't catch the hint.

"I don't think so, Aunt Kay. I want to get home. I'll see you later."

"Kay," Mom said in a weakened tone, "there won't be an anniversary. It's canceled, indefinitely."

Chapter 46

Angela wasn't able to garner stamina sufficient to lift her frame from the seat at the kitchen table. She wasn't reeling from her mother canceling the anniversary again. To be honest, she hadn't been able to adequately focus on the planning in weeks. She replayed her mother's words, stopping, rewinding and replaying repeatedly in her mind.

Reese waltzed into the kitchen and grabbed the refrigerator door. "How about going out for breakfast?" he asked with the orange juice container in his hand.

Food was her last priority.

"Did you hear me, are you up for breakfast?"

She let her gaze slowly rise, struggling to keep her eyelids open. "No," she said barely above a whisper.

"Are you feeling okay?" he said, pouring juice into a glass.

"No."

"What's wrong?" he asked with a halfhearted voice.

"I spoke with Mom this morning and she told me they saw Sylvia yesterday."

He rubbed one side of his face. "Really, that's good. Is she okay?" he asked with more concern than he'd shown in weeks toward her.

"Sylvia is fine, but my parents aren't. They aren't doing well at all."

"Well, another two months and the trial will be over. Having the trial behind them is bound to help some."

"The trial is going to be a disaster. At first I was confident Dad would be acquitted, but I'm not sure now."

"Why?"

"Because Sylvia isn't testifying on his behalf, that's the first part. The second part and the worst is that Sylvia's claiming Dad molested her."

"Wow."

"You don't have anything else to say? When Mom told me, I was floored. I can't wrap my brain around the concept. It can't possibly be true."

"I know your Dad and he's a good man, but I also know your sister and Sylvia wouldn't lie about something so important."

"I don't know anymore. My husband, my mother, and uncles, and my aunts have kept secrets from me. Why not my father, too, and Sylvia, for that matter." She pulled herself from the table.

"My code for time to go," Reese said.

"No, you don't have to go," she said, "I'm going back to bed. I have a headache."

Reese heard the bedroom door close upstairs. She had finally done it. Sylvia had confronted her father. He dialed a number from his cell phone and Sylvia answered on the second ring.

"Hey, sis, I figured you needed a friend right now. I heard about your conversation with your parents. Are you all right?"

"Not by choice. They caught me at Aunt Kay's and what could I do?"

"Took a lot of courage for you to speak up and I'm proud of you, sis."

"Reese, you have been absolutely wonderful to me. You've been a great friend and I couldn't have gotten through this past month without you."

"Well, I can't take any credit here. I came to you for help from the beginning and you've been there for me, too. We're just two people trying to survive in this game of life. You're all right with me, sis. I'll stop by later on today if you're going to be home."

"I'm going out during the day but I'll be back around five."

"Five, that's perfect, just in time for the game. I'll see you later, and, Sylvia, take care of yourself. You have enough to deal with as it is."

"Who were you talking to?" Angela said, causing his heartbeat to race.

He knew better than to use the phone in the house. She'd never understand his friendship with Sylvia, so why bother to explain? He had two options: tell the truth and let her spaz out or lie and avoid an argument.

"A buddy."

"Are you going to stand there and lie? I heard you say Sylvia. You can't mean my sister, Sylvia?"

"It's not what you think. Sylvia has been nothing but a good friend to me."

"I was stupid about Felicia the first time around. Wasn't she your friend? You got me the first time, but don't take me for a two-time fool."

"This isn't that kind of situation."

"Exactly what kind of situation is this, Reese? What are you doing, spying on the family and running to Sylvia with information?"

"No, Angela."

"You're doing something. I caught you whispering on the phone to my sister, the one who doesn't talk to anyone else in the family, but she talks to my husband. Come on now, what do you expect me to think? Do you really think I'm stupid? You and Sylvia are a piece of work. How dirty and disgusting can you be, and to think I was actually beating up on myself for not working harder at getting over your mistake. You deserve what you get, but I can tell you now, it won't be my sister."

"What are you talking about?"

She stomped up the stairs not wanting to hear a word slither across his lips. They were perfect for each other, he and Sylvia, a cheater and a thief, but he still wasn't ending up with her. Sylvia had everything—friends, job and her parents' unconditional love. Dad was a trial away from going to prison and his primary concern was Sylvia, Sylvia, Sylvia, but then she was his only daughter, actually only living child. Supposedly he had no knowledge of Uncle Sam, but maybe his close relationship with Sylvia was instinctive. Either way, Sylvia wasn't coming out on top this time. Whether Angela stayed with Reese or not, he wasn't going to Sylvia for sure. She'd rather Felicia have him before her sister.

"Angela, wait."

She stopped midway up the staircase. "That's the problem, Reese, I've waited too long. It's time for me to get on with my life. Everybody else seems to do whatever they want to, have whatever they lay their eyes on, and I'm always the one sitting back and dealing with the crappy leftovers. Well, those days are over. I'm reclaiming me."

"What does that mean?"

"For once, you'll have to wait and see what my next move is. We'll see how you feel for a change," she said, ascending the stairs with a newfound zeal.

Chapter 47

Angela ran into the bedroom, closed the door and stood in the center of the room, not sure what to do next. She had to do something, but what? Thoughts were orbiting in her head. She heard Reese's voice talking to Sylvia, mixed with Felicia's voice playing with the baby, her mom's pleas and the attorney's instructions. She heard other voices but wasn't able to identify them.

Reese busted into the bedroom. She wanted space, alone time to think, to reflect and to maintain control. The force he used to open the door indicated he was intent on having his say. "Angela, we've got to stop playing these games. I'm done," he said, tossing his hands into the air. "I love you, Angela, I do, as crazy as it sounds, I love you. I want to be with you, but I can't make you want me. That's the real deal. Yes, I've said it a thousand times, I slipped up. I was wrong and I'm sorry, but this isn't about me anymore, Angela. This is about you," he said, pointing in her direction but staying near the door.

"About me?"

"Yes, you, Angela, you," he said, pointing both index fingers at her. "You have to decide if you're going to forgive me."

"I've already forgiven you."

"No, you haven't. You might say you have, but your attitude toward me most of the time says different." She knew exactly what he meant and felt an inkling of guilt. "This is it for me, Angela, for real."

"Why, do you have somebody else already?"

"No," he said with an annoyed expression. "And for the record, you're wrong about me and Sylvia. We are friends, period. I mean, give me some credit. I would never go there."

"You went there with Felicia."

"Forget about Felicia. I would never go there with your sister or your cousin or your friends. You know what I mean."

"Humph."

"All right, Angela, if this is how you want it. I'm tired of slamming into your brick wall. You let me know what you want to do," he said, and turned, facing the door, "but I wouldn't wait too long if you want me to stay."

Baffled and mad were a nasty mix. He was right. She was tired of the back-and-forth tussling in their marriage, too. Her thoughts were swirling again like a tornado, out of control. She could hear Reese, Mom, Sylvia, Aunt Mabel, Uncle Sam and Aunt Ida's wisdom, but the voice ringing louder than any other was Aunt Kay saying, "If you want your husband, don't give him a reason to go hunting elsewhere." Reasons, what reasons had she given him to go cheating with

Felicia? Reese was a grown man. He knew right from wrong. As far as Sylvia was concerned, she would give him the benefit of the doubt and accept whatever they were doing as friendship. She couldn't bear the implication of any other scenario, anyway.

Reasons, what reasons? Okay, the baby thing was an issue, but there wasn't anything wrong with her waiting to have children. Maybe she did put her family ahead of Reese's needs every now and then. Maybe she could show him a little more support like she so freely gave to the family. Perhaps there were a few areas she could work on, but then again, Reese was grown, and had to own up to his mistakes regardless of her contribution, she wanted to believe.

Angela let her thoughts glide back more than a month ago, to the evening she and Mom sat in the car. The night she'd promised to read a scripture but hadn't. She schlepped to the nightstand and extracted her Bible, something that hadn't happened in months. She pulled the sticky off the page containing the scripture Mom wanted her to read. Her fingers didn't stop until she landed on Romans 5 beginning at verse three. "But we also rejoice in our sufferings, because we know that suffering produces perseverance; perseverance, character; and character, hope. And hope does not disappoint us, because God has poured out His love into our hearts by the Holy Spirit, whom He has given us."

She read through verse five and closed the Bible, gently, only to find herself opening it again and rereading over and over. Mom's advice made sense. God's love was bigger than her problems. All she had to do was maintain hope, realizing that truly nothing was too hard for Him.

For the first time in a while, she decided to talk with Him, openly and honestly, putting her feelings and desires out in the open, barring resistance from guilt, hurt and shame. She dropped to her knees and started a dialogue of prayer with God, which she hadn't done in far too long.

Chapter 48

Easter was like Christmas. Mount Calvary was stuffed with holiday worshippers, making it nearly impossible to find a seat thirty minutes prior to service. Reese included. Next week the congregation would shrink back to normalcy, eight people per fifteen seats. Mom and Dad sat on the end, one row in front. Sylvia didn't attend. She wasn't expected, but her absence was weird. Despite their squabbles, Sylvia always attended family functions. There was a void, a sadness. Her sister was off base about Dad, but something serious was going on with her. Sure, Sylvia had friends, sorority sisters, plenty of them who adored her, most likely, but they weren't family. They weren't her sister, her only blood sister, half or whole.

Hats and "amens" colorfully decorated the sanctuary. Families were together; it didn't get any better.

"Jesus died on the cross that we might have life and life more abundantly," Reverend Jacobs preached.

Reese gestured twice to stretch his arm along the pew behind her, but aborted his attempts both times, probably afraid of her reaction. Had she become too difficult, not the Angela Jones he knew? Angela leaned forward, giving the signal she wouldn't resist.

"Do you know what kept Jesus on the cross?" The congregation was fired up, tossing answers toward the pulpit. "It was His love for us, for you, for me. That's what kept Him there. Aah, but wait, the story gets even better, amen," he uttered, slightly lowering his tone and peering into the Bible.

Reese's arm was outstretched behind her. He drew his arm in tighter, a real embrace. She didn't resist.

"After He hung His head and died on the cross, they buried Him in the tomb," Reverend Jacobs said, slamming his hand on the podium, and the church was as loud as a pep rally. "He stayed there Friday night, Saturday night, but come Sunday morning," he belted, "He rose with all power in His hands. Hallelujah."

The congregation was on their feet, cheering like a football stadium of fans. Angela was renewed, her spirit, her faith. Easter was proof that miracles happened. Reese eased his arm around her waist.

"That's what love can do, saints," Rev. Jacobs concluded. "How deep is your love? Are you willing to sacrifice yourself, your pride for the love of another?" He motioned for the congregation to sit, but they remained perched on the edge of their seats, ready to stand at a moment's notice. "First Corinthians 13 teaches us about love. I'm here to tell you, don't give up on your loved ones. Sometimes they can get on your last nerve." Laughter roared through the church.

"Anybody have relatives like that? You know who I'm talking about. We all have one, somebody who just isn't right until they make you mad. You know who I'm talking about. The people who would have gotten an earful if they'd approached you before you became a born-again believer."

The congregation laughed some more. "Well, there is good news. First Corinthians is your answer. Starting with verse four, the Word says 'Love is patient, love is kind. It does not envy, it does not boast, it is not proud. It is not rude, it is not self-seeking, it is not easily angered, it keeps no record of wrongs. Love does not delight in evil but rejoices with the truth. It always protects, always trusts, always hopes, always perseveres.' Verse eight, 'Love never fails.' Did you hear me, Mount Calvary? Never fails. Amen. So the next time a person gets on your last nerve, whip some 1 Corinthians 13 on them and love them right off your nerves. You see, church, sometimes you have to get on your knees. Prayer is necessary, but you also have to get up off those knees and put some effort into working out your situations. Don't wait for God to part the Red Sea for you every time. Do you always need a miracle? He's equipped you with love, use it and get your relationships healed. Amen."

Sylvia lay on her mind. Truth was, Angela loved her sister and she missed her, dearly. Easter was a miracle. There was hope.

Chapter 49

A nice dose of spirituality in the morning was polished off with a feast at Aunt Kay's afterward. Easter dinner was supposed to be at Aunt Mabel's this year, but with Deon's recent passing, who could turn down Aunt Kay's request to host the dinner. People, plates, food, makeshift seating and laughter were in abundance, the first in a long time.

Angela allowed herself to become absorbed in the festivities, relishing a rare family scene based on the past three months. No one was arguing or fighting, but then Denise and Aunt Mabel hadn't arrived. They were so much alike, stubborn, in control, but loved their family. Wasn't a surprise when they battled over who would host the dinner, holiday after holiday for the past three years. Once the power struggle was so fierce, both hosted Thanksgiving dinner simultaneously, requiring the Reynolds to track from one house to the other, both Denise and Mabel later claiming to have had the better meal. The family eventually tired of the constant dueling and settled on Easter being the one group family holiday, and Denise would alternate with Aunt Mabel. Before the two feisty ladies arrived, Angela was determined to forget about the trial and Uncle Sam for one meal.

"Where are your parents?" Aunt Kay asked.

"Dad complained about having a headache, so they went home after church. Actually, Dad hasn't been feeling too well for the past week."

"What is it, a cold?" Aunt Kay asked, placing more carved turkey on the platter located in the center of the table, surrounded by stuffing, fresh cranberry sauce, string beans, steamed cabbage, mixed greens and too many other dishes to hold on one plate.

"I saw him leave during the service. He was gone for a good while before he came back," Aunt Ida commented.

"Well, I'll be sure and set two plates aside for them. What about Reese, is he coming?"

"Reese ran by his mother's house."

"Good seeing him in church with you today," Aunt Ida said. "You talk to Sylvia lately?"

"Not recently." The festivities were quickly dissolving into drudgery. Parents, siblings, cousins and children blanketed the house. She felt like an orphan and a single woman, might as well have been with no husband, parents or sister to share dinner with her.

Aunt Kay had left the dining room and returned from the kitchen with a fresh pot of sweet potatoes. "I remember when you, Denise and Sylvia were growing up and you'd sit on my front porch during the summer, laughing and playing until I made you come in. Remember that?"

Hopscotch, double-dutch, jacks, Hula-Hoop and Mary Mack were the games of choice back when Sylvia was her little sister and looked up to Angela as if she was the queen. She didn't want to get emotional. She'd have to explain herself in front of fifty family members.

"Angela, come into the kitchen with me?" Aunt Kay asked, and she obliged. Aunt Kay set the empty pan on the counter and her embrace was a comforting hand to a child lost in the woods of life.

"Don't you worry about a thing. Your family is going to be okay. Just keep doing what I told you to do."

Angela pushed back and grabbed a paper towel. "What?"

"Keep working on your relationship with Reese. You're a smart girl. Don't let your man get away if you want him," Aunt Kay said, placing the pot in the sink. "And reach out to your sister. No matter what happens, she's your sister and you need to support each other. You're both going through a lot right now and sisters can help each other."

Aunt Kay verbalized what Angela felt. She was mad and had been angry at Sylvia for so long for different reasons, mostly because her sister was living out her dream. She dared step out of the Wilmington box and go where her heart led. Blaming Sylvia was easy. Angela leaned against the counter and grabbed another paper towel to wipe her cheeks.

"Come on out when you feel up to it."

"How deep is your love?" was the question Reverend Jacobs asked in service earlier, and she wasn't able to answer.

Who was she? Anger, bitterness and revenge weren't characteristic of the woman she wanted to be.

"Hey, cuz, what you doing in here? Everybody's out there," Lee said, setting his plate in the sink. "You okay?" he asked.

The lump in her throat, the fur ball of shame was lodged deep. She let her gaze fall.

"Come here, cuz, I'm here for you." he said, reenacting the same hug Aunt Kay had freely given earlier. "Uncle Herbert is going to be okay. We know he's innocent. Plus Sylvia got that good lawyer. Uncle is going to be all right."

She let a few sobs escape. Lee assumed her anguish was the culmination of preparing for the trial and watching her dad fade, but he was wrong. Her tears were as much for him as they were for anyone. There he was, one of her many crosses to bear, a person who would be a constant reminder of why faith, forgiveness and love were key to survival.

"Come on in and grab a plate," Angela heard Aunt Kay tell someone. She stuck her head in the door. "Get on out here. Your husband is here," she said, grinning ear to ear.

Aunt Kay and Lee were a blessing, a sorely needed source of encouragement, but Reese, the old Reese, the one she married six years ago long before Felicia, was her husband.

"I'll catch you later, cuz," Lee said, returning to the dining room. "What's up, man?" he asked as he ran into Reese on his way out. "Take care of my little cousin, man."

Reese stood in the doorway. She prayed silently, asking God to forgive her for having a hard heart and for courage. Neither made a move toward each other.

"Thought you were going to your parents'?" she said, clearing her voice.

"I did," he said, coming closer. She wiped her cheeks one more time with a soaked paper towel. Reese snatched a fresh one from the roll, lifted her chin gently and wiped her cheek. "But I wanted to be with you today." Maybe it was God, maybe it was Reese taking charge. She wasn't sure, but whatever was enabling her to have a moment of security and to experience the love of her husband again, she was gladly accepting. She threw her arms around his waist and collapsed into him. Today was the first time in three years, at least, where she felt hopeful, truly hopeful, and that much she acknowledged was definitely from the Lord.

Denise bobbed in and out of the kitchen, with bare minimal disturbance.

"You two in there," Aunt Mabel hollered, "come on out here. You can get back to your lovey-dovey stuff later. I have a big announcement to make. Some of you might need to take your seats for this one."

"Mabel, what is it, because we can't stand another bit of bad news," Aunt Kay commented, handling Aunt Mabel's signature sock-it-to-me cinnamon cake and banana pudding. "We've had our share," Aunt Kay said, with affirmations pouring in from the dining room, adjacent living room and family room.

"Hush up, everybody," she said, flapping her arms like a bird in midair. "This is great news for me. Tony is getting married, June 23, so mark your calendars."

Screams and hollers abounded. Denise stormed out the room in the direction of the bedrooms. One out of fifty applauding was as close to perfect as Aunt Mabel could expect. Angela leaned her back into Reese's frame as he stood in the kitchen doorway behind her. The Reynoldses were finally experiencing trickles of happy times, and her marriage, which was all but dead, might be in the midst of a resurrection.

Chapter 50

He wanted to pace around the bedroom, but his legs were tired, worn, as was his spirit. The primary job God had appointed him to do, he'd failed, not once but twice. First when he let Donny get killed in the war. Louise didn't want Donny to go, but he had been honored to have his son follow in his military footsteps. He hadn't accepted the full blame, but an amount sufficient to plague him for fifteen years. He'd sent one child to his death, now his baby girl was struggling with the backlash from the upcoming trial.

"Herbert," Louise called out, entering the bedroom. "Are you hungry? Would you like a bite to eat?"

"No thanks, honey, I'm not hungry," he said, fighting off the pounding in his head. Speaking was laborious with excruciating pain bombarding his temples.

"Herbert, you haven't eaten a full meal in three days.

Starving yourself is not good," she said, approaching the bed and sitting on the corner.

"I'm not trying to avoid eating. I'm just not hungry."

"You have the same headache?"

He gave a slight nod of affirmation.

"You've had it almost two weeks. We shouldn't have gone to church yesterday. You know how loud Mount Calvary can get on holidays. We should have kept you home and in bed yesterday."

"Church was the best place for me."

"Normally, I would agree, but in this case, the Lord will need to meet you right where you are, in this bed. I'll get you some pain reliever, but what you really need is to go to the doctor."

"A doctor can't help what's ailing me."

"What is it, the trial?"

"The trial I can handle. Sylvia is what has my mind running here and there. My heart is heavy," he said, caressing his temples. "I never would have dreamed my daughter could believe I was capable of abusing her. You know I would never hurt those girls, never, not Latoya and definitely not Sylvia."

Louise rubbed his legs, which were underneath the sheet. "I know you wouldn't," she said in her consoling voice, but with the throbbing in his head, every word, no matter how soft, sounded like a scream. "Deep down, Sylvia knows, too. She'll come around, you'll see. We have to keep the faith, and not be swayed by what we see in the natural. God is in control and I'm staying on the Word. This, too, shall pass. All we have to do is hang in there and see the manifestation of God's faithfulness."

Words were limited now, expensive, too painful to utter, but he had to try Sylvia one more time. She had to believe him. Having her on the other side of the river and alone with no family to help her through this struggle was unacceptable. He was her father, and until his last breath was taken, he'd look out for his baby girl, no matter what.

"Why don't you rest, and I'll check on you later," she said, kissing his cheek.

"Yes, I need to rest. I will, but can you please dial Sylvia's number for me first? I have to hear my child's voice. I have to try one more time."

Louise retrieved the phone from the dresser, dialed the number and handed the handset to him. He'd called countless number of times in the past three days with no success. The headache that was bouncing in and out prior to Sylvia accusing him of abuse was planted and raging. He laid his head on the pillow, unable to continue sitting up in bed but determined to complete the call.

The voice mail again. He'd leave another message, what else could he do? "Sylvia, this is Daddy. Baby girl," he said, with speaking becoming too much of a strain and his words transforming into a drawl.

"Herbert, let me have the phone," Louise insisted.

Against his wife's wishes, he continued, had to. "I want you to know that I love you. No matter what happens, I love you. You'll never know how sorry I am," he uttered, and took a pause.

"Please let me have the phone," Louise pleaded, this time putting her hand on the handset but not pulling it away.

"Your whole life my job was to protect you from hurt,

harm and danger. I've failed you. I've failed God, and I've failed myself," he said, hearing a rapid series of beeps on the other end.

Louise's eyes welded with tears, and she gave a weak tug to the handset. "Don't do this honey, don't. You're breaking my heart," she said, sobbing.

"Baby girl, Daddy loves you. That's what I wanted you to know, no matter what you say or do." He was prepared to say more, but the voice mail clicked off and the call was disconnected. The heaviness of the call caused him to drop the handset, which Louise retrieved and was about to return the phone to the dresser. "Can you dial Angela for me, too, please?"

"Why do you want to call Angela now? Let me get you the pain reliever and you can take a nap. The medicine will help your headache."

"The nap can wait. I need to call my daughter before I go to sleep, then I'll take the medicine and eat a bite later, too, if that will make you happy."

She didn't smile or display a halfhearted grin. Louise was determined to take care of him even when he was resistant. He was blessed to have her for a wife. Many wrong and some right decisions he'd made in his life, but marrying Louise was by far the smartest action he'd taken in his entire life.

"Wait before you dial Angela. Louise, I haven't gone to church as much as you over the years, but I do believe in Christ."

"I know you do, Herbert. You're a good man."

"I mostly go because you go, but I've never truly made a commitment to the Lord, not really."

"I hope you don't feel like the problems we're having now are because you haven't been going to church?"

"No, no, nothing like that, although going to church more probably wouldn't hurt, but no. I'm saying that after all these years of you gently nudging me closer to the Lord, I'm finally ready to make a true commitment."

"What are you saying?" she asked, gripping the handset but letting the light in her eyes brighten. He hadn't seen joy quite as vibrant in her face since December, a distant time.

"When I was coming up, the Reynolds children had to get baptized by six. So, I've been baptized and gone to church most of my life, but I don't know God like you do. You're amazing at how you pray and believe, and things happen for you. I'm in a bad spot, Louise. Your prayers are my only hope. With Sylvia feeling the way she does about me, I don't think I can make it."

"Don't you dare talk that way, Herbert Reynolds. Remember, you are a child of the King, and as your Heavenly Father, He loves you the same way you love your children, endlessly. The Lord won't leave you and I won't, either. We're going to make it."

"See what I mean?" he said, speaking a little too loud and reengaging the roaring and pounding in his head. "Your faith is solid," he said in a low but clear voice. "I love you, Louise," he said, mustering energy sufficient to caress her free hand.

She reciprocated with an embrace, and then dialed Angela's number, the last call he would make before resting.

Chapter 51

Sylvia relaxed in the den, her private retreat, with a stack of books and a bowl of popcorn. She was determined to block out the week and force herself to have a pleasant evening, but life wasn't cooperating. She had listened to the fifteen messages Daddy left since Easter and the three from Mom. His message an hour ago sounded strained, and the part of her that loved and longed for her father was suffering. To hear the ache in his voice and realize the agony he was most likely enduring threatened to draw her back into the closet, the place of secrets, lies, endless fear. She couldn't regress. She'd garnered the courage to confront her abuser. The "C" in ACE was done and she could look forward to "E," embracing the future. Relief was slow coming, but at least she'd taken the first step toward freedom. The nightmares hadn't tapered off, but they would cease. She was sure of it.

Stop procrastinating. She sat at her desk and pulled out

the checkbook. The sooner she wrote the check, the sooner she could get back to popcorn and leisure reading. She scribbled Jackson, Greene, Schaffer and Horowitz on the "pay to order of" line. Three checks in, writing the $2,000 amount didn't get easier and spelling out two thousand was worse. A few strokes and the check was signed and ready to mail, a process she would have to do for months to come. After all, she had selected Attorney Jackson over Aunt Mabel's discount attorney. Herbert Reynolds was her father. The part of her who would always be his offspring couldn't turn her back on him, no matter what he'd done. The adult who was "trying to get her mental health stable without medication" aspect of her life couldn't support him.

The doorbell rang, sending her body into instant panic. The last call from her parents came an hour ago, about the amount of time it took for them to fumble around the roads in Jersey and land on her doorstep. On the other hand, could be Reese. She hadn't spoken to him since last Thursday or Friday. No way to tell if he was at the door. The den didn't have windows. The beveled glass framing both sides of the front door posed a problem. She couldn't exit the den without her shadow being detected in the foyer, since the front door was a few yards off to the side. She was stuck.

The doorbell persisted, and then the phone rang. Denise's number appeared on the cordless phone's caller ID.

"Denise, hello, girl," Sylvia whispered.

"Why are you whispering? Open the door, I knew you were in there hiding."

Sylvia hustled to the door. One click and Denise was inside.

"You should call me ahead of time so I'll know you're coming," she said, closing the door and taking Denise's coat.

"Hello," Denise said animatedly, "I tried to call but the line was busy the first time and then your mailbox was full."

"Oh," Sylvia said, hanging the coat in the closet, then directing Denise to the living room. "Go on in and make yourself at home," she told her cousin. "I'll be right there."

Denise rushed into the living room as if intense heat was being applied to her feet. Sylvia returned to her desk, dated the check and stuffed it into an overnight-delivery envelope. She left the den and met Denise in the living room with the envelope in her hand. "Can you please place this in the box at the front of the development for me when you leave?"

"Sure, no problem," she said, with eyelids squinted and an air of agitation.

"So what's up with you looking mean and everything?"

"I should have called, but no matter what, I was going to come, anyway," she said in an anxious tone. "Can you believe Tony is getting married?" She spewed the words past her clenched teeth.

"You're kidding, really married, or 'engaged without a ring' kind of getting married?"

"A real marriage with a date. I'm not so sure about the ring, but I doubt there is one," she said, unable to sit still. "Tony doesn't have any money, unless the woman bought her own ring."

"That's a definite possibility," Sylvia said, chuckling for the first time in ages. "How did you find out?"

"Aunt Mabel couldn't wait to share the news with the family Sunday. You know how she is, bragging and everything," Denise said, teetering on the edge of the sofa, not visible from the front door.

"Well, at least she can finally get her shot at a wedding. I won't be going."

"Me, neither, as far as I'm concerned he doesn't have the right to get married," Denise yelled with her neck twisting. "Ooh," she moaned, and flopped back onto the sofa, "I am so mad I don't know what to do."

Sylvia had her issues with the family, but Tony wasn't her battle. He was Denise's. She'd listen and be supportive, as Denise had unconditionally done for her over the past two months.

"What right does he have to get married and have a family? My brother is dead and it's Tony's fault."

A decent counselor, semi-churchgoer or a reasonable cousin would have inserted words of wisdom leading ideally to a shifting in Denise's anger toward Tony, but for the moment, Sylvia opted to be none of them. She had snatched her opportunity to speak her mind with Mom and Daddy a week and a half ago. Denise's loss had earned her a right to vent, too. A listening ear was the only role she would play this evening.

"He has to pay."

"What do you mean?" Sylvia asked.

"I mean he has to pay."

"You don't mean like kill him or anything drastic, do you?" Even a listening ear had to speak at some point.

"No, just because I don't want to go to jail, but he deserves what he gets. I want him to suffer."

The doorbell rang and both women were motionless, no

sound. Ten seconds later, the bell rang again, followed by a forceful rapping on the door.

"Whoever it is knows you're here, plus they can see my car in your driveway."

"Oh, boy," she winced, acknowledging Denise was right. She was caught and was going to have to face her parents, who were most likely on the other side of the door. She trudged to the door, organizing her thoughts and potential words. Her hand gripped the doorknob. She sucked in a deep breath, released it, opened the door and relaxed. "You."

"What, you were expecting somebody else?" Reese asked, sliding past her and entering the foyer. "If you answer your phone sometime I wouldn't have to pop up."

Denise came from the living room. "Hi, Reese."

"What's up, Denise? I thought that was your car in the driveway."

"I guess I'm not the only one who pops up on your doorstep."

"Somebody has to check on this woman, since she won't answer the phone. She got me driving across the bridge on a weeknight."

"How's Angela?"

"Angela is Angela."

"Umph, let me leave that alone," Denise said, going back inside the living room.

"Where have you been for the past week?"

"Chilling at home, trying to get your sister to take me back," he said in a low voice. "Your advice helped. We're actually making progress and it feels good."

"Good to hear."

"And you need to know how much your sister misses you."

"Yeah, right."

"Seriously, check this out. She's the one who asked me to come and check on you."

"What a surprise."

"Hard to believe, this is truly a miracle. So you never know what can happen, sis."

"You staying?" Sylvia asked Reese.

"No, I'll catch you later."

"Sure you don't want to stay?"

"No, I just came to check on you. I know this thing with your father can't be easy, but you're a tough sister. Keep your head up," he said, resting his hand on her shoulder and peering around the corner into the living room but not having a view. "Call me if you need me," he whispered, and gripped her shoulder. "And thanks."

"For what?"

"For being a true friend to me and to your sister. You really did give me some good advice about how to deal with Angela. So, thanks," he said, and left.

Sylvia retuned to the living room.

"Reese is cool," Denise said. "I didn't know he was checking on you, too."

"Every now and then he stops by for free counseling," she said, laughing it off. "Seriously, he's been a good friend. He's supportive like family should be without the baggage. Sometimes he'll come over and watch the game, but mostly we sit and talk about how much he loves Angela."

"I had heard the two of you were tight."

"How'd you hear that?" Sylvia inquired.

"You know how this family is. Everybody is in everybody else's business, and rumors have a way of becoming fact. Anyway, forget about Reese and Angela. I'm upset about Tony, with his molesting self. They should have laws against people like him."

"They do," she said, reflecting on Daddy's trial.

"I mean laws against them ever being happy. I wonder if he told his so-called fiancée about his past. She has the right to know."

"Denise, do you really want to get into a battle with Tony?" He was older and always a little scary to Sylvia.

"Somebody has to step up to him. Let me ask you something," she said, perching on the edge of the sofa. "Are you positive Uncle Herbert was the one who touched you?"

Sylvia had blocked out Daddy for a rare moment and Denise's question caught her without a rapid-fire response. After careful consideration of her answer, she said, "I think so. I hope so," unable to imagine the possibility of wrongly accusing her father.

"Why do you ask?"

"I don't think Uncle Herbert is the one. I think it was Tony."

Sylvia sat tall in her seat, yielding no ground in her fight to stay in control, to not let her emotions and building sense of confusion and uncertainty direct her words. Denise couldn't be right, no way, could she? Would the nightmare ever end? She had identified an abuser from the pool of viable candidates, certain the man towering over her in the closet was Daddy. It was like finding a man guilty based on eyewitness testimony and DNA evidence exonerating him later, after a conviction, sentencing and unlimited humiliation.

"Mom said he used to babysit you and Angela when you were little."

"A long time ago."

"I know, and I'm not trying to stir up a bunch of bad feelings, but if Tony is the one who abused you, Uncle Herbert shouldn't take the blame."

"You talked to Aunt Kay about this?"

"We talked some, but you know how the old people are. Let sleeping dogs lie, that's what they say whenever an old topic comes up nobody wants to deal with. Well, Tony is not getting away with what he did to Deon. There is no statute of limitations as far as I'm concerned. His sleeping dogs better get ready to wake up, because the only thing lying around here will be me waiting for the right time to make my move," Denise said, latching her hands behind her head.

Chapter 52

Sylvia wanted to hack at her dreams, kill them. There was no way she could have erroneously blamed her father for such a disgusting act, but the feeling of having made a gross mistake wouldn't leave her alone. Peace eluded her in sleep and not much came while she was awake. What was she going to do? She would try sleeping one more time. She rolled to the middle of the bed, drifting in and out of sleep, dreaming, but able to hear the sounds in the room: the clicking of the furnace going on and off, ticking of the alarm clock, wind against the windows, each amplified, intense.

Donny wasn't home much when they had the babysitter. He got to stay late at school and afterward he got to go over to his friends'. Angela didn't like when the babysitter came to the house. She wanted to go with Mom but couldn't. So she sat on the couch and watched cartoons the whole time until Mom came home. She wasn't like Angela. Sylvia liked visitors. She would sit on his lap and sing songs, draw pictures and play with her dolls. He would give her ice cream and cookies, her favorite. That was fun. Angela never wanted to play upstairs. Upstairs was fun, except for the dark room, the place where he'd tell her a secret and she'd promise to never, never tell Angela, Donny, Mom or Daddy, because they would be mad at her. She reached for his hand, looking up, and it was him.

Sylvia sprang up, breathing heavily and struggling to gain her bearings, squinting at the clock, trying to bring three-fifty into focus. Instinctively she reached for the bottle of water sitting on the nightstand next to her bed. The bottle was in the same general area she'd left it at two-forty, one-fifteen and twelve-thirty. She rubbed her neck, contemplating whether to lie down or get up, neither of which were appealing.

Why did Denise have to go and mess with her head? She'd made the startling revelation about her abuse. She'd faced the demon of her closet. She'd acknowledged it, confronted her father, and she was supposed to be embracing the future, but the last and possibly the most critical aspect of her therapy model wasn't working. How could it not have been Daddy—why else would "daddy's little girl" bear so much discomfort? She didn't have an answer. Confusion and more despair was the only element she was embracing. How could she make such a horrible mistake?

She knew Herbert Reynolds, the father who loved her endlessly, unconditionally. Yet, she didn't have faith in him at the most tumultuous time in his life. What he was enduring now was worse than being in the war. At least during the war he had somewhat of a cause and a supportive home front. Today he was on the front line defending himself against the Latoya Scotts and Sylvia Reynoldses of his world with limited backup. Shame and agonizing remorse crawled into the bed and bounced in and out of her emotions. She wailed and wiped her eyes incessantly until the clock displayed a quarter to five.

Toughen up. She had to face him, the man she had accused in error, the man whom she had single-handedly destroyed. She went to the bathroom, unable to look at herself in the full-body mirror. Latoya wasn't the culprit. She was. No matter how nice Daddy was to Latoya. She didn't have the benefit of growing up nurtured, loved and cared for in his house. She didn't know what an incredible and honorable man her father was. Latoya didn't truly know the man she was accusing and the impact it would have on his soul. Sylvia did, and no mirror or introspection could reverse or justify the damage she'd done to the best man on earth, her daddy.

Chapter 53

Sylvia lingered in the bathroom. There was nowhere else to go. Being alone, truly alone, separated from family, carried almost the same amount of despair as being in the closet. She would build her confidence and see Dad before evening, asking for his forgiveness, his and Mom's, Angela's, too. She was wrong and had to step up and take responsibility.

The phone rang. At 5:00 a.m.? She dashed from the bathroom and snatched the phone from the nightstand. Herbert Reynolds, the caller ID read. Wow, God worked fast. Her father had called relentlessly for days with no response from his baby girl, but her rejection didn't stop him from reaching out. This was her chance to start mending broken fences. She pressed the talk button and let her words fly. "Daddy," she said with a surge of relief, like water building behind a dam and finally breaking free.

"Sylvia, it's me."

"Angela?"

"Yes, I'm glad you answered the phone. Mom and Dad have been worried about you, me, too."

She owed Angela an apology, too, but first Daddy. "You're at Mom and Daddy's awfully early," she said, hoping Angela and Reese hadn't torn their relationship again, not so soon in the reconciliation phase.

"Sylvia," she said, and stopped, letting silence continue the conversation.

"Angela, hello, Angela," she said, getting louder.

"You need to meet me at the hospital."

"Why?" she said, heart rate and blood pressure rising.

"It's Daddy."

Sylvia let her behind fall onto the bed. "What about Daddy?" she said, clutching the handset, bracing for the worst and daring only to think the best.

"The ambulance just took him to the hospital. I'm on my way, but Mom wanted me to call you."

"I'm on my way," Sylvia said, leaping to her feet and not stopping until she was extracting a pair of pants from her closet.

"What happened?"

"Don't know, maybe a heart attack. Listen, I have to go. I'll see you when you get there. Sylvia," she yelled out before disconnecting, "I love you."

Chapter 54

Angela rested her head on Reese's shoulder, gripping the chair with her free arm, dazed by the new challenges dropped at their feet. She had watched her mother stay close to the gurney when the paramedics loaded Dad into the ambulance back at their house. Seeing Mom show tremendous courage, episode after episode, time after time, challenge after challenge, and heartache after heartache gave Angela a newfound respect for her mother. Louise Reynolds truly was a woman of faith. She was grounded in the Lord. Circumstances didn't shake her hope or her faith. No matter what storms came into their lives, and since January hurricanes, tornadoes and tragedy of tsunami proportion had overrun them, at least her, but not Mom. She didn't waver. The mistake Mom made with Uncle Sam didn't seem to cripple her, either. How she was able to put the past behind and march on, with dignity and no guilt was a lesson

Angela hoped to learn one day. Who was she not to forgive her mother when she was in need of forgiveness herself? Avoiding Uncle Sam and Aunt Mabel was another issue, wouldn't be easy—as a matter of fact, downright awkward.

"Are you cold?" Reese asked, briskly rubbing her arm.

"Not really. To tell the truth, I'm not thinking about myself. All I can think about is Mom and Dad."

"Your parents are fighters. You know that," he said, easing her head back on his shoulder.

The wide emergency room doors slid open and Sylvia ran in, making a beeline for the counter, not looking into the seating area.

"Sylvia," Angela called out, jumping to her feet and moving toward the counter. Sylvia ran to Angela. They paused for a second and then embraced. Words couldn't articulate the joy her heart felt, seeing her sister, knowing she was all right. Standing together, bonded, seemed like ages. She didn't want to let go, afraid their connection would once again slip beyond her reach. Sylvia gestured to pull away, but Angela held on for a few extra seconds, hoping to deposit enough of her love to last her sister in case she decided to claim distance again.

Angela finally released her little sister.

"Where is Daddy?"

"Back there," she said, nodding her head in the direction of the examining rooms.

"Do you know what happened?"

"They're running tests, but they're not sure. I guess Dad fell and hit his head on the kitchen counter."

"Fell, how did he do that?"

"I'm not sure. They're checking to see if he had a heart attack or a stroke before he fell. We just don't know."

"Is he conscious?"

"He wasn't when the ambulance came to the house."

"I want to see him." Sylvia approached the counter with no haste. "Can we go back to see Herbert Reynolds? He's our father."

The nurse gave the okay. Sylvia took a few steps, determined to see Dad. She had to see him, to talk to him, to make him know how sorry and how wrong she was. She had to.

"Do you want to go back there with us?" Angela asked Reese before Sylvia whisked her beyond the doors.

"No, it will be too many people. Go ahead. I'll wait out here."

"Oh, Reese, I'm sorry. I didn't see you there," Sylvia said, walking toward him and talking simultaneously. Reese stood and gave Sylvia a hug of compassion.

"Nice to see the two of you together," Reese said.

"Nice to see the two of you together," Sylvia said.

"Let's go. You need to see your father."

Sylvia, who was in full stride, stopped, beamed directly into Angela's eyes, and said, "We need to see our father."

Angela locked arms with Sylvia and patted her sister's hand. "You're absolutely correct, our father. Herbert Reynolds has been our father from the day we were born."

Sylvia chimed in, "And will be until the day we die. And we were sisters from the day we were born."

"And will be until the day we die."

"I'm sorry," Sylvia said.

"I know," Angela said, flicking away a lone tear streaming down her cheek. "Me, too."

"You know we have to talk."

"I know," Angela acknowledged.

"We've had far too many misunderstandings."

"And fights," Angela added.

"And hurts, secrets and who knows what else."

"But we're still sisters, and we're going to do better. I promise," Angela affirmed, with words that sounded like they were carrying the weight of commitment and would not just vanish into the air.

Their arms locked tighter.

"I promise, too," Sylvia said.

The two hit the big green button positioned on the wall next to the huge double doors leading into the examining room. They waited until the doors slowly swung open, arm in arm. Whatever was awaiting them on the other side of the door would have to be powerful in order to beat two determined Reynolds sisters.

Chapter 55

Sylvia had run home, showered, dressed, swung by the office and was back at the hospital by two o'clock. "Where is Daddy?" she asked her Mom and Angela, who were alone in his private room.

"I just got here a few minutes before you walked in," Angela said.

"Both of you just missed him. They took him down for more tests," Mom answered.

"What kind of tests? He had an MRI last night."

"They're giving him an EKG."

"But I thought they weren't concerned about his heart. Why would they give him an EKG?"

"To tell the truth, Sylvia, I'm not sure what all they're doing. What I do know is he was awake and talking a little. I was so happy. I didn't hear everything the nurse said, but she did say he was doing better. No sign of a stroke or a seizure. Oh, yes, and they said he might need a transfusion."

"Why?"

"You didn't see him at the house this morning, but there was a lot of blood."

"From hitting his head on the counter, that seems odd. I can understand the swelling I saw in the emergency room this morning, but how could he lose enough blood to need a transfusion?" Sylvia wondered.

"I'm not sure but your father is B negative and they're low on blood supply. She asked if any of us were B negative," Mom said. "I'm O positive and apparently he can't use my type. He needs B negative. Blood type A won't work. They'll have to use O negative as a last resort if it comes to that. I can't remember your blood types. She asked if the two of you would be willing to donate blood for your dad."

"I must have your blood, then. I'm O positive, too," Sylvia said without thinking.

"I don't know if I can get tested," Angela said.

The three knew the implication of having Angela's blood types defined. Burying the truth had been the method used for coping with the past. Once a secret was uncovered that had lingering consequences, ignorance was the next stage of coping. So long as Angela didn't know her blood type or ever have to deal with the harsh reality that she didn't share Herbert Reynolds's blood, she could perhaps find a way to live with the deception, but the look on her face didn't exude confidence.

"Can't they get blood from the blood bank? Why do we have to take a blood test?" Angela continued.

"They must not have the kind he needs. I'm praying he doesn't need a transfusion, in the name of Jesus."

"Excuse me, I'm going to the cafeteria and get a cup of hot tea," Angela said, dashing for the door.

"Want me to go with you?"

"No, you can stay with Mom. I'll be back," she said, rushing hurriedly into the hallway.

"I'm so sorry for what I've put my child through. She doesn't deserve this, but there's nothing I can do now but pray for her to find peace with my mistake. I hope she'll be able to move on with her life and leave the past in the past."

"It's not easy to leave the past alone, Mom, when the consequences are in front of you every day." Mom fidgeted in her seat. Voices approaching the door were getting louder, but she kept talking, determined to release the truth about Tony in one rapid movement, swift, done. "I'm not talking about you, Mom. I'm talking about…" was the extent of her revelation. The door was instantly filled with too many people. Aunt Mabel busted inside first with Uncle Sam, Lee and Lee's fiancée, whose name was difficult remembering. Why bother making the effort to commit his friend's name to her memory when most likely she'd be replaced with a new face next month?

"Hello, hello, hello," Aunt Mabel sang, entering the room like the pied piper with her family trailing.

"Where's Herbert?" Uncle Sam asked.

"Having a few tests done."

"How's he doing?" Aunt Mabel asked with a recognizable tone of concern.

"Much better, no stroke or sign of a heart attack."

"Amen," Aunt Mabel cried out in the middle of a packed hospital room, where keeping quiet was the law.

Angela arrived to find a room full of family members who couldn't read the occupancy sign on the door. She squeezed past Lee and Uncle Sam, avoiding eye contact.

"Herbert might need a blood transfusion, but they're short on his blood type."

"Sam, he's your brother. Shouldn't the two of you have the same blood type. Give him some of yours," Aunt Mabel suggested.

"Are you B negative?"

"No, I'm A negative."

"I don't believe A will work, only B."

"What about you girls? Did you get your mother's blood or did at least one of you get your father's?" Aunt Mabel said in a joking way, oblivious to the extent of actually how not funny her comment was. Secrets and lies were a wildfire, always burning, never truly under control, a constant threat.

"We both took after Mom, I guess," Sylvia said, refusing to let Angela suffer in silence while the blood test issue dragged on.

"Well, we can all get tested if need be. You don't have to worry. If there's a drop of B negative blood in this family we're going to find it," Aunt Mabel assured. She meant well. Sylvia couldn't deny her commitment to the family. If it wasn't for Aunt Mabel, the family reunion probably would have died ten years ago, but she made sure the event was scheduled, location secured and communication went out year after year, sometimes with help, sometimes not. The price for her love was cheap. Yet, Sylvia had paid the premium time and time again.

Chapter 56

The two-visitor rule was ignored by the Reynoldses with the room swelling to ten visitors at times and another ten in queue in the waiting room. The Reynoldses were going to show up whether asked or not. At any minute the nurse and Daddy would return and a whole bunch of people were going to get kicked out. No sense in clearing the room just yet, Sylvia decided. Wait and let the nurse do her job. Sylvia planned to serve as reinforcement if necessary.

"I almost forgot. Kay, Arthur and Aunt Ida are coming around five. They told me to tell you," Aunt Mabel said to Mom. "Tony and Linda are on their way, too."

Oh, no, he wasn't. Sylvia wasn't ready to confront him. She hadn't determined how to handle him, but whatever and whenever she decided, he wasn't going to sit in her father's room breathing the same fresh air as the man who'd been erroneously blamed for Tony's crime. He had no right showing up.

"Speaking of the devil," Aunt Mabel said as Tony and a woman entered.

"Hey, hey, hey," he said, strolling to a few feet inside the doorway, the only unclaimed space in the tiny room.

"We have too many people in here. Somebody will have to leave," Angela suggested.

"Man, cuz, you're always handling your business," Lee teased.

"I'm serious. The nurse is bringing Daddy down any minute and there are too many people in here. He won't be able to breathe."

"We'll make do, don't worry. A person can't have too much love especially when they're in the hospital."

Sylvia shot out of her seat. "We mean it, somebody has to get out." She clamped her teeth together, letting the words squeeze past.

"She's right," Mom agreed, "we have too many people. I'll go to the waiting room and let someone have my spot. We shouldn't have more than four at a time. Herbert will be tired and we don't want to stress him with a lot of talking."

"Angela, are you staying?" Aunt Mabel asked.

"Yes, we're both staying," Sylvia jumped in.

"Okay, Tony, why don't you and Linda stay so you can introduce her to your uncle," Aunt Mabel directed.

"He's not up for introductions. Daddy's in the hospital, not on the golf course," Sylvia hurled back at her aunt.

"Sylvia," Mom called out in a tone Sylvia had heard repeatedly during her rambunctious childhood.

"You're awfully snippety, young lady. I'm only trying to help work out the room situation," Aunt Mabel said. Uncle Sam and Lee kept quiet as usual. Lee followed his mother around, jumping to her orders like a lapdog. Uncle Sam ignored her. Whenever she asked him a question, she always had to repeat it twice after echoing her signature phrase, "Sam, did you hear me?" She said, "I'll walk to the waiting room with Louise. Come on, Lee. We'll let Tony and Linda wait with the girls."

Anger was a surge of water, searching for a path to be released and creating havoc when unsuccessfully finding an outlet. "Tony is not staying in this room," Sylvia said, peering into the floor and letting her gaze rise, focused, fierce, and met her abuser where he stood, in shock and dismay. She wasn't a five-year-old girl anymore. She was a woman taking charge of her life and emotions, no longer suffering at the expense of someone else's poor choices. "I don't want you anywhere near me or my father."

"Sylvia," Mom said, pulling her daughter's arm, trying to get her attention. Sylvia freed the hold Mom had on her arm.

"What is wrong with you?" Aunt Mabel asked, standing in the middle of the room, with the others looking on but silent. Uncle Sam walked out along with Lee and his fiancée.

"Ask Tony. He knows."

"I have no idea what's wrong with you. I haven't done anything to you."

Sylvia broke toward him with Aunt Mabel stepping in front of her. Angela grabbed one arm and Mom the other.

"Child, you have lost your mind, you and Denise. Louise, I don't know what's wrong with this girl, but this is not how you treat visitors. We're here to visit your father. The least you can do is show some manners and respect. You'd think with all of your degrees you would have learned how to treat people by now. You don't see your sister throwing a fit. She knows how to act around her people," Aunt Mabel preached.

Aunt Mabel was not her concern at the moment. "Tony, either you get out of here right now or you'll have some explaining to do to my father and to the rest of the family."

"What are you talking about?" Aunt Mabel asked. "What is she talking about?" she asked Tony.

He hunched his shoulders. Sylvia knew he knew the secret was no longer a buried product of the past. She was grown and couldn't be ignored.

"Mama, I'm leaving. This is crazy," he said, grabbing his woman's hand and bolting out the door.

Battle lines were drawn with her on one side and Aunt Mabel on the other, neither giving an inch. After a minute, Aunt Mabel caved, giving Tony time to escape. "Louise, we're leaving, too. Sylvia is losing her mind. Please don't plan to show up at Tony's wedding in June acting like this. I won't stand for it."

"We'll see if there's a wedding once Linda finds out Tony is a child predator."

"What did you say? What kind of a lie are you telling? You've let Denise suck you into her nonsense talking. Deon is gone. Leave it alone with these lies."

"I'm not talking about Deon. I'm talking about me, when I was five years old, in that big closet in my parents' room."

Mom sighed, which sounded like she was drawing her last breath—Angela, too. She had wanted to tell Mom in a more discreet fashion, but the opportunity for openness had arrived and she had to partake. Better out than in.

Aunt Mabel's mouth flew open and she slung her pocketbook under her arm. "You and that Latoya Scott must be working together. When are you going to stop trying to tear down the reputation of good men? I'm surprised at you, Sylvia. I didn't think you'd do such a thing, try to start trouble in the family," she said, walking toward the door. "You and Denise are causing a whole lot of trouble, more than you're going to be able to handle, I can guarantee you that much."

"If you don't believe me, ask Tony," she cried out, slamming the truth into Aunt Mabel's ears despite her attempt to escape through the doorway. Tony didn't have to make restitution to her, too late, but Linda would find out. She'd make sure he didn't get free access to a set of innocent children and tarnish their future and maul their memories like he'd done to her for twenty years. Her nightmares were ending. Tony and Aunt Mabel's were just beginning.

Chapter 57

The ruckus had dissipated along with Aunt Mabel. Lee and his girlfriend wanted to stay, but Aunt Mabel put up a fuss, so he left the hospital, too. Uncle Sam didn't leave with them, but Sylvia suspected that Angela probably wished he had. The rest of the family came around five, stayed for a short visit and offered to leave so Daddy could rest, leaving his immediate family.

The nurse had changed Daddy's bandages and given a good report on his vital signs. His medication was reduced, but he was still groggy and had been most of the day. Thank God he was all right. She couldn't have lived if he'd died due in part to her wrongly accusing him of a crime so awful most people didn't feel comfortable saying the word. How did she dare entertain the notion of the gentle, kindhearted, loving soul lying in the bed hurting a child, not his or anyone else's? She didn't deserve him as her father, but God had seen fit to bless her with him, anyway.

"I'm going to get a cup of coffee," Reese said. "Does anybody want anything?"

"No, I'm fine," Mom said. "The food you brought was plenty. Thank you so much."

"Nothing else for me, either. This was fine. Thanks," Sylvia said, lifting an empty bag.

"I'll go with you," Angela said. Reese was a decent man. He made his mistakes like everybody else. Reese and Angela looked happy, as if they enjoyed being together. Sylvia hadn't seen them express as much affection in at least a year. Her sister's marriage was looking up. At least one Reynolds couple would survive the frigid winter and enjoy a renewed beginning, a fresh spring. More than she could say for Tony Reynolds. Forget about letting sleeping dogs lie. He was a predator, had been for almost three decades. Well, she wasn't exactly sure when he began his attacks or when they ended, but what if he was still abusive? His fiancée, the mother of three children, had a right to know what kind of man she was marrying and surrendering her babies to. If his attacks were all relegated to the past, then perhaps she could forgive him and they could move on, but the choice was hers.

Daddy was drifting in and out of sleep. He was aware of his family's presence in the room but unable to stay awake and engage in a conversation.

"Daddy looks so much better."

"He does. He's glad to see you. Once his little girl walked through the door, you were all the medicine Herbert

Reynolds needed. Your father loves you and Angela. You mean the world to him."

Keeping her voice lowered, Sylvia responded. "I know he does, and, Mom, I'm so sorry."

"Shhh, no need to apologize anymore. What's done is done and we move on, like family. God's mercy has gotten us through a hard time, and we're here, standing and pressing on. So, release your guilt," she said, patting her on the hand. "Let it go. You've already asked God to forgive you." Dad groaned, drawing instant attention from her and Mom. False alarm, he was sound asleep. "You've asked for my and your father's forgiveness and you know you have it, but even if we didn't forgive you, the one who counts is God. Once He forgives you, you're forgiven with your offense never to be slung in your face again by the Almighty. And you can't let anybody else throw it in your face, either. You have to learn to shake it off and keep going once you're forgiven and have tried to seek the forgiveness of those you offended. That's all you can do, and you've done that already. Now you have to forgive yourself. Let this go or your mistake or guilt will eat up every shred of joy and happiness you possess."

"I've forgiven myself, but not Tony. I can't let this go," she said with her tone escalating.

"Not so loud," Mom said. "We don't want to wake your father."

"Right, I'm sorry, but Mom, Tony has to be held accountable. Why should he be able to get married and roll on with life while others suffer at his expense? That's not fair."

"Sylvia, life isn't fair. Why do you think we need Christ in our lives? To make it right, that's why."

"Mom, I'm all for religion, but Tony needs a good old-fashioned dose of reality. Denise and I are both telling his fiancée together. If I was a mother, I'd want someone to tell me. Wouldn't you?"

"We're back," Angela whispered, entering the room with Reese following close behind.

"We'll talk later," Mom said.

Chapter 58

Latoya lay sideways across her twin bed, the single spot in the house she could call her space, one not violated by her meddling nine-year-old sister, her clumsy five-year-old brother or her twelve-year-old twin brothers, who were always playing too much and breaking her stuff. She envisioned having her own place, but her dream wasn't going to happen. She raised her loose-fitting sweatshirt, leaving her turtleneck and T-shirt intact. She let her fingers span out and delicately pressed into her stomach. Thank goodness for winter. Two months and still safe. She would never have been able to fool her mother for this long in the summer. She pulled the XL sweatshirt down, covering her pouch.

Mr. Reynolds was a nice man. A rush of guilt surrounded her. He was one of the few men in her life who hadn't tried to take advantage of her. He actually gave her extra tutoring after class. She'd made her first B last year in math. She remembered carrying the test paper around in her book bag for three solid months, taking a peek daily. He told her she was smart and she had the test to prove it.

The door flew open and her baby brother ran in.

"Get out of my room," she yelled, and tossed her pillow from the bed. He narrowly missed the attack and ran out with the door slamming behind. She wanted to scream for privacy. Guilt leaped in and wrestled her iron disposition into submission. She picked up the newspaper one more time, having read the headline and story at least fifteen times in the past twenty-four hours.

"Local Principal Hospitalized." What if she was the reason for him being in the hospital? Maybe he had a heart attack like her father had four years ago. Mama said Daddy died because he had too much pressure from work and from life. Her life had changed for the worse when her dad died. Mama worked two jobs: bookkeeping at the factory during the day and cleaning offices at night. Three Saturdays a month she worked at Macy's. She got a discount, but the people there didn't realize how broke Mama was all the time. Having gas money for the ride to Macy's was her treat.

What would Mama do when she found out about this baby, that her daughter wasn't a virgin? She wouldn't be able to keep it a secret forever. When she accused Mr. Reynolds, there was no concept of a pregnancy. Her lie seemed like the perfect solution at the time, since he had turned down the other options she'd offered. No other man had. He was the first. She had no choice. He had threatened not only to suspend her, but to also tell Mama about her seductive behavior being inappropriate for a fourteen-year-old.

Ever since her birthday in December, she'd promised herself no man would ever force her to feel so badly or ashamed again. Nobody was taking anything from her without permission. She'd vowed to fight harder next time, maybe even scratching their eyes out if she had to, but the time in January was supposed to have been different. She was in charge, fixing a problem the best way she knew how. A few weeks before getting into trouble with Mr. Reynolds, she had already worked out a problem with the owner after he caught her stealing and again at her babysitting job a week later when the father caught her smoking and threatened to tell her mother. She was able to keep them both quiet. Their silence came easy, wasn't so bad. The only reason she lied was to shut the principal up, but not like this.

Wasn't right for him to pay for what others had done to her from the time she was eight. Mama felt badly about having to work so hard and having to leave her children alone most of the time, trusting others to babysit. She never had the heart to tell Mama about the first time, and then she lost count after that time. She wanted to protect her mother from the heart attack.

Latoya reread the article, rubbing her stomach again. Eventually she had to deal with Mama, and eventually the couple Latoya babysat for was going to have to deal with Mama, at least the husband. Probably another set of charges, another trial, more newspapers. Her mind was weighed down, heavy, throbbing, but she had to do right by Mr. Reynolds. She mustered courage and dragged her resisting body from the bed. Her mother would know the truth. Last week the calendar said it was time for spring. Her secret was going to be discovered, anyway. Maybe one day Mr. Reynolds could forgive her for ruining his life the way hers would soon be, once the full truth surfaced.

Chapter 59

After the first blowup, Aunt Mabel and Tony kept their distance. If they were visiting the hospital, it had to be late at night, which didn't bother Sylvia so long as they weren't in the room when she arrived. If she had her druthers, he and Aunt Mabel would deposit their goodwill elsewhere.

Mom sat on one side of the hospital bed and Sylvia on the other. She stayed overnight with Mom instead of running back and forth across the bridge for a fifth night straight. She'd go home tomorrow. Run by the office. Have her secretary reschedule patients the entire week. Sylvia hated having to reshuffle the schedule, especially for her critical patients, but there was no choice. She was needed in Delaware and her place for the next week would be by the side of Herbert Reynolds.

Daddy began stirring. "Daddy," she whispered, and leaned close to him. "Daddy," she called again.

"Herbert," Mom said, joining in.

The nurse walked in, causing both to abort their attempts to wake him. "Mr. Reynolds," the nurse called out, much louder than Sylvia and her mother were doing. "Mr. Reynolds," the nurse repeated, fumbling with the gadgets on the IV and the machine tracking his heart rate and blood pressure.

Daddy started to come around.

"How's he doing, Nurse?" Mom asked.

"His vital signs are good. We just have to deal with the trauma to his head and this nasty cut," she said, pulling a pair of plastic gloves over her hands.

"What's next?" Sylvia asked.

"The goal is to keep reducing the swelling around his brain. He's doing very well, extremely well, actually. The way he looks now compared to when he came in here, it's a miracle."

"So you don't know what happened before he fell?"

"No, and that's the mystery," the nurse said, jamming the box of bandages back into the supply cabinet after extracting one almost the size of a small paperback book.

"We'll step out while you change the bandage," Mom told the nurse.

"Would you prefer for the aide to come in and give him his bath now or wait a little later in the morning?"

"She can bring the tub and I'll do it," Mom said.

They retreated to the hallway and took the short walk to the waiting room. The bandage change took about ten minutes and then they could return.

"Finally, things are looking up, one miracle after another. I still can't believe Latoya came forward and told the truth."

"I knew the Lord would work this out," Mom said confidently.

"Once this is over, I'm considering offering my services to Latoya and her family for free."

"Sylvia, that would be wonderful."

"Really, you wouldn't be offended?"

"Absolutely not. What a way to turn a bad situation into something good. You see, you never know how God is going to use a situation."

"God didn't have Latoya lie on Daddy."

"No. He sure didn't, but if He allowed the situation to happen, we have no choice but to grow spiritually from the experience, otherwise we waste precious time in our lives with problems that bear no fruit. Every experience in your life has to make you stronger and increase your faith. You begin to learn that if God worked it out once, He'll do it again, and again. I'm a witness."

"I don't have a lot of faith."

"Yes, you do. Everyone does. Your faith is not the same like mine. God gives each of us the amount necessary to live out our life, following the path He has set for us."

"Mine is little and not getting bigger."

"Then, young lady, if you're not growing your God-given measure of faith, then you better work on tolerance."

"Not too good with tolerance, either."

"That's not true. You're willing to work with Latoya Scott, someone who has caused you pain."

"Yes, but she's a child. Tony is different. He's a grown man. I can't believe this doesn't bother you?"

"Oh, I'm bothered, don't get me wrong," Mom said,

twisting her neck slightly toward her shoulder. "I'm angry, very angry and hurt that I allowed someone to harm you. I can't change what he did to you. To be honest, your father and I will deal with Tony soon enough. I'm too upset to approach him right now. I might say the wrong thing, but in due time, he is going to deal with me, after your father is out of the hospital and we can approach him together. Trust me, he's not getting off totally free. And, I have to apologize to you and to Angela for leaving you with someone who hurt and abused you. Baby, I'm so sorry," Mom said. "I had no idea. It's good for Tony that I didn't catch him. Back then I probably would have killed him."

Angela felt her eyebrow arch.

"What, don't look at me like that. I didn't know the Lord then like I do now, and Tony better be awfully glad I know Him now. Rest assured that this isn't over. I'm not sure what we're going to do or say to him, but we will approach him. Your father and I owe you that much. It was your father's and my job to protect you and we didn't. I'm sorry, honey."

"I don't blame you or Dad, not even a little bit. You trusted Tony. He's the predator."

"I don't want to harp on this, but you'll be better served talking to him in private. Tell him you know what he did. If you want me to be there, I'll be there."

"Mom, I can't keep this quiet. He's been allowed to hurt too many children. He has to be exposed, publicly."

"But by talking to him in private, you'll get the results you're looking for without humiliating him in front of other people. Exposing an old secret bears more punishment than you think."

"He humiliated me. I'm not doing any more or less than he did."

"He's not your barometer for right and wrong. You can handle yourself better than he did."

"I have to speak up. He might hurt his fiancée's children if I don't. As a practicing psychologist, it's my duty."

"I understand where you're coming from. I agree you should speak up, especially for the sake of the children, but not in public. That's my point. Sometimes I believe it's better to let some secrets stay secret, leave the past in the past. You know Aunt Ida Mae believes it's best to let sleeping dogs lie."

After the fallout about Angela's paternity, she had to agree. If she could, Sylvia would gladly take back the revelation about Mom and Uncle Sam. Angela's knowing had made their family situation worse. "But in this case, you need to come forward for the right reason. You have to ask yourself, are you doing this to protect the children or to seek revenge?" Mom asked.

Sylvia wanted to immediately answer "protect the children," but couldn't. "Mom, he deserves what's coming to him, and Denise is planning to stand up at his wedding when the minister asks for objections."

Mom's face turned flush red. "Sylvia Mariah Reynolds, you can't possibly think of doing such a thing. Please don't. You have to know exposing him in front of a group of people is wrong. You're a smart girl. You can find another way to do what's right."

"Exposing a predator is right."

"It's not what you're doing, young lady. It's how you're going about it, but okay, just be prepared."

"For what?"

"For the same to happen to you or to someone you love." Sylvia didn't speak, but the words were chipping away at her resolve. "When you sow good seeds, good follows you. When you set traps for someone, you end up falling, too. Be careful, young lady. Having your say is one thing. Plotting revenge is another."

Sylvia had longed for mother-daughter conversations, but hearing Mom's nuggets of wisdom was awful. They made too much sense. Daddy went along with her quirky comments. Mom was steadfast and challenged her ideas. And to think this mother-daughter bonding was what she thought she wanted. One earful and her longing was satisfied for at least a good year. Almost too embarrassed to speak the words, she told Mom, "Denise is planning to expose him at the wedding. I'll just be there."

"How far are you planning to go with this?"

"I don't know. Actually, I haven't figured out what I'm going to do yet. I have considered taking legal steps."

"It happened so long ago. Isn't it too late to press charges?"

"Probably not. Normally the statute of limitations is seven years, but in cases like this, the clock begins when the victim knows or remembers the crime occurred. If I had my way, sexually violating or physically abusing a child would be treated just like murder with no statute of limitations. If you abuse someone at eighteen, they could arrest you at eighty, pull you out of the retirement home kicking and screaming if they have to. I'd love to nail a bunch of perverts to the wall."

"Sylvia, I don't understand you sometimes."

"What?"

"You have amazing compassion on one hand and such hard-heartedness on the other. You need to find a balance in your life, honey, otherwise you're going to drive yourself crazy."

"Too late," she said humorously, trying to retain the awkward but open dialogue with her mother, a gift she longed to have, now possessed and was grateful to have.

"Mrs. Reynolds," the nurse interrupted. "I've changed your husband's bandages, but he's getting cleaned up and I'll be back with his meds."

"Thank you," Mom said, and the nurse left. "I was going to clean him up."

"Mom, take a rest. You'll have plenty of time to take care of Daddy." Sylvia paused before speaking again. "Do you think you'll ever tell Dad?"

Mom held back her response, as though she was meditating, and finally began to answer. "Yes, I am going to tell your father. You need to know that the Lord delivered me from my adultery a long time ago. So I'm not telling him because of guilt."

"What made you decide to tell him after all these years?"

"Because of something your sister said—secrets can't live in a marriage. She was right and I have to live the same advice that I give to others. Your father deserves to know. I'll tell him after he's recovered and strong again."

"Are you worried about how he will react?"

"No, I'm not. Our marriage is covered in the blood of Jesus and is stronger today than it was thirty years ago. With Christ in our lives, your father and I can handle anything, and so can you, Sylvia. Take a lesson from your mom, when

you get married, never share information with others that
you wouldn't be willing to share with your husband. Never
let secrets enter your marriage. A marriage is too precious
and too much of a blessing to jeopardize."

Chapter 60

Sylvia hadn't been to church, but her absence didn't seem to stop God from hunting her down and sending Mom's reinforcements. The elevator door opened and out stepped Aunt Ida Mae. By now she'd heard the gory details about what had happened the other day with Aunt Mabel and Tony.

"Aunt Ida Mae," she and Mom greeted. "Did you come on your own?"

"Kay dropped me off on her way to work. She'll stop by and get me on her lunch break or I can stay until she comes by this evening."

"Aunt Ida Mae, you don't have to wear yourself out staying here all day."

"Well, I'm here if you need me," she said, taking a seat.

"She should be able to go back in the room in a few minutes. They're getting him cleaned up," Mom told her.

Mom gave Aunt Ida Mae an update on Daddy's improving condition and small talk followed.

"Feels good to get off my feet, thank you, Jesus," Aunt Ida Mae said, rearing back in her seat. "Sure feels good taking a load off."

"I bet it does," Mom responded.

"I guess you both heard," Aunt Ida Mae said with her arms resting across her stomach and eyes closed.

"What?"

"Mabel called off Tony's wedding."

"What?" Mom said.

"Uh-huh, sure did, called it off. She said there was too much confusion in the family for a wedding."

"Good, he shouldn't be getting married, anyway," Sylvia said, feeling a sense of relief, mostly because she wouldn't have to confront him in public. Mom didn't know it, but she'd gotten her rethinking about how to approach Tony.

"I believe they canceled the wedding but not the marriage. If I understood Mabel correctly, Tony and Linda are getting married at the courthouse."

"Courthouse," she yelled, catching herself, realizing she was in the hospital quiet zone. Aunt Ida Mae's eyes opened. "That's exactly where he should be, in court for what he did to me and to Deon."

"I heard about what happened at the hospital the other night with you, Mabel and Tony."

"Aunt Ida Mae, I know what you're going to say. I should forgive Tony and let this go. Let sleeping dogs lie. I know, I know. Mom has already told me, but Mom agreed with me that I should talk to Tony and I plan to. He's not getting married before I talk to him and Linda."

"Is that right?"

Sylvia was prepared for more retort from the Reynoldses' designated angel but was shortchanged. "He has to acknowledge what he did to us."

Aunt Ida Mae nodded her head, still no response.

Sylvia slid to the edge of her chair. "He was wrong and he should be a man, step up, confess and take responsibility."

"Is that what you want?"

"That's what I want." She sat back in her seat, finally getting a response from Aunt Ida Mae.

"What if he doesn't?"

"Th-then," she stammered, "he gets what he gets."

"So you're in the judgment business now," Aunt Ida Mae said, closing her eyes again. Mom could have jumped in anytime to save her drowning daughter but didn't. Mom knew Aunt Ida Mae was too much spiritually for Sylvia to handle, but she didn't lend a helping hand. Mom relaxed in her seat and let Aunt Ida Mae do the talking, what little she did. They were working together, had to be.

"I'm not passing judgment on Tony. He abused me and Deon, and somebody has to stand up to him and make him pay. He shouldn't be free to walk away without any consequences, should he?"

"What Tony did was wrong and I told Mabel so. Make no mistake about it, there are consequences for what he did, but don't you let his sin cause you to stumble."

"That's right, Ida Mae, exactly what I've been telling my daughter. She's better than this."

"God has brought this family through a lot of tragedy this year and we're only two days into April. We have to be thankful and humble. Some battles we don't choose, but we have to fight them. Some fights we create."

"What are you saying, that I'm starting an unnecessary battle with Tony?"

"No, I'm saying let God handle Tony. He's bigger and more powerful than you. It's okay if you talk to Tony, but don't do it with revenge and malice in your heart. You never know, maybe he's not the same person today that he was then, and trust me, I'm not making excuses for him. Nothing can justify what he did, but as a family, we have to find a way to keep moving. In Galatians, in the fifth chapter, somewhere around the fourteenth or fifteenth verse, the Word is very clear. It's says, 'If you keep on biting and devouring each other, watch out or you will be destroyed by each other.' If a family keeps trouble brewing, they'll end up destroying one another and that's not the way to be. Doesn't mean you won't have some arguments, doesn't mean people won't fall short and it doesn't mean family won't have to deal with consequences from their actions, but don't you always be the one keeping up the fight."

"You're real church-going women. You let people get away with everything because you're able to forgive like that. I'm definitely not there and may never get there."

"Just because we believe in the Lord doesn't mean people can walk all over us. Don't be misled. I don't fly off the handle, but I'm not a pushover. You know that," Mom added.

"Me, neither, but I know how to choose my battles and how to speak loud with a soft voice. That's what age and wisdom will do for you. I'm not talking about Tony, but I'm saying in general, you have to give your family room to fall and get up," Aunt Ida said.

"Remember, God gave me grace and I'm not the same person I was thirty years ago," Mom said.

"The same grace God gave your mother He might choose to give to Tony, if he repents and deals with his mistake like your mother did. You have to allow room for God's mercy in Tony's life and in yours. Sylvia, you never know when you're going to make a big mistake in your life and need somebody to forgive you and let go of how much you hurt them and broke their spirit. Don't get too self-righteous. None of us are perfect, except Jesus. Trust me. You'll need grace somewhere down the line like Tony needs now."

Ugh, she wanted to scream, but they were double-teaming her. She didn't want their words to make sense, but they did. She would talk to Tony, in private. Depending on his reaction, she would determine the next step. How Linda found out, from her or from him, would be up to Tony. She was at peace with her intended plan.

"Mr. Reynolds is all cleaned up now. You can go back in his room if you'd like," the nurse told them.

Chapter 61

Hope was in the air. Dad was on his way home with Sylvia and Mom. Reese was getting the prescription filled downstairs in the hospital pharmacy. She was the only one left in the room. Angela folded Dad's last two hospital gowns and placed them neatly on the windowsill and stared out the window into the sunshine. A dose of light recharged her soul, generating energy sufficient to pack her father's few remaining items. She held the photo containing all five of them: Dad, Mom, Sylvia, Donny and her. The world she'd known for thirty years was no longer, but Dad was still Dad. No paternity test or dead secret would keep her from her father's love.

A smile eased its way onto her face as she reflected on the kind of mother God had blessed her with, one of tremendous courage, integrity, faith—an all-around good person who made mistakes but had a heart for those she loved.

Angela placed the picture inside the small overnight duffel bag gently, unwilling to bring additional harm to the family of five represented in the photo. Angela was startled by the rapping on the door. She turned to find her father's nurse, the one who had cared for him during his eight-day stay.

"I'm sorry, I didn't mean to startle you," the nurse said with a clipboard in her hand, holding a small stack of papers. "I stopped by to see if your Dad needed anything else before leaving, but I see he's already left."

"Yes, my sister took him home. Thank God he got better. We're very happy."

"He's a wonderful man, very polite. We were glad to take care of him, but I'm sure you're glad to have him going home."

"Definitely, he had us worried a week ago."

"Well, his recovery was miraculous. The swelling diminished on its own. His blood cells replenished without the need for a transfusion. All went well."

"I'm so glad he didn't need the transfusion, especially since no one in my family matched his blood type."

"We were glad he didn't need a transfusion, as well, but the matching part isn't true."

"What do you mean?" Angela stopped fumbling with the bag of items and directed her attention to the nurse.

"There was one person who matched perfectly, not only type but also some of the other indicators that we use."

Angela returned to her fascination with the bag. "My sister Sylvia, right?"

"No, not your sister. You were the perfect match."

"What?" she asked, ready to fall on the floor. "There must

be some mistake, I'm not, I mean I couldn't. Are you sure you didn't get my results mixed up with my sister, Sylvia Reynolds?"

The nurse combed the charts. "No mistake, see, says right here," she said, showing the chart to Angela. "You and your father are a perfect match. At least if either of you ever need blood in the future, you know where to go."

"Thank you, thank you," Angela cried out as Reese returned with a pharmacy bag.

"You're welcome," the nurse said, walking away. "Take care, Mrs. Jones, and take care of your father."

"I will," Angela said, watching the nurse leave. "My father," she said to Reese, falling into his arms, "Dad is my father."

"Of course he is—nothing changed."

"No, he's really my father. Thank you, Jesus."

"What do you mean?"

"Come on," she said, taking the prescription and letting him carry the duffel bag. "I'll tell you the great news on the way to Dad's," she said, with an overwhelming portion of joy she thought would never graze her path again. Hope and miracles were in the air. She locked onto Reese's arm and sailed into the hallway, proud to be his wife, proud to be a legitimate child of Herbert and Louise, proud to be a Reynolds and proud to be a child of the King.

* * * * *

READING GROUP GUIDE
by Patricia Haley

ABOUT THIS GUIDE

The questions and discussion topics that follow are
intended to enhance your group's reading of
Let Sleeping Dogs Lie by Patricia Haley. We hope the
novel provided an enjoyable read for all your members.

MAKES YOU GO HMMM!

Thought-Provoking Questions for Discussion

Now that you have read *Let Sleeping Dogs Lie,* let's talk about some of the issues addressed. Grab your reading friends and have fun.

1. When, how or what should Louise tell Herbert about the affair with Sam? Should she have told him thirty years ago? How would you have expected him to react back then versus now—the same or differently? Would you want to know, if it was your spouse? Would knowing help or hurt the relationship?

2. What was appropriate or inappropriate about the relationship between Sylvia and Reese? Can a married man befriend a single woman without presenting a problem for his wife? If so, how? If not, why? Can a married woman befriend a single man and still have her husband feel okay about the relationship?

3. Herbert made reference to a secret early in the prologue and recounted memories from the war prior to his meeting with Latoya. What do you think his secret was?

4. What's the difference between forgiving and forgetting? What was Aunt Ida's opinion? Do you agree?

5. Denise is put in a tough situation—having to divide Deon's estate, with her parents fighting each step of the way. Should she sell the town house to her father, knowing his girlfriend will most likely occupy the

home with him, or should she side with her mother and not sell the place to him?

6. Why did the words *daddy's little girl* bug Sylvia so much?

7. When did you realize Tony was the culprit and not Herbert?

8. Denise is angry at Tony and blames him for Deon's death. What will she gain by exposing Tony as a molester at the family event? What other way might she deal with her anger and loss?

9. Why and how should Tony be forgiven by Sylvia? By Herbert and Louise? By Denise? What would Jesus do? How?

10. Should Tony face criminal charges for his twenty-five-year-old transgression? What's best for the family? What's best for Sylvia?

11. Did Keisha (Arthur's mistress) belong at Deon's funeral?

12. The Reynolds family was a mixture of unity and dysfunction, love and bitterness. In times of need they came together, and at other times they drove one another crazy. What did you like and dislike about their family?

13. Reese and Angela have struggled with issues surrounding their marriage. Is there any hope for them? What can they do to make it work? What have they done right? Wrong?

14. You don't know much about Deon, but based on what you do know, do you think he committed suicide, or was the overdose an accident? Aunt Mabel implied that Deon was sick, although no one else in the family

acknowledged her comment. She also implied that suicide was a more acceptable tragedy for the family than having to deal with certain illnesses. How or why would a person make such a distinction?

15. Who's your favorite character(s)? Excluding Tony, who's your least favorite? Who would you like to see in a sequel?

16. How would you describe the marriage between Arthur and Kay? What's the source of their underlying tension? What about the marriage between Mabel and Sam? Both marriages had issues. Which would you prefer: Arthur and Kay or Sam and Mabel? (You have to pick one—☺)

17. How do you feel about Arthur? Sam? Lee? Do you consider them to be strong or weak men? Why?

AUTHOR'S NOTE

Dear Reader,

Thank you for obtaining a copy of *Let Sleeping Dogs Lie*. I hope you enjoyed the story. Take a moment and join my mailing list or post a note on my Web site letting me know your thoughts about the story.

For your reading enjoyment, included is an excerpt of *Still Waters*…another story dealing with a family challenged with secrets and the unwillingness to forgive past hurts.

As always, thank you for the support. Keep reading, and I look forward to hearing from you online at:

www.patriciahaley.com

Other New Spirit titles by Patricia Haley
No Regrets
Blind Faith
Still Waters

The following is an excerpt from Patricia Haley's previous novel STILL WATERS. This book is available wherever trade paperbacks are sold.
ENJOY!

Chapter 1

"I don't want a divorce." Mrs. Williams didn't flinch, not so much as a whimper. If the thought of divorce was offensive, she didn't let on. "I didn't get married to end up divorced. I don't want to be one of those women who ends up alone, and I definitely don't want my kids to grow up without their father, but I'm tired," Laurie continued. "I'm just tired of trying to make him happy. If he would just act right, everything would be fine," she said as three of her sons came running up the aisle. "Junior, wait in the lobby for me and watch Baby Rick. I'll be right out," she told her preteen before turning back to the church mother. "That two-year-old can be a handful at times."

"I know six boys and a husband keeps you busy. I don't know how you find so much time to spend here at church with a husband at home."

"To be honest, I used to love working here at the church.

It was my only time away from the house, the kids, and Greg, especially when he gets into one of his moods like he's in right now. That's why I'm in no rush to get home today."

"Men need their space, that's all."

"Space? I'm the one who needs space. Don't get me wrong, I love my children, but six is a lot. I couldn't handle another one."

Baby Rick came charging in with Junior in pursuit.

"That's okay, I got him," Laurie said, corralling Baby Rick as he tried to breeze by. "Take your brothers and go to the car," she told Junior. "I'll be right out."

Mrs. Williams laughed openly. "You're still young, Laurie. How are you going to stop another child from entering this world if that's the plan God has for you?"

She'd stayed in the marriage believing it would settle down and get back to the way it used to be, back to when they were happy. If they were to have a chance, Greg had to get his anger under control. The more explosive he became, the more difficult it became and the less interested she was in concealing their issues from outsiders. In the meantime, she couldn't allow another child to sneak into the household, not through her womb. She had a plan, and it was to keep avoiding Greg's intimate advances until her body said the coast was clear. Menopause was far off, but avoidance was the best she could do for now, although there was a good chance that Greg's frustration wouldn't hold out much longer; with no backup plan in sight, fear whisked in.

"Got to take the good with the bad, honey. Marriage isn't easy, but stick it out and let God get the glory." Easy to say for a deacon's wife married forty-five years. Mrs. Williams wasn't married to Greg Wright, a man whose moods swung like a roller coaster—fast, slow, up, down, winding, scary, and at other times sprinkled with sheer exhilaration. Those were the times she was drawn to Greg, like when she first met him. Back then they couldn't stand being apart for more than a day. Now it was hard being around him for more than an hour. Something had to change. She knew it and hopefully God did, too.

Chapter 2

At least Sunday only came once a week. A reasonable person could endure three hours of just about anything, barring concentration camp torture, which was the closest analogy he could render for the weekly pilgrimage to his parents, the almighty Mr. and Mrs. Wright. Greg sat at the table nestled between two booster seats. His troubles swirled around, unbridled. Cheek resting on this tightly clasped fist, he plopped a pay stub and a few bills on top of the chipped veneer tabletop. Jolted back into reality, he felt his body stiffen for a fleeting moment when the garage door opened. Greg knew he'd have to work hard in order to stay calm.

A millisecond was the only separation between keys jiggling in the back door and a stream of kids filing through the laundry room, making enough noise to put the Atlanta Falcons stadium of fans to shame. Greg eased to his feet but was overcome with a flood of Sunday-school drawings thrust in his face.

"Daddy, see what I made?" six-year-old Keith said, pushing the paper into his father's view.

"Mine is better than yours," followed his seven-year-old brother.

"I got one, too," said a younger child.

Mitchell bypassed the bombardment of his father and went straight to the refrigerator. He was tall for a nine-year-old, particularly with a short mother and a father of average height. But tipping the scale at 175 pounds nullified any statuesque presence Mitchell might have commanded.

Junior stood at a distance.

"Boy, get out of that refrigerator. Get upstairs and get your clothes changed," Laurie yelled, lugging her purse, book bag, and the toddler.

"Okay, boys, I'll look at everybody's paintings one at a time," Greg said, sorting through the papers, trying to put them in some type of coherent order. "I can see that you've all done a really good job," he said to his pack of budding artists, sealing the accolade with a group hug, tight, not wanting to let go. This was his paradise, the family he'd created. They were the morphine that kept him going. "I'm proud of you."

"Are you going to take mine to your work again?" one of his sons asked.

"He's not taking yours," Mitchell said, gulping down a kiddy container of juice. "If he takes anybody's, it will be a real picture that I made, not some little finger paint thing you made at church."

"Mitchell, I said get upstairs," Laurie shouted. "That mouth of yours is going to get you into more trouble than you can handle."

"Stop yelling at the boy all the time. He didn't mean anything by it," Greg roared.

Silence rolled into the eat-in kitchen like a Caribbean summer shower—brief, noticeable, and just enough drizzle to put a harmless damper on the festivities. Laurie bent over to set the baby down. Her eyes screamed back at her husband as their gazes met before she stomped out of the room.

Anger swelled in Junior. He caught up to his brother on the stairs, bumping him hard. "You're always starting stuff." He bumped him again. "I'm sick of you. Why don't you just leave?"

"You talking to me, Junior?" Mitchell said with voice cracking.

"Who else you think I'm talking to? You don't see anybody else on the stairs, do you?"

Mitchell shrugged his shoulders and kept quiet.

"Maybe I hate somebody else around here, too; maybe I don't."

"You hate me, Junior?" Mitchell whispered with tears forming.

"Nah, now get out of my way and leave me alone. Just stop starting stuff, then I won't have to hate you and I won't have to hurt you, either."

Mitchell ran to his room.

The fight on the stairs didn't stop the laughing and kiddy

talk going on in the kitchen until Daddy made everybody go upstairs to their bedrooms. Daddy carried Baby Rick. When they got to the top of the stairs, he handed him over and said, "Take off Rick's suit and put that outfit on that your mother laid out for him this morning."

"What outfit?" Junior asked, mad inside that he got asked instead of somebody else.

"Boy, what's wrong with you? You saw that outfit lying on his dresser this morning."

Junior swallowed hard and sighed loud enough to feel he'd retaliated, but not enough to let his father hear. "Come on, Rick. Let me help you get your clothes changed." *You're the only one who doesn't get on my nerves around here,* he reminded himself.

Before Greg walked away from Junior and Baby Rick, he added, "And get that room cleaned when we get back from your grandparents. That's too much mess for a two-year-old and a twelve-year-old to be making."

Two brothers per room swallowed the 2,200-square-foot house, which was a nice size 8 years ago for the young family, before the boys started coming and wouldn't stop. But there was always room for one more child. The boys wouldn't agree, especially Junior. Being the oldest, he had his own room before Rick was born. Against his will, last year Junior was forced to share his bedroom with his baby brother. The age difference was a consideration at first, but it hadn't made sense to switch the other four boys around since they were already adjusted. The situation could be worse. He felt pleased that at least every one of his sons had his own bed. Not bad for six boys.

* * *

Greg opened the door to the master bedroom and found Laurie undressing. His eyes danced over her as he pushed the door shut, tight.

Laurie kept silent.

"What do you think about another child—a girl this time?" Greg caressed her bare shoulders. Preempting his hands from clawing at her any further, she jumped up.

"We need to get over to your parents. You know how mad they get when we're late."

"Forget my parents," he said, flicking his hand in the air, then breaking its force and letting it fall like a feather onto her shoulder, which was still in arm's reach. She dipped her shoulder and let his hand fall off. Crisscrossing her arms, she covered herself, hoping that would be enough to get him moving along another line of thinking. "Please let me get dressed so I can help the kids get ready."

Towering over her at five-foot-ten, his body easily nudged her until she fell back onto the bed. His slim physique with no hint of muscles sprouting from any region followed suit, completely covering her size-sixteen body, compliments of her back-to-back pregnancies. "You never spend any quality time with me anymore," he said, stretching her hands out above her head and kissing her neck. "What happened to us? We used to be all over each other when we first got married. Now I can barely touch you without you pulling away."

Look around here, she wanted to tell him. "Greg, we're not twenty years old anymore. I have more to worry about, like the boys and taking care of the house. By the time I finish with my list of stuff to do every day, I'm tired."

"It's always the kids, the house, your church, your family, or something."

"Don't blame the church. You complained so much about me being involved over there that I stopped pretty much everything except Sunday service. So you can't blame God. I don't spend as much time with Him anymore, thanks to you."

"Okay, so you eased up on church, but you're always busy with the kids. You don't have any time left for me, and I'm your husband. I should come before the kids."

The kids, she thought. *I didn't make them by myself.* But she wouldn't dare broach that subject.

He continued lining her body with tiny smooches, despite her frigid response.

"Greg, please, let's go. I really don't want to be late."

"Shoot, come on, Laurie, what's the problem now?" He snapped to his feet. She watched the blood vessels in his temples swell like a cresting river, then contract. "What's wrong with you? You act like you don't want to touch me half the time. News flash, woman—you're my wife, which means I'm committed to you and you're committed to me. That includes everything," he preached. "What do I have to do to get some affection from my wife?" he howled with temples pulsating.

Laurie eased off the bed, careful to stay out of arm's reach of the brooding storm. Speaking up was good, but at what price? Fumbling to get her clothes on, she said, "Greg, why do we have to go through this? I'm not saying I don't want to be with you like that."

"Like what, Laurie? Like a husband and wife should be,

as one, connected? You act like it's a bad thing," he screamed, taking a step toward her.

She compensated by taking a step back and rushed to pull the shirt over her head, leaving her view impaired for only a brief moment. "Greg, the kids can hear you."

"So what—those are my kids. They know Mommy and Daddy have disagreements. Don't worry about them; this is about you and me."

She knew he was approaching the red zone. The place on the thermometer where overheating was inevitable; the spot where the hose burst, sending molten liquid spurting every-where and painfully burning all in its path. "Greg, look," she said, slapping her hands against her thighs, "can we go to your parents, and then when we get home tonight, I'll do whatever it is you want me to do? Is that okay?"

He scratched his head with eyelids closed. "My goodness, you make it sound like I'm some kind of an animal. I'm not trying to force you to do anything. This has to be something you want, too. Don't do me any favors," he said, slamming the door on his way out.

Laurie breathed a sigh of relief. It hadn't been pretty, but the little thunderstorm had blown in and out without any major damage, preserving enough energy to handle the upcoming phase two—dinner with the Wrights.